The Stone Light

Also by Kai Meyer

Dark Reflections, Book 1: *The Water Mirror*

The Wave Walkers, Book 1: *Pirate Curse*

The Stone Light

KAI MEYER

TRANSLATED BY ELIZABETH D. CRAWFORD

MARGARET K. McELDERRY BOOKS
NEW YORK   LONDON   TORONTO   SYDNEY

Margaret K. McElderry Books
An imprint of Simon & Schuster Children's Publishing Division
1230 Avenue of the Americas, New York, New York 10020

Originally published in German in 2002 as *Das Steinerne Licht*
by Loewe Verlag
Published by arrangement with Loewe Verlag
First U.S. edition, 2007

Book design by Ann Zeak
The text for this book is set in Stempel Garamond.

Manufactured in the United States of America
2 4 6 8 10 9 7 5 3 1

Library of Congress Cataloging-in-Publication Data
Meyer, Kai.
[Steinerne Licht]
The stone light / Kai Meyer ; translated by Elizabeth D. Crawford. — 1st U.S. ed.
p. cm. — (Dark reflections ; bk. 2)
Summary: While Merle and the Flowing Queen travel to Hell to enlist Lord
Light's help in Venice's fight against the invading Egyptian army, Serafin joins a
resistance group that is led by an ancient sphinx.
ISBN-13: 978-0-689-87789-6 (hardcover 13)
ISBN-10: 0-689-87789-7 (hardcover 10)
[1. Magic—Fiction. 2. Sphinxes (Mythology)—Fiction. 3. Orphans—Fiction.
4. Mirrors—Fiction. 5. Fantasy.] I. Crawford, Elizabeth D. II. Title.
PZ7.M57171113 Sto
[Fic]—dc22
2006002252

The Stone Light

Contents

1

SON OF HORUS

FAR BELOW, THE LANDSCAPE, LOOKING LIKE A SEA OF ashes, steadily passed beneath the wings of the obsidian lion. Vermithrax's pitch-black stone body glided along under the thick cloud cover, almost weightless. The girl on his back had the feeling that if she simply stretched out her arm, she could touch the puffy undersides of the clouds.

Merle was clutching the flying lion's mane with both hands. Vermithrax's long coat was of stone, like his entire body, but for some reason Merle didn't understand, his fur felt soft and flexible—only one of the countless marvels the stone lion concealed in his mighty obsidian body.

The wind at this height was bitterly cold and cutting. It effortlessly penetrated Merle's coarse, calf-length dress. The skirt had hiked up and uncovered her knees, so her legs were exposed to the wind. The goose bumps on her legs had come to seem just as matter of course as her growling stomach and the earaches she was having from the height and the cold air. At least her heavy leather shoes protected her feet from the cold, a feeble consolation considering their desperate situation and the empty countryside that was moving along a hundred yards below them.

Two days had passed since Merle had escaped from her native city of Venice on Vermithrax's back. Together they'd broken through the Empire's siege ring and were flying north. Since then they'd seen nothing beneath them but ravaged wilderness. Empty, ruined cities of jagged remnants of burned-out walls; abandoned farms, many burned down or ground to dust under the heels of the Egyptian army; villages in which only stray cats and dogs were still alive; and, of course, those places where the soil looked as if it were turned inside out, churned up, and devastated by powers that were a thousand times greater than any ox-drawn plow.

Only Nature resisted the brutal power of the Empire, and so it happened that many fields were sparkling with springtime green, blooming lilac bushes rose over the deserted walls, and trees wore dense, succulent foliage.

The strength and life in all these plants stood in mocking contrast to the abandoned farms and settlements.

"How much farther?" Merle asked glumly.

Vermithrax's voice was deep as a well shaft. "Before another full day passes."

She said nothing in reply but waited for the ghostlike voice inside her to make itself known, as it usually did when Merle needed comfort or just a few cheering words.

But the Flowing Queen was silent.

"Queen?" she asked boldly. Vermithrax had long ago gotten used to the fact that Merle occasionally spoke with someone he could neither see nor hear. He could easily tell when her words weren't addressed to him.

"Did she answer?" he asked after a while.

"She's thinking," came out of Merle's mouth, but it wasn't she who spoke the words. The Flowing Queen had once again made use of Merle's voice for herself. For the time being, Merle tolerated this rudeness, even though she was silently angry about it. At the moment she was glad that the Queen was at least showing a sign of life.

"What are you thinking about?" Merle asked.

"About you humans," the Queen said and then changed into her mind-voice, which only Merle could hear. *"How it could come to this. And what would bring a man like the Pharaoh to . . . do something like this."* She didn't have a hand of her own to gesture toward the wasteland on the ground, but Merle knew very well what she meant.

"Is he one, then? A human being, I mean? After all, he was dead until the priests brought him to life again."

"The mere fact that a man rises from the dead still need not mean that he engulfs all the countries in a war such as the world has not seen for a long time."

"For a long time?" Merle mused. "Was there ever a war in which someone succeeded in conquering the entire world?" Except for Venice, whose hours were numbered, only the Czarist kingdom had withstood the attacks of the Empire for three decades. All other countries had long since been overrun by mummy armies and scarab swarms.

"People tried. But that was thousands of years ago, in the time of the suboceanic cultures."

The suboceanic cultures. The words resounded in Merle's ears long after the Queen's voice was silent. After she'd freed the Flowing Queen from the hands of an Egyptian spy, she'd first assumed that the strange being was a survivor of the suboceanic kingdoms, which, according to the stories, had once been inconceivably powerful. But the Queen had denied that, and Merle believed her. It would have been too simple.

No one was able to see through a being like her completely, not even Merle, who was closer to the Queen than anyone else since their joint flight from Venice.

Merle snatched herself from her thoughts. Thinking about Venice meant thinking about Serafin, and right now that simply hurt too much.

She peered out over Vermithrax's black mane. Before them rose the rocky crags of high mountains. The landscape had been hilly for some time, and now it was rising ever more steeply. Soon they would reach the mountains. Supposedly their destination lay only a little bit beyond them.

"There's snow down there!"

"What did you expect?" asked the obsidian lion with amusement. "Look how high we are here. It's going to be quite a bit colder before we get to the other side."

"I've never seen snow," Merle said thoughtfully. "People say there hasn't been any real winter for decades. And no summer. Spring and fall just melt into one another somehow."

"Apparently nothing changed at all while I was locked up in the Campanile." Vermithrax laughed. "The humans are still always complaining from morning till night about the weather. How can so many heads busy themselves with so many thoughts about something they can't influence at all?"

Merle couldn't think of an answer. Again the Queen made use of her voice. "Vermithrax! Back there, at the foot of this mountain . . . what is that?"

Merle swallowed, as if she could just choke down the unwelcome influence that was controlling her tongue. She immediately felt the Queen withdraw from her mouth, a feeling as if, for the blink of an eye, all the blood left her tongue and her cheeks.

"I see it too," she said. "A flock of birds?"

The lion growled. "Quite large for a flock of birds. And much too massive."

The dark shadow floating like a cloud over part of the mountain's flank was sharply outlined. It might be several thousand yards away yet, and in comparison to the huge rock giant in the background, the thing darkly silhouetted against the slope didn't seem particularly impressive. But even now she suspected that this impression would change if they were to come nearer to it. Or if the thing came to them.

"Hang on!" cried Vermithrax.

He lost altitude so abruptly that Merle felt as if her insides were being expelled through her ears. For a moment she felt like throwing up. She was about to snarl at the obsidian lion when she saw what had prompted him to undertake the maneuver.

A handful of tiny dots were whizzing around the large silhouette, bright spots that glowed in the light of the setting sun as if someone had sprinkled gold dust over a landscape painting.

"*Sunbarks,*" said the Queen in Merle's mind.

Now they've got us, Merle thought. They've blocked our way. Who would have guessed we're still so important to them? Granted, she was the bearer of the Flowing Queen, the protecting spirit who lived in the waters of the lagoon and who saved Venice from the Egyptian conquerors. But that was past now. The city was irrevocably in the tyrants' power.

"It must be coincidence that we are meeting them," said the mind-voice of the Flowing Queen. *"It does not look as though they have noticed us."*

Merle had to agree she was right. The Egyptians couldn't have overtaken them so quickly. And even if they'd succeeded in alerting a part of their armed forces, they certainly wouldn't have been waiting for the fugitives so very visibly on the snow field of a glacier. "What are they doing here?" Merle asked.

"The big thing must be a collector. One of their flying mummy factories."

Vermithrax now shot away over the top of a dense forest. Occasionally he had to avoid towering firs and spruces. But otherwise he was heading straight toward their adversary.

"Perhaps we should avoid it," Merle said, trying not to sound too anxious. But in truth her heart was racing. Her legs felt as if they belonged to a rag doll.

So that was a collector. A real, actual collector. She hadn't ever seen one of the Egyptian airships with her own eyes, and she would gladly have missed out on the experience. She knew what the collectors did, even *how* they did it, and she was only too painfully aware that each collector was under the command of one of the dreaded sphinx commandants of the Pharaoh.

Quite a dark outlook.

And yet it got worse.

"That is really a *crowd* of sunbarks flying around it," said Vermithrax tonelessly.

Merle, too, could now make out that the golden dots were nothing other than the smallest flying units of the imperial fleet. Each of the sickle-shaped sunbarks had places for a troop of mummy soldiers, besides the high priest whose magic held the bark in the air and in motion. If the Egyptians should become aware of Vermithrax and his rider, the setting of the sun would be their only chance: The darker it grew, the clumsier the barks became until, at night, they finally became completely unusable.

But the side of the mountain was still flooded with bloody red; in the west, the sun was only half sunk behind the peak.

"Avoid it," said Merle again, this time more urgently. "Why aren't we making a wide arc around it?"

"If I am not mistaken," said the Queen through Merle's mouth, for the words were also addressed to the lion, "this collector is on the way to Venice, to take part in the great battle."

"Assuming there is one," said Merle.

"They will give up," said Vermithrax. "The Venetians were never especially courageous. Present company excepted."

"Thank you very much."

"*Vermithrax is right. There will probably not be any fighting at all. But who knows how the armies of the Empire will fall on the city and its inhabitants? Venice has led the Pharaoh around by the nose for more than thirty years, after all.*"

"But that was you!"

"*To save you.*"

They had now come to within just a few hundred yards of the collector. The sunbarks were patrolling at a great height over them. The barks glowed red as the light of the sinking sun caught their golden armor. Merle's only hope was that from above, the obsidian lion was invisible in the shadows among the treetops.

The collector was massive. It was in the form of a pyramid whose top point was cut off. Framed by a crenellated battlement, there was an extensive observation platform with several superstructures, which were arranged so that they were higher toward the middle and created a kind of point. Merle made out tiny figures behind the battlement.

The forest grew thinner as the land rose slightly. Now they could make out deep furrows in the forest floor, a labyrinth of protective trenches, which still, after all the years, had not been completely grown over. At one time a bitter battle had raged in this place.

"*Here men are buried,*" said the Queen suddenly.

"What?"

"The land over which the collector hovers—there must have been a large number of dead buried there during the war. Otherwise it would not be hovering so steadily in one place."

In fact, the massive body of the mummy factory was hanging completely motionless over a meadow on which the high grass bent in the evening wind. In another time, this could have been an idyllic picture, a place of rest and peace. But today the collector cast its threatening shadow over it. It floated just high enough over the meadow for a Venetian palazzo to have found room under it.

"I'm going to land," said Vermithrax. "They'll see us without the tree cover."

No one contradicted him. The obsidian lion set himself down at the edge of the forest. Merle felt a hard jolt as his paws touched the ground. Now for the first time she became conscious of how very much her backside hurt from the long ride on the stone lion's back. She tried to move, but it was almost impossible.

"Do not dismount," said the Queen. *"We might have to take off again in a hurry."*

Lovely prospect, Merle thought.

"It is beginning."

"Yes . . . I see that."

Vermithrax, who knew no more about the Empire and its methods than what Merle and the Queen had told him after they freed him from his tower prison in the middle of the Piazza San Marco, let out a deep snarl. His mane stiffened. His whiskers suddenly stood out as straight as if they'd been drawn with a ruler.

It began with the leaves of the trees around them withering so fast that it seemed as if the autumn had decided to carry out its work a few months too early and within a few minutes. The foliage turned brown, curled, and gently fell from the branches. The fir tree under which they'd taken shelter lost all its needles, and from one moment to the next, Vermithrax and Merle were covered with a brown mantle.

Merle shook herself and blinked up toward the collector. They weren't directly beneath it, Heaven forbid, but they were near enough to be able to see its entire underside.

The gigantic surface was suddenly covered with a network of crisscrossing dark yellow glowing stripes, with multifold angles and following no recognizable pattern. A round area in the center, half as large as the Piazza San Marco, was all that remained dark. Merle had to clutch Vermithrax's obsidian mane more tightly when suddenly the ground trembled, as in a strong earthquake. Very close by, several trees were uprooted and tipped over, tearing out other trees as they fell and crashing to the ground in the midst of a thick cloud of flying dirt and needles. The air was so filled with dry splinters and bits of the withered foliage that, for a moment, Merle found it hard to breathe.

When her eyes stopped tearing, she saw what had happened.

The field over which the mummy factory hovered was gone. The soil was churned up as if by an army of invisible giant moles. The glowing net was no longer attached to the underside of the collector, but was unraveled into an immense number of glittering ropes of light and hooks, no one formed like the next. They were all aimed downward, approaching the ravaged ground and pulling something out of it.

Bodies. Gray, fallen-in corpses.

"So that's how they get their mummy soldiers," whispered Vermithrax, and his voice was faint with the horror of it.

Merle pulled at his mane. She had averted her eyes, could no longer look at what was taking place before her. "Let's get out of here!"

"*No!*" said the Flowing Queen.

But Vermithrax had the same feelings as Merle. Just get away from there. Away from the suction of the collector before they themselves ended on one of the glittering hooks and were pulled up into the mummy factory, where slaves and machines would turn them into something that was satisfied by a *different* kind of life, of submissiveness and obedience and the will to kill.

"Hold on!" he roared. The Queen objected loudly in Merle's voice, but the obsidian lion paid no attention to her. In no time his wings raised them into the air. In a daring stratagem, he turned to the east, against the fast-approaching darkness. At the same time he shot forward, careless of all the sunbarks and high priests who might become aware of them at this moment.

Merle clung so tightly to Vermithrax's coat that her arms vanished up to the elbows in his mane. She bent deep over his neck, to offer less wind resistance, but also to avoid the shots of the Egyptians. She hardly dared look up, but when she finally did, she saw that half a dozen sunbarks had detached from their formation around the collector and taken up the chase.

Vermithrax's plan was as simple as it was suicidal. He had surmised that in the massive body of the collector there must be weapons that could easily shoot a flying lion from the sky. But if he got close to the vicinity of the sunbarks, the commanders on board the collector would perhaps think twice about shooting at a target in the midst of their own people.

It wouldn't work, Merle thought. Vermithrax's plan would have been a good one if they were dealing with ordinary opponents like the ones the winged lion knew from his own times, when he was not yet a prisoner of the Venetian City Guard. But the sunbarks were occupied by mummy soldiers, each of them only too easily replaced, and they would even sacrifice one or two priests.

Vermithrax cursed when he came to the same conclusion.

Only a little way ahead of them, a wooden bolt the length of a man whizzed through the air past them, fired from one of the ports in the collector body. The mummy factory itself was too cumbersome for a pursuit, but its weapons were vicious and long-range.

Merle felt sick, worse than ever as Vermithrax kept doubling back and maneuvering turns that she would not have believed possible for his heavy stone body. Up and down, often in such quick succession that Merle soon lost any feeling for over and under. Even the Queen was silent with concern.

Once, Merle looked back. They were now almost at the level of the observation platform. Several figures stood behind the battlement. Merle could see their robes and their grim faces. High priests, she guessed.

Among them was one who caught her eye especially. He was a good head taller than the others and wore a ballooning cloak that looked as if it were woven of pure gold. His hairless skull was covered with a network of gold-colored filaments, like a jeweler's engraving on a brooch.

"The Pharaoh's vizier," whispered the Flowing Queen in her head. *"His name is Seth. He is the highest priest of the cult of Horus."*

"Seth? Isn't that the name of an Egyptian god?"

"The priests of Horus have never been known for their humility."

Merle had the feeling that the eyes of the man were boring into her forehead across the distance. For a heartbeat it seemed to her that the Queen groaned in pain inside her.

"Everything all right?" she asked.

"Look away! Please . . . not into his eyes."

At the same moment a whole swarm of bolts rushed over their heads. Two of them struck sunbarks that were quite close to the lion. Smoke billowed from one as it went down in a tailspin of jerky spirals. The other fell like a stone and smashed on the ground in showers of steel splinters. The rest of the sunbarks pulled back a little so as not to be caught in the hail of shots from the collector.

This was the chance Vermithrax had been waiting for.

With a wild cry he plunged down. On his back, Merle screeched as the ground shot up toward them. She already saw them lying smashed beside the debris of the bark.

But a few yards over the rocks, Vermithrax pulled out of the dive, swept across the ground and the edge of a wall of rock, then sank down deep again, behind the wall and out of the collector's line of fire. Now they had to deal only with the four remaining barks, which would follow them over the rock wall at any moment.

The Flowing Queen had recovered from the penetrating eyes of the vizier. *"I know now why I chose Vermithrax for our flight."*

"Because you had no other choice." Merle hardly

heard her own words; the headwind tore them from her lips like scraps of paper.

The Queen laughed in her mind, which was a strange feeling, for it seemed to Merle as though she herself was laughing, entirely without her own effort.

The lion flew across a labyrinth of ravines before he discovered one that was broad enough to hide in. Shots were striking to the right and left of them, steel bullets this time, fired from barrels in the noses of the sunbarks. But none came close enough to them to be dangerous. Stone fragments were raining on them from all sides. Sparks flew when ricocheting shots skidded over the rock walls and ate furrows in the stone.

The ravine was not deep, with hardly more than twenty feet or so to the surface level. It narrowed as they went farther into it, the walls just far enough apart so that Vermithrax could fly through at a lower height. Two sunbarks had followed them into the rocky labyrinth, while the other two were gliding over the maze of ravines and lurking, in case the obsidian lion surfaced again. It wasn't difficult for Vermithrax to fly around sharp corners and curves, while the long sunbarks had to slow down before each bend in order not to crash against the rocks.

Beneath them the gorge filled with water, the blind arm of a brook or mountain lake. Vermithrax followed its course, and soon they were racing over the surface of a river. The rock walls were farther apart now, offering the sunbarks enough room to maneuver. But Vermithrax's lead was still too big, and the two barks overhead had not yet discovered the ravine.

"We cannot keep flying so low if we want to get to the other side of the mountain."

"We have to survive first, don't we?"

"I am only trying to plan things, Merle. Nothing else."

It was hard for Merle to concentrate. Not at this speed, not with death hanging over her. They might have escaped the collector, but the sunbarks were still after them.

"Vermithrax!" She bent toward the lion's ear and tried to talk over the noise of the wind. "What do you have in mind now?"

"Sundown," he replied shortly. His tone revealed that he was more exhausted than she'd realized. In fact, it hadn't occurred to her at all that a creature like Vermithrax could also just run out of breath.

The river under them grew faster. Merle saw that the water no longer glowed red, as it had a few minutes before, but only reflected the shadowy rock walls. Also, the sky had lost its glow and changed to violet blue.

She felt like screaming with relief. Vermithrax was right, his plan had worked. He'd outsmarted the Egyptians. The sunbarks had vanished. Merle imagined the sickle-shaped flying ships going back to the collector at a creeping pace, crippled by the failing daylight, as useless as pieces of iron salvage.

The stream became faster, wilder, and above all louder, and soon a crown of white foam rose up before them, spreading across the entire span of the water. Behind it there was nothing but darkness.

With a jubilant cry, Vermithrax raced out over the waterfall, which crashed to the ground about a hundred yards below. The obsidian lion maintained his level so that Merle could look out over the country at the foot of the mountain, over forests and fields slumbering in the darkness of the falling night. The lion slowed his wing beats, but he continued flying forward unswervingly. Merle stared silently at the landscape passing below for a long time before she again addressed the Queen.

"What do you know about this Seth?"

"*Not much. Followers of the cult of Horus recalled the Pharaoh to life over thirty years ago. Since then they appoint the high priests of the Empire. That means that Seth has been their leader since then.*"

"He didn't look that old."

"*No. But what difference does that make?*"

Merle thought about how she could make clear to someone who was timeless like the Queen that a human being's exterior should give information about his age. When it didn't, it could mean two things: Either the person was not showing his true face or, though he might look like a human, in reality he was not one. At least not a mortal.

When Merle showed no sign of answering the question,

the Queen went on: *"The Horus priests have much power. In truth, they are the ones who steer the fortunes of the Empire. The Pharaoh is only their puppet."*

"That would mean that Seth, if he is the leader of the priests of Horus and in addition the vizier of the Pharaoh, that he also—"

"Is the true ruler of Egypt. Indeed."

"And the world."

"Unfortunately."

"Do you think we'll meet him again?"

"You should pray that it does not happen."

"Pray to the Flowing Queen? The way all Venice is probably doing right now?" She was immediately sorry for the words, but it was already too late.

In the hours that followed, the Queen was silent and withdrew herself into the farthest corner of Merle's consciousness, wound into a cocoon of her cool, alien, godly thoughts.

They crossed the mountains a little bit farther to the east without meeting an adversary again.

At some point, it must have been after midnight, they saw the other side before them in the gray icy light of the stars, and now finally Vermithrax allowed himself a stop to rest. He landed at the top of an unapproachable needle of rock, just wide enough for him to lie down and for Merle to climb from his back.

She ached all over. For a while she despaired of ever being able to walk again at all without every step, every bone, every muscle hurting.

In the darkness she kept looking for signs of pursuers, but she could discover nothing suspicious. Only a predatory bird circled in the distance, a falcon or a hawk.

No sound came from the broad lands at the foot of the mountain, not once the cry of an animal or the fluttering of the wings of birds. Her heart shrank, and apprehensiveness overwhelmed her. With alarming certainty she realized that there was nothing alive down there anymore. No human beings, no animals. The Egyptians had even abducted the dead, to man their galleys, sunbarks, and war machines.

She lowered herself down at the edge of the tiny plateau and stared out into the night, lost in thought. "Do you think Lord Light will help us?" It was the first time in hours that she'd addressed the Queen. She didn't really expect an answer.

"I do not know. The Venetians treated his messenger badly."

"But they didn't know what they were doing."

"Do you think that makes a difference?"

"No," said Merle dejectedly. "Not really."

"Exactly."

"All the same, Lord Light did offer to support Venice in the fight against the Empire."

"That was before the Body Guard killed his messenger. Besides, it is not in the nature of humans to enter into a pact with Hell."

Merle grinned mirthlessly. "I've heard entirely different stories about that. You really don't know much about us humans."

She leaned back and closed her eyes.

In the year 1833, the English explorer Charles Burbridge had discovered that Hell was anything but an old wives' tale. It existed as a real, subterranean place in the center of the earth, and Burbridge had led a series of expeditions there. He was the only one to return from the last one. Many of the things he saw and experienced were documented and, up to the beginning of the great war, were taught in school. But there was no doubt that this was only a fragment of his actual discoveries. According to the rumors, the remainder were too dreadful, too shocking, for him to reveal them in public. Therefore, after Burbridge's last expedition, no one else had dared the descent. Only since the outbreak of the war had new signs of life come up from below, which finally climaxed with Lord Light, the storied ruler of Hell, offering the Venetians his support in the battle against the Pharaoh. But the City Council, in its arrogance and self-satisfaction, refused his help. Merle herself had become a witness when Lord Light's messenger was murdered in the Piazza San Marco.

And now Merle, the Flowing Queen, and Vermithrax were on their way to ask Lord Light personally for help, in the name of the people of Venice, not its city councillors. But it was questionable whether—even if their mission were successful—they'd be in time. And who could say anyway that Lord Light wouldn't do exactly the same to them as had been done to his messenger in Venice?

But the worst thing was that there was nothing else left for them to try except to climb down into the abyss on Burbridge's trail. And none of them, not even the Queen, had any idea of what they would find down there.

Merle opened her eyes and blinked over at the sleeping Vermithrax. She was dog tired herself, but she was still too excited to be able to rest.

"Why is he helping us?" she whispered thoughtfully. "I mean, you're the Flowing Queen and somehow a part of Venice—or the other way around. You want to protect what belongs to you. But why Vermithrax? He could simply fly back to his relatives in Africa."

"Assuming he would still find them there. The Empire has not only spread to the north."

"Do you think the other talking lions are dead?"

"I do not know," said the Queen sadly. *"Perhaps. Possibly they have just moved farther on, so far away that the Egyptians will not find them for the time being."*

"And Vermithrax knows that?"

"Perhaps he surmises it."

"Then we're all he has, right? His only friends."
Merle stretched out a hand and gently stroked one of the
lion's stone paws. Vermithrax purred gently, turned on
his side, and stretched all four feet toward her. His jowls
fluttered each time he took a breath, and Merle could see
that his eyes were twitching under the lids. He was
dreaming.

She pulled her dress more closely around her body to
protect her from the cool wind, then snuggled up close to
Vermithrax. Again he purred blissfully and began to snore
softly.

The Queen is here, she thought, because she and
Venice belong together in some sort of way. One can't
exist without the other. But what about me? Really, what
am I doing here?

Her closest friends, Junipa and Serafin, her master
Arcimboldo, and the mermaid Eft, they were all still in
Venice, where they were exposed to the dangers of the
Egyptian invasion. Merle herself was an orphan. She'd
been found in a basket on the canals as an infant and had
grown up in an orphanage. Today the thought that she had
no parents who might have been concerned about her was,
for once, a comforting one.

Still, it wasn't that simple. Sometime she'd find out
what sort of people her mother and her father had been.
Sometime, most certainly.

Lost in thought, she pulled the magic hand mirror

from her pocket. The surface consisted of water that could never leave the mirror, no matter how she held it. Sometimes, when Merle thrust her arm inside it, she could feel her fingers enclosed by those of a gentle, warm hand. The water mirror had lain beside her in the basket when she'd been found. It was the only thing that bound her to her parents. The only clue.

There was something else in the mirror: a milky veil, which constantly flitted over the surface. The phantom had escaped from one of Arcimboldo's magic mirrors and settled itself in the small hand mirror. Merle would have been glad to establish contact with it. She only wondered how. Serafin had told her that the phantoms in Arcimboldo's mirrors were humans from another world who'd succeeded in crossing to this one—without, however, realizing that they appeared here only as phantoms, blurry hazes trapped inside mirrors.

Serafin . . . Merle sighed inaudibly.

She'd hardly begun to know him and then they were separated by the Body Guard of the city councillors. They'd spent only a few hours together, wearing, dangerous hours, in which they'd snatched the crystal vial with the essence of the Flowing Queen from the Egyptian spy. And although they knew so little of each other, she missed him.

She fell asleep with the thought of his smile, of the roguishness in his eyes.

In her dreams it seemed to her that she heard the scream of a falcon. She was awakened briefly by a gentle draft of air on her face, the scent of feathers, but there was nothing anywhere near them, and if there had been, it concealed itself in the darkness again.

2

THE MASTER THIEF

THE TOWER CLOCKS OF VENICE HAD STRUCK MIDNIGHT long ago. Deep darkness lay over the city and the waters of the lagoon. The streets were empty, nothing was stirring except stray cats hunting their prey, untroubled by the threat of the Empire.

It was quiet on the bank of the narrow canal, alarmingly still. Serafin sat on the stone curbing and let his feet dangle. The soles of his shoes were a mere handsbreadth above the water. The alley between houses that he'd followed here was narrow and dark; it dead-ended at the water's edge.

Not so many hours ago he'd come here with Merle and shown her the reflections on the surface—reflections that might not really be there and were only to be seen between twelve and one o'clock at night. They showed the houses on the bank of the canal, and yet they weren't reflections of the reality: Some of the windows mirrored in the water were illuminated, although in reality the buildings were abandoned and dark. Now and again something moved, such as the reflections of pedestrians who didn't exist at all—not in *this* Venice, the city in which Serafin and Merle had grown up. Instead, there were rumors that a second Venice existed in another world, and perhaps even a dozen or a hundred of them.

Feeling melancholy, Serafin crumbled bits of a small loaf of bread into the water, but no fish came to receive the unexpected delicacies. Since the Flowing Queen had been driven from the waters of the lagoon by the poison of the Egyptian high priests, one rarely saw fish swimming through the canals. Instead of them, algae now thrived in the waters, and Serafin wasn't the only one who had the feeling that it was growing worse with each passing day. Dark green strings, amorphous and twisted, like wet spiderwebs. It could only be hoped that they didn't really come from one of the great sea spiders, which no one had ever seen but were rumored to be living in the Mediterranean in the ruins of the suboceanic kingdom, there where the water was deepest.

Serafin felt miserable. He knew that Merle had escaped from Venice on the back of a stone lion, and for all his confusion, he was still grateful for that. At least at the moment, she was in no danger from the Egyptians—provided she'd been able to get past the siege ring of the Empire without being caught by the sunbarks.

It wasn't the impending invasion that caused his concern either. The fear of the Egyptians went deep, certainly, but in a peculiar way that frightened him, he'd resigned himself to it. The capture of Venice was inevitable.

No, something else was gnawing at him, hardly letting him sleep and making him restless all day long. His stomach felt like a hard ball that wouldn't let him take any nourishment. He had to force himself to take each bite, but even that didn't always succeed. The crumbs of bread on the water below him were his evening meal.

He was concerned about Junipa, the girl with the mirror eyes. And of course about Arcimboldo, the magic mirror maker on the Canal of the Expelled. It had been Arcimboldo who'd taken Junipa and Merle from the orphanage and made them apprentices in his workshop. Arcimboldo who—as Serafin had learned shortly before—had entered into an agreement to soon surrender Junipa to Lord Light, the master of Hell.

Serafin had demanded explanations from Arcimboldo, and the magic mirror maker had answered most of his questions.

Arcimboldo seemed to be a beaten man. For years he'd secretly supplied Lord Light with his magic mirrors. Time after time, he'd met with Talamar, Lord Light's courier, to hand over new mirrors. And one day Talamar had made a special proposal, to which, after a long hesitation, Arcimboldo had agreed. He should restore sight to the blind Junipa, of course with the help of his magic mirrors. A noble gesture on his part, and since then, Junipa learned a little faster each day how to manage with her new powers of sight.

But that wasn't all.

Lord Light had not directed Arcimboldo's attention to Junipa out of altruism. Serafin had had to probe for a while before the mirror maker finally told him everything.

"Junipa can also see in the dark with her new eyes," Arcimboldo explained over a glass of tea, while the moon shone through a skylight in the workshop. "Merle has probably told you that already. But it doesn't end with that."

"End?" asked Serafin with irritation.

"The magic mirror glass with which I replaced her eyeballs will give her the power to look into other worlds at any time. Or better: through the *mirrors* of other worlds."

After a long silence, Serafin finally found words again. "Such as the ones that are reflected in some of the canals around midnight?"

"You know about those? Yes, into those, and also

others. Junipa will look through her mirrors at those who live there, and they'll never know it. She'll observe kings and emperors making important decisions in their mirrored halls, and she'll see when fully laden ships are reflected in the waters of distant oceans. That is the true power that her mirror eyes give her. And it is she whom Lord Light is after."

"Control, isn't it? That's what he's all about. Not only does he want to know what's going on in this world—he'll only be satisfied when he knows everything. About all worlds."

"Lord Light is curious. Perhaps we should say 'thirsting for knowledge'? Or 'interested'?"

"Unscrupulous and vicious," said Serafin angrily. "He's exploiting Junipa. She's so happy that she can see after a life of blindness—and she has no idea what's behind it."

"She does," contradicted Arcimboldo. "I've spoken with her. She now knows what power she will have at her command in time. And I believe she has accepted it."

"Did she have a choice?"

"Lord Light gives none of us a choice. Not me, either. Had I not taken his gold, the workshop would have closed long ago. He's bought more magic mirrors than anyone else since the Guild expelled me. Without him I'd have had to send all my apprentices back to the orphanages. Merle and Junipa wouldn't even have come here." The little old man shook his head sadly. "Serafin, believe me, my own fate is not the issue here at all. But the children . . . I couldn't allow that."

"Does Junipa know where she's going to go?"

"She suspects there's more behind it. Even that she won't be staying here with us for long. But she knows nothing of Talamar and Lord Light. Not yet."

"But that can't be allowed to happen!" Serafin exclaimed, almost overturning his tea. "I mean, we simply can't allow her to . . . to go to Hell. In the truest sense of the word."

To that Arcimboldo had said nothing, and now Serafin was sitting here on the canal and looking for a solution, for some sort of way out.

If Venice had been a free city and there had been no Egyptians threatening it, perhaps he might have been able to flee with Junipa. He'd once been one of the most skillful master thieves in Venice, of whose existence most of the city's citizens had no inkling at all. But the Empire's siege ring enclosed them on all sides, a hangman's noose of galleys, sunbarks, and umpteen thousand soldiers. There was no way out of the city, and to hide from Hell *and* the Egyptians somewhere in the alleys was a futile undertaking. Sooner or later they'd find them.

If Merle were still in Venice, together they might perhaps have found a solution. But with his own eyes he'd seen her fly over the Piazza San Marco on the back of a stone lion—over the lagoon, out of the city. And for reasons he didn't know himself, he doubted that Merle would be back soon enough—if ever—to save Junipa from her fate.

Where was Merle? Where had the lion taken her? And what had become of the Flowing Queen?

The reflection of the other world faded as a clock in a nearby church tower struck one, followed by quite a few others. The hour after midnight was past, and with it the lighted windows on the water vanished abruptly. Now the waves reflected the dark housefronts only very vaguely, unlit, a reflection of the reality.

Serafin sighed softly, stood up—and suddenly bent forward again. There was something in the water, a movement. He'd seen it clearly. Not a reflection, from this or any other world. Perhaps a mermaid? Or a big fish?

Serafin saw a second movement, and this time it was easier to follow it with his eyes. A black silhouette glided through the canal, and now he discovered a third. Each was about fifteen feet long. No, fish were certainly not *that* big, even if these were shaped something like sharks. They came to a point in front, but the width was the same along the rest of their length, like a thick tree trunk. Serafin saw no fins, either, as far as he could make out in the dark water.

The last silhouette slid along just under the surface, not so deep as the others, and now the moonlight broke over its surface. No doubt about it—metal! With that, there was really no more doubt about where they came from. Only magic could move objects of iron or steel through the water like feathers. Egyptian magic!

Serafin ran. The surrounding houses came right down to the water, so he couldn't run directly along the canal. He had to take a roundabout way to follow the three vehicles. He quickly ran back through the blind alley, went around several corners, and finally came to a piazza that he knew only too well. Forty steps away from him, a little bridge led over the canal into which he'd just scattered his supper. In a narrow house on the left, he and Merle had met the three traitors from the City Council and the Egyptian spy. Here they'd thwarted the delivery of the Flowing Queen.

Now the house stood there abandoned and inconspicuous. No one would have supposed that the invasion of the Empire had begun precisely here, behind boarded-up windows and a gray, crumbling façade.

On the bridge stood a figure in a long, dark cape. Its face was hidden under a deep hood.

For a moment Serafin had a sense of walking through an invisible door into the past. He'd already seen this same man once, at the same hour of the night, in the same place: the Egyptian envoy, the spy, from whom they had wrested the crystal vial containing the Queen. Merle had burned his hand with the help of her magic mirror, while Serafin had set a horde of angry street cats on his neck.

But now the man was here once more, and again he was hiding himself under a hooded cape like a street robber.

Serafin overcame his shock quickly enough not to be discovered. He swiftly pressed himself against a house-front. The moon was illuminating the opposite side and a large portion of the narrow piazza; but the part through which Serafin was moving lay in deep shadow.

Protected by the darkness, he approached the bridge. The envoy was waiting for something, and after Serafin's recent discovery, there was little doubt as to what that was. In fact, there now sounded a hollow metallic sound, which was irregularly repeated. Something was striking against the wall of the canal under the bridge.

Something was coming alongside.

The envoy hurried to the foot of the bridge and from there looked into the water. Meanwhile, Serafin was still thirty feet away from him. He hid behind a small altar to the Virgin Mary that someone had attached to the house wall a long time ago. Very likely, no offerings had been placed there for a long, long time. In recent years most people had prayed to the Flowing Queen; nobody believed in the power of the Church anymore, even though there were still some holdouts who attended church as a matter of form.

Serafin watched the envoy move back a few steps, away from the edge of the canal. He was making room for six men climbing up the narrow steps from the water.

Men? Serafin bit his lower lip. The six figures had been men once. But today they bore no likeness to their former selves.

Mummies.

Six mummy soldiers of the Empire with faces dried up and fallen in, so that they resembled each other like twin brothers. Any characteristics that might once have differentiated them had vanished. Their faces were those of skeletons, covered with gray skin.

All six wore dark outfits that glittered metallically in the moonlight now and then. Each held a sword such as Serafin had never seen before: The long blade was curved, almost half-moon-shaped, but the edge—unlike that of a scimitar—was on the inside of the curve, which led to a completely different way of wielding it. Egyptian sickle swords, the feared blades of the imperial mummy soldiers.

There must have been room for two of them in each of the strange vehicles in the water. They had sat in them one behind the other, as in a hollow tree, unable to move. But mummies, Serafin thought cynically, probably didn't have to scratch at all; that would only have peeled the desiccated skin from their bones.

So that was what the Egyptians made of the dead. Slaves without will or mercy who sowed death and destruction. Presumably there were similar scenes playing out all over Venice at this moment. The invasion had begun.

But there was a difference between being conquered by flesh-and-blood opponents and by . . . something like that. You could talk with humans, ask for mercy, or at least hope that they retained a portion of their humanity. But with mummies?

Serafin could no longer bear the idea of a Venice emptied of all life, in which an inhuman Pharaoh ruled. He knew that it would be best for him to keep still, not move, not even breathe, but that was impossible. At last, when it became clear to him that the Egyptian envoy had command of the six soldiers, he could not creep away. He had to do something, had to act. Even if it was madness.

He let out a sharp whistle. For a moment nothing happened. But then the envoy whirled around so fast that his dark cloak billowed out. His hood slid back for a moment, long enough so Serafin could see what the cats had done to him. The spy's face was furrowed with crusted wounds, not harmless scratches but deep gouges, which would soon scab over to an ugly wasteland of scars. And the man knew whom he had to thank. He remembered the sound that had set the cats on him.

He remembered Serafin.

The envoy called something in a language that Serafin didn't understand and pointed toward the altar, as if his eyes could see through the massive stone. Faster than Serafin would have thought possible, the mummies began moving, their sickle swords raised. One of them stayed behind, near the envoy. The man pulled his hood up again, but first he threw Serafin a hate-filled look in which there was a promise—of pain, of misery, of long torture.

The mummies had covered half the distance. Serafin had just leaped from his hiding place when the cats finally came.

Thirty, forty, fifty stray cats, from all directions, from all openings, from the roofs and out of the sewers. And with every second there were more, until the piazza swarmed with them.

The envoy shrieked and retreated backward up the bridge, while he ordered one of the other soldiers back with a shrill command so that he could keep the cats from getting at him. But the other four mummies paid scarcely any attention to the animals, who fell on them from all sides. Claws sank into the paper skin. Teeth bit into clothing and armor, snapped at fingers, and tore dusty scraps from cheeks and arms.

None of it stopped the mummy soldiers.

They kept single-mindedly on their way, stamping through a sea of fur and claws, each hung with a dozen cats like living Christmas tree decorations. The sickle swords whistled through the air and in blind rage struck their victims, some on the ground, some in mid-leap. Meowing and shrieking echoed and reechoed from the houses. But the animals learned quickly. More and more often they fastened themselves to the sword arms of the soldiers, until the mummies sagged under the weight.

Serafin was immobilized with horror. Not for long, only for a few instants. It was enough for him to realize that the cats were sacrificing their lives for him. With all the danger that threatened him, he couldn't permit that. Cats were the friends of the master thieves, their allies, not their meek slaves. He hesitated a moment, then let out a new succession of whistles. Immediately the wave of cats surged back; only those who were biting and hooked into mummies stayed a few seconds longer. Then they also gave up, let themselves drop, and whisked away.

Serafin's command meant that the cats should run away, back to wherever they had come from. But they didn't obey. They fell back from the mummies for only a few yards, stopped at the edge of the piazza, and watched their opponents with glowing eyes.

Meanwhile, Serafin had run to the other side of the piazza. From there he looked back and saw the cats clumped in front of the buildings like a wave of fur. He also saw that the mummy soldiers were hard on his heels.

The cats waited for him to call them to attack again, but he didn't have the heart to. Nearly a dozen animals lay dead or dying in the lane that the four mummy soldiers had plowed. The grief that overwhelmed Serafin at this sight shook him even more strongly than fear for his life.

Ten more yards and the four soldiers would reach him. Silently they rushed toward him. In the background, up on the bridge, stood the envoy, his arms crossed, barricaded behind his two guards.

"The cats!" cried a light voice suddenly out of the shadows behind Serafin. "They should pull farther back!"

Serafin whirled around. A torch burned in the recess between the houses, but he couldn't recognize who was holding it. He whistled again, moving toward the source of the light as he did so.

This time the cats obeyed. In the wink of an eye, they climbed the houses and windowsills, drainpipes and steps, wooden beams and balustrades.

"Watch out!" bellowed a second voice, this time from the left.

Serafin turned and ran. The mummy soldiers had almost reached him. He looked back over his shoulder—and saw two garish tongues of flame leap out of the street openings in the direction of the mummies. There was a crackling snarl, then the four mummies were alight. Flames licked over their dried-out bodies, sprang from one limb to the other, ate along under the steel of their armor. One soldier sank to its knees, while the other three still ran on. Two struck wildly about themselves, as if they could drive off the flames with their sickle swords. But the third rushed straight at Serafin without stopping, its weapon raised, ready to deal the deadly blow.

Serafin was unarmed except for his knife, which he tore from his belt. He knew he hadn't a chance with it.

Nevertheless, he stood there as if his boots had taken root. He'd been a master thief of the Guild, the youngest ever, and had learned that you don't run away from an opponent. Not if others were ready to risk their lives for you. And as he saw it, not only had the cats done that, but also the mysterious helpers who came to his aid with their fire breath.

Now he saw three figures leap out of the recesses on both sides of the street. Two flung their torches to the ground, while the third rushed at one of the burning soldiers with his drawn saber. Very briefly the idea flitted through Serafin's mind that he knew this face, all three faces, but he had no time to make sure.

The burning mummy threw itself at him like a demon, a towering column of fire, from which the razor-sharp blade of the sickle sword struck at him. Serafin avoided the blow and at the same time tried to put some distance between himself and his opponent. He could perhaps escape the sword, but if the flaming creature fell on him, he would burn miserably.

Out of the corner of his eye he saw the fighter with the saber strike the head of his mummy foe from its shoulders, with an elegant turn that showed either long practice or enormous talent. The two others had also drawn their blades and fought with the remaining mummies, nowhere near so skillfully as their leader, but the fire assisted them. It consumed the undead soldiers with such speed that they literally fell apart before they could become dangerous. Serafin's adversary, too, in spite of all its determination, became ever weaker, its movements more uncontrolled, until its legs gave under it. Serafin took a few steps backward and watched as the mummy was consumed by flames like a heap of straw.

"Watch out!" cried a voice.

Serafin looked hastily around. The two bodyguards of the envoy had rushed forward, followed by their master. They rushed at his saviors. Serafin's eyes were tearing from the smoke of the numerous fires. He still could not clearly see who was standing with him. Earlier he had seen their faces . . . but no, that was impossible.

He quickly ran around the first fire, jumped over the second, and lifted a sickle sword from the ground. One of the mummies had lost it before it was entirely burned up. The grip was warm, almost hot, but not so bad that he couldn't hold it. The weapon felt clumsy to him, the balance of the blade with a will of its own. But he wouldn't allow others to fight for him while he stood by doing nothing. He grabbed the weapon with both hands and rushed into the fight.

The leader of the three rescuers sprang skillfully forward and back, avoided sword blows, and inflicted numerous wounds on one mummy soldier. Then the saber flashed through the defenses of the soldier in an explosion of blows and thrusts and beheaded it. Again, dust billowed out in all directions, but no blood flowed. The torso collapsed. Serafin quickly realized that this was the best way to conquer a mummy: The magic of the Egyptians affected the dead brain; without skulls they were ordinary corpses again.

And then, when he finally recognized who'd saved him, he didn't believe his eyes. He would have expected anyone else, but not *him*.

The two other fighters had their hands full to keep the last mummy off their necks. Serafin supported them with the heavy sickle sword as well as he could, while the leader pressed forward, avoiding a revolver shot from the envoy, pursuing him to the bridge and there striking him down with slashing saber blows.

Finally the last mummy also fell. Serafin looked across the plaza, his breath rattling. The traces of dead cats were clearly to be seen in the flickering light of the fire. He swore to himself never again, under any circumstances, to ask the cat folk for help. He had used them selfishly, without considering, and bought his life with those poor creatures lying there in front of him.

One of his fellow fighters laid a hand on his arm. "If what I've heard about the friendship of thieves with the cats is true, they made their decision themselves."

Serafin turned and looked Tiziano in the face. Arcimboldo's former apprentice smiled crookedly, then bent and wiped the dust off his saber blade on the uniform of a mummy torso. Boro, the second fighter, walked up next to him and did the same thing.

"Thanks." Serafin himself thought it could have sounded a little heartier, but he was still too astonished that it was they who'd come to help him. Although Tiziano and Boro had probably never been bad fellows at the bottom of their hearts—at least that's what Merle thought; her problem was much more that they were too closely allied with Dario. Dario was the oldest of Arcimboldo's apprentices and Serafin's archenemy from the time he'd given up master thievery, and the two hated each other's guts. One time Dario had even attacked Serafin with a knife in Arcimboldo's workshop on the Canal of the Expelled.

And of all people, Dario, who was more detestable to him than almost anyone else, whom he considered underhanded, lying, and cowardly, this same Dario now came straight across the piazza to him, carelessly shoving his saber back into its sheath, the saber with which he'd just saved Serafin's life.

Dario bowed to Serafin, looked him over, then grinned. But it didn't seem especially friendly, only arrogant and unmitigatedly insufferable. Entirely the old Dario.

"Looks as if we came just in time."

Tiziano and Boro exchanged looks that seemed embarrassed, but neither of them said a word.

"Many thanks," said Serafin, who still could think of nothing better. To deny the help he'd desperately needed from the three would have been foolish and transparent—and besides, it was just the sort of answer Dario would have given in his situation. Instead, and in order to differentiate himself even more strongly from his former adversary, he added a compliment with a sincere smile: "You can handle a saber really well. I wouldn't have expected it of you."

"Sometimes you can be wrong about others, hmm?"

"Very possibly."

Boro and Tiziano gathered up their torches and rubbed them on the housefronts until the flames were extinguished. Now for the first time Serafin noticed the bulbous flasks they wore at their belts. There must be a fluid in there they'd used to spit fire. Certainly he'd heard that Arcimboldo's apprentices had left the magic mirror workshop two days ago in order the join the resistance fighters against the Empire. But he was astonished at how fast they'd learned to handle the flames. On the other hand, it was possible that they'd learned it earlier. He knew much too little about them.

"I thought you'd have turned tail sooner," Dario said. "Thieves aren't fighters, are they?"

"Not cowards, either." Serafin hesitated. "What do you want with me? You certainly didn't cross my path by accident."

"We were looking for you," Boro said. Dario repaid him with a dark side glance. But the sturdy youth took no notice of him, wholly in contrast to the past. "Someone wants to see you."

Serafin raised an eyebrow. "Oh?"

"We're not mirror makers anymore," said Dario, before one of the others could come forward again.

"Yes, I'd already heard that."

"We've joined the rebels."

"Sounds fabulous."

"Don't get funny."

"Your performance was quite impressive. You just polished off six of those . . . brutes."

"And the fellow in the cape," said Dario.

"And the fellow in the cape," Serafin repeated. "I wouldn't have been able to deal with them alone. Which perhaps means that I wouldn't be a particularly good rebel, right?"

They all knew better, for although Serafin wasn't a skillful fighter with a saber, like Dario, as a former master thief he possessed a whole list of other talents.

"Our leader wants to speak with you," said Dario.

"And I was thinking that was you."

Dario's look grew as dark as the empty eye sockets of a mummy soldier. "We don't have to be friends, no one's asking that of you. You should just listen. And I think you owe us that, don't you?"

"Yes," said Serafin. "I guess I do."

"Good. Then just come with us."

"Where?"

The three exchanged looks, then Dario lowered his voice conspiratorially. "To the enclave," he whispered.

3

LILITH'S CHILDREN

MERLE SAW THE STATUES EVEN FROM A DISTANCE, AND they were bigger than anything she had ever seen in her life. Very *much* bigger.

Ten figures of stone—each at least four hundred feet high, although that was a rough estimate, and they might actually have been even a little higher—standing around a gigantic hole in the landscape. That was what it was, in fact: a hole. Not a crater, not a deep valley. The closer they came to the opening, the clearer it became that it had no bottom, as if a divine fist had simply smashed a piece out of the earth's crust like a splinter from a glass ball. The hole had an irregular shape and must have been larger than Venice's main island.

As Vermithrax flew closer to it, the edges blurred in the moisture drifting across the landscape like a very fine drizzle. Soon Merle saw only the vast edge in front of her, as if the lion had brought them to the end of the world. The opposite side of the abyss was no longer visible. Merle was seized by a feeling of great emptiness and desolation, in spite of the Queen inside her, in spite of Vermithrax.

For hours now they'd been noticing a strange smell — not of sulfur, like the time Hell's messenger had appeared in the Piazza San Marco, but sweeter, hardly less unpleasant, as if something were decaying in the innards of the earth. Perhaps the heart of the world, she thought bitterly. Perhaps the entire world was just dying from the inside out, like a fruit on a tree in which rot and parasites had spread. The parasites were the Egyptians. Or, she corrected herself, maybe even all the people who had no better ideas than to plunge into a war of mythical dimensions.

But no, *they* were not the ones who had begun this war. And also not billions of other people. At this moment, for the first time, she became aware of the whole magnitude of the responsibility she'd undertaken: She was looking for help in the battle against the Egyptians, for help for an entire world.

In the battle against the Egyptians. There it was again.

And she was right in the middle of it. She was no better than all the others in this war.

"Do not talk such nonsense," said the Queen.

"But it's the truth."

"That it is not. No one wants more war, even more bloodletting. But the Egyptians will not let anyone talk to them. There is no other way. The fruit on the tree is helpless when it rots—but we have a choice. We can make our own decisions. And we can try to defend ourselves."

"And that means more war. More dead."

"Yes," said the Queen sadly. *"It probably does."*

Merle looked out over Vermithrax's mane again. To her left and right, the obsidian wings were rising and falling. The soft swishing swelled and receded, gently, almost leisurely, but Merle hardly heard it anymore. The sound had long ago entered into her flesh and blood, just like the lion's throbbing heartbeat; she felt it beneath her as if she were herself a part of this stone colossus, merged into him the way the Queen was now a part of her. She wondered if things would all come to the point when they, who had once been three, would more and more become one, just like the Egyptians, who numbered in the millions but followed only one brain, one hand, one eye—that of the Pharaoh.

Yes, said a cynical voice that wasn't the Queen's, and at the end the shining prince is waiting for you on his white horse and will carry you to his castle of flower petals.

Vermithrax's voice snatched her back to reality. "That is so . . . gigantic!"

Merle saw what he meant. The closer they came to the statues, the more titanic they seemed to her, as if they were continuing to grow right out of the soil, until the stone skulls broke through the clouds somewhere and swallowed the stars with their mouths.

"They are watchmen. The Egyptians built them," said the Queen with Merle's voice so that Vermithrax could hear too. "Here the Egyptian forces clashed with the armies of the Czarist kingdom for the first time. Look around you—everything is wasted and destroyed and uninhabited. Even the birds and insects have flown away. It is said that the earth itself finally convulsed in pain and distress, a last act of strength, to make an end of the fighting, and it swallowed all that it found on it."

"It really looks as though the ground fell in!" Vermithrax said. "Simply collapsed on itself. No earthquake could do something like that."

"There has only twice in history been something comparable. For one, the landslide that swallowed Marrakesh a few years ago—and perhaps the same powers were at work there as here—and then of course the wound that the fall of Lucifer Morningstar made in the earth."

"Morningstar?" asked Vermithrax.

"Even a stone lion must have heard of him," said the Queen. "An infinitely long time ago—so the humans tell it—a burning light from Heaven was supposed to have fallen directly to the earth. Many stories are told of its origins, but most people still believe that it was the angel Lucifer, who turned against his creator and was thrown out of Heaven by him. Lucifer fell burning to the depths, tore a hole in the earth, and thence plunged into Hell. There he rose to become ruler and the most powerful antagonist of his creator. So the angel became the devil—at least the old legends say so."

"Where is this place where Lucifer hit the earth?" Vermithrax asked.

"No one knows. Perhaps it is somewhere at the bottom of the sea, where no one has looked—except for the inhabitants of the subterranean kingdoms. Who knows?"

Merle felt her tongue loosen, and finally she herself was able to speak again. "I can't stand it when you do that."

"Excuse me."

"You're only saying that."

"I am dependent on your voice. We cannot exclude Vermithrax."

"But you could ask politely. How about that?"

"I will take pains to."

"Do you believe that story? I mean, about Lucifer Morningstar and all that?"

"It is a legend. A myth. No one knows how much of it corresponds to the truth."

"Then you have never seen that place in the sea yourself?"

"*No.*"

"But you know the suboceanic kingdoms."

"*I know no one who has seen the place with his own eyes. And no one who knows for certain whether it ever existed at all.*"

She'd never get anything more out of the Queen this way. But what did she care about the suboceanic cultures at the moment, anyway? A much more pressing problem lay directly in front of her, now stretching from one horizon to the other.

They were still some forty feet away from the edge of the Hell hole. In front of them rose one of the ten statues, more impressive than the Basilica of San Marco. It was the figure of a man with naked upper body and legs. According to the manner of ancient Egypt, he had only a loincloth wound around his hips. His skull was hairless, smooth as a polished ball. This head alone must have weighed several tons. The figure had both elbows bent and the palms laid together in front of its chest so that the arms formed a large triangle. The stone fingers were intertwined in a complicated gesture.

Merle suppressed the impulse to imitate it with her own hands; she would have had to let go of Vermithrax's mane to do it.

"*Ask him to fly past two other statues,*" said the Flowing Queen.

Merle passed the request on to the obsidian lion. Vermithrax immediately flew a loop and turned east, where the next stone giant was, a few hundred yards away. Each of these monumental figures stood with its back to the abyss, its pupilless eyes gazing rigidly into the distance.

"And the Egyptians built them?" Merle asked.

"Yes. After the battlefield sank into the ground, the remaining armies of the Czarist kingdom used the opportunity to flee. They retreated many thousand of miles to the northeast and established a new boundary there, which they still hold today. The Egyptians went around the area and continued their advance, while their priests had these statues erected to watch over the entrance to the interior of the earth."

"Only symbolically, I hope."

The Queen laughed. *"I do not believe that the statues will suddenly come to life when we fly past them. In case that is what you meant."*

"I was thinking of something like that, yes."

"Oh, well, I have of course not been here myself before, and—"

Merle interrupted her by clearing her throat.

"Yes?"

"Please hold your tongue."

"If I had one, I would not always be needing yours."

"Did anyone ever tell you that you're a know-it-all?"

"No one."

"Then now is the best time to do it."

"What is a know-it-all?"

Merle let out a groan and addressed the lion. "Vermithrax, was she always like this?"

"Like what?" asked the obsidian lion, and she had the feeling that he was smirking, even though from her place on his back she couldn't see his face.

"So difficult."

"Difficult, hmm? Yes . . . yes, I think you could say that."

Again the Queen laughed inside her, but she dispensed with any remark. Merle could hardly grasp that for once the Queen did *not* have to have the last word.

The second statue was not appreciably different from the first, with the exception that the fingers were inter-twined in a different way. The third figure displayed yet another gesture. Otherwise they were all as alike as peas.

"Is that enough?" Vermithrax asked.

"Yes," said the Flowing Queen, and Merle passed it on.

Vermithrax flew around the statue without it awakening.

"Did you really expect that all at once it would start moving so as to catch us out of the air with its hand?"

Merle shrugged her shoulders. "I think for a long time I haven't known what to expect anymore and what not to. I also didn't think that I would free Vermithrax from his prison. Or fly over the countryside on his back. Aside from all the other things that have happened in the last few days."

She tried to catch a glimpse over the edge of the abyss, but she saw only rocks and fine, vapory veils, bathed in a reddish shimmer. She wasn't sure if that was caused by the sun, which stood high over the wasteland, or if the source of the diffuse glow was inside the earth.

"Do you think that's really Hell down there? I mean, like in the Bible or the pictures on church altars?" Her skeptical tone surprised her. Hadn't she just declared that after all their experiences there was nothing left that could astonish her?

Vermithrax didn't answer, perhaps because he was still thinking, or he had no clear opinion about it. But the Queen answered, *What do you think?*

"I don't know." Merle's eyes swept over the expressionless face of the nearest statue, and she wondered if the artist who had created these features would actually have made them so utterly emotionless if gravest danger lay in wait there below. "Anyway, Professor Burbridge never wrote of gigantic fires roasting the damned. Or of chains and torture chambers. I guess we should believe him. Besides—," she broke off.

"What?"

After a short pause Merle took up the thread again. "Besides, a Hell like the one in the Bible wouldn't make sense. Inflicting pain on someone for all eternity is so . . .

so unreasonable, isn't it? After all, we punish a person so he won't do something bad again. And, of course, to scare off anyone else. But if the good are incapable of sinning, and at the same time the sinners have no chance to do good because, after all, they're imprisoned forever in Hell . . . I mean, what sense would there be in it?"

The Queen said nothing to that, but Merle had the feeling that she silently agreed with her, was even a little proud of her. Emboldened, she went on: "If God is in fact infinitely good, the way it says in the Bible, then how come he sentences some people to eternal damnation? How do the two fit together, good and punishment?"

To her surprise, Vermithrax now joined in. "You're right. Why should we punish a guilty person if the punishment can't change him anymore?"

"Sounds like quite a waste, I think."

"We might call that down there Hell," said the Queen, *"but I do not think it has anything to do with what your priests preach. Neither with God nor with the Devil."*

"But?"

"Only with our own selves. We survive, or we die. That depends on us alone."

"Can anyone like you actually die?"

"But of course," said the Queen. *"I live and die with you, Merle. Whether I want to or not."*

Merle grew dizzy at these words—and to her astonishment, she again felt something like pride. But at the same time she felt the invisible weight on her shoulders grow a little bit heavier.

"What do you think?" cried Vermithrax over his shoulder. "Should we try it?"

"That is what we came here for, after all."

Merle nodded. "Let's try it!"

Between her knees she felt the lion draw in a deep breath and once briefly tense all his muscles. Then he turned sharply, flew a narrow arc, and shot out over the edge.

The sweetish odor became even stronger as they found themselves over the abyss, but there was still nothing to see except the steep rock walls and a sea of mist. The reddish glow of the vapors became more intense now, as if there were a sea of lava hidden under the layer of fog, which would evaporate into hot air any minute.

Obviously the same thought was on Vermithrax's mind. "What's under the clouds?"

"May I?" the Queen asked. Merle thought she sounded slightly too ironic, too sure of herself.

"Go ahead." And before she knew it, the Queen was already speaking with her mouth. "It is only ordinary fog, nothing more. It has to do with the fact that two different levels of air density come together here. You will probably have to get used to breathing under there at first."

"What are air densities?" asked the lion.

"Just trust me." Then she withdrew into herself again.

"She says things like that all the time," Merle said to the lion.

"How do you stand it?"

Merle had a dozen caustic remarks on her tongue, but she suppressed them. Secretly—and she only reluctantly admitted to it—she was even a little glad that she had the Queen in her.

Sometimes it was good to have someone who knew all about you share everything and have an answer to many questions.

And sometimes it was a scourge.

Vermithrax began the descent. He didn't head down in a straight line but turned in wide circles. As he did so, he tilted dangerously to the side, so that after a short time Merle could feel her stomach rebel once again. She would never get used to this accursed flying.

The obsidian lion stayed close to the southern wall. The stone was dark and appeared to be full of cracks. Once Merle thought she made out a kind of groove leading down from the upper edge; it looked like a makeshift staircase or a road that someone had hewn out of the rock. But at the next turn she lost sight of the narrow ribbon again. Anyway, she had her hands full just holding on tight and keeping her eyes more or less rigidly on the back of Vermithrax's head in the hope of being able to keep her nausea and dizziness halfway under control.

The fog lay a few yards below them, smooth as a

frozen lake. Only, its center was filled with incessant motion, wafting veils that turned around themselves like lone dancers of water vapor. The red glow was brighter in some places than others. Whatever might await them down there in the depths, it wouldn't be long before they came face-to-face with it.

It had been cool high up in the air; but now, the farther down they moved, the warmer it became. Not hot, not humid, in spite of the moisture, but warm in a comfortable way. However, Merle was much too tense to be happy about it. Only a few minutes before, when Vermithrax had been circling the statues, the wind had cut through her clothes like a knife through parchment, but the cold wasn't what was occupying her mind. Other thoughts claimed her attention, concerns and speculations, premonitions, and an appropriate measure of confusion.

Then they broke through the fog.

It was only a short moment, certainly not a minute, until Vermithrax's descending flight had borne them through the layer of mist and thrust them out on the underside in a star-shaped eruption of steam and gray vapors. Merle had automatically held her breath, and now, when she tried to take in a deep breath, she was overcome with panic: It wouldn't work! She couldn't breathe! Her throat closed, her chest burned like fire, and then there was only fear, pure, instinctive fear.

But no, there *was* air, and now she filled her lungs with

it, yet it seemed to be different somehow, perhaps thinner, perhaps heavier, it didn't matter. Gradually Merle grew calm again, and then for the first time she became aware that Vermithrax had also gone into a wobble, seized by the same terror of suffocating, by the certainty that it had all been a bad, even fatal, mistake. But now his wing beats steadied, became gentler again, more regular, and the winding course of their descent stabilized.

Merle leaned forward a bit. Not too far, because she already guessed what she would see—an abyss, a bottomless abyss—but the reality exceeded her fears by a great deal.

If a term such as *depth* had ever applied to anything—pure, frightening, reason-transcending *depth*—it was this shaft into the vitals of the earth. The mist was now gone completely and replaced by a clarity that seemed to Merle wrong somehow, somehow inappropriate. She had last experienced this feeling when she swam through the Venetian canals with the mermaids, protected by a glass globe that provided her with a remarkably sharp view of the world under the water. Nonetheless, it was a sight for which the human eye wasn't created; really, everything ought to have been blurred and cloudy, a wavering curtain on her retina.

Here below, in the interior of the abyss, something similar was happening to her. This was no place for human beings, and it astonished her that still she perceived it with all her senses, took it in, if she could not also comprehend it.

The rock walls fell away vertically to the deep, but it seemed to Merle that she saw every indentation, every projection, a little more clearly than above the fog. She could also make out the opposite side better now, although she didn't at all have the impression that the walls were any closer together. Everything was bathed in red golden brightness, which came from the rock itself, from a hair-fine network of veins of glowing lines, in some places clumped, in others almost invisible.

"*Impressive,*" said the Queen, and Merle thought that was an utterly inadequate description, a modest, empty word in the face of this marvel.

Suddenly she became aware that this place must be a facet of the real, true Hell. Something that, except for Professor Burbridge and a small number of select people, no human being had ever seen.

Then she caught sight of the tents.

"Do you see that?" Vermithrax bellowed.

"Yes," whispered Merle, "I see them."

A ways below them and about eighty yards sideways, there was a ledge in the rock wall, a protruding cliff, like the nose of a giant upside down. The upper side was flat and, estimating roughly, twenty by twenty yards wide. There were three tents on it. One was in tatters, although the poles still stuck up in the air like the branches of a dead tree. Something had slit the canvas. A knife perhaps. Or claws.

The two other tents looked undamaged. The flap at the entrance of one was thrown back. As Vermithrax neared the camp, Merle could see that the rock ledge was abandoned.

"What do we do now?" she asked.

"You are curious, are you?"

"Aren't you?"

"A mind can only take in a limited amount of knowledge, and to mine, those things there make no difference."

Show-off, Merle thought. "Then aren't you interested in what happened to the people?"

"It is of interest to you. *That is enough."*

Vermithrax circled several times in front of the rock cliff. Merle noted how carefully he inspected the tents and the other remains of the camp. There was a fireplace; a row of chests, which were piled behind at the rock wall; a dish right beside the burned-out campfire; also three rifles, which were leaning against the wall as if their owners had just vanished behind the rocks for a moment. Whatever might have happened to these people, they hadn't even had time to grab their weapons. An ice-cold tingle ran down her back.

Finally the obsidian lion had seen enough; he made an abrupt swerve and landed on the rock ledge, only a few yards away from the destroyed tent. Now Merle could also see that the path she'd already noticed above opened onto this plateau, and to the right of them it led on farther down into the abyss.

She leaped from Vermithrax's back, landed on both feet—and at first fell right onto her backside. Her knees were weak, her muscles stiff. It was almost an accustomed feeling by now, but it had never been so bad before—possibly also a result of the changed air conditions, just like the weariness that she now felt more strongly than in the past few days. And the rest on the plateau where they'd spent the night wasn't even six or seven hours ago.

Maybe, it occurred to her suddenly, they'd lost time in some way when they entered this other world by crossing the fog, or even earlier, when they'd passed the stone watchers. Had they in truth traveled not just a few seconds but several hours through the layer of mist?

Nonsense, she told herself, and *"Nonsense!"* said the Flowing Queen in her mind. But somehow it seemed to Merle not entirely convincing either time.

After she'd limbered up her legs and her knees would again bear the featherlight weight of her body, she began to search the tents. Vermithrax begged her to be careful, while he sniffed the rifles and rooted through the chests with nose and paws. Even the Queen warned her to be careful, which really was something totally new.

Ultimately they found little that would be useful to

them. In one of the undamaged tents Merle found a thin leather band on which dangled a dried chicken claw as a pendant. At the top, sticking out of the severed limb, were several sinews like the wires of a puppet. When Vermithrax challenged her to pull on them, the chicken's claw closed, as if all at once there were life in it. Merle almost dropped the hideous thing in terror.

"Yucky." She let go of the claw and only held on to the leather thong.

"*It is a good luck charm,*" the Queen explained.

"Oh, yes?"

"*The inhabitants of the Czarist kingdom carry them. You do know that they are under the protection of the Baba Yaga?*"

Merle nodded, although she was aware that the Queen couldn't see it, only feel it at the most.

On the other side of the plateau, Vermithrax rooted through another chest with his front paws and poked around in it with his nose.

"*What do you know about the Baba Yaga?*"

"Not much. She's a witch. Or something like that."

The Queen was clearly smirking. "*A witch. A goddess. The people have seen very much in her. It is a fact that she has protected the Czarist kingdom, as I*"—she stopped, as if pain and guilt welled up in her and in some strange way rubbed off on Merle—"*as I protected Venice.*"

"Do you know her? Personally, I mean."

"No. She is not like me. At least I guess that. But what I want to say is this: Since time immemorial the Baba Yaga has had a certain form with which the people identify her. An old woman who lives in a little house—but this house stands on two chicken legs as tall as trees and can run around on them like a living creature."

Merle swung the pendant. "Then this thing is a sort of symbol?"

"It is. The way the Christians wear a cross to protect themselves from evil, so the inhabitants of the Czarist kingdom wear such a chicken foot—at least those who believe in the protection of the Baba Yaga."

"But that would mean—"

"That these are the remains of an expedition that was sent here by the Czar."

Merle thought over what that might mean. The armies of the Egyptians had overrun the entire world within a few decades—with the exception of Venice and the Czarist kingdom. However, there had never been contact between the two, at least none of which the common folk had learned. Nevertheless, the sight of the destroyed camp filled her with a remarkable feeling of loss, as if an important opportunity had been missed here. How did it look in the Czarist kingdom? How did people there defend themselves against the attacks of the Empire? And, not least, how did the Baba Yaga protect them? All questions to which they perhaps could find answers here, if someone didn't prevent them.

"Do you think they're dead?" Merle directed the question to both the Queen and Vermithrax.

The lion trotted over placidly. "The tent wasn't slit with a knife, at any rate. The edges are too rough and frayed for that."

"Claws?" Merle asked, and she guessed the answer already. Gooseflesh crept along her arms.

Vermithrax nodded. "There are traces of them on the ground."

"They scratched the *rock*?" Merle's voice sounded as though she'd swallowed something much too large.

"I'm afraid so," said the lion. "Pretty deeply, too."

Merle's eyes slid to the obsidian lion's paws and inspected the ground. His own claws left no traces in the stone. The creatures the Czar's expedition had encountered—what kind of claws must they have?

Then she knew. The answer popped up from her memory like the head of a sleeper who unexpectedly awakens. "Lilim," she said immediately.

"*Lilim?*" the Queen asked.

"When Professor Burbridge discovered Hell sixty years ago and encountered its inhabitants for the first time, he gave them this name. The teacher in the orphanage told us about them. Burbridge named them after the children of Lilith, the first wife of Adam."

Vermithrax cocked his head. "A human legend?"

Merle nodded. "Perhaps the oldest of all. I'm surprised you don't know it."

"Every people and every race has its own myths and stories about its origin." The obsidian lion sounded a little offended. "You don't know the old lion legends, either."

"*I know who Adam was,*" said the Queen. "*But I have never heard of Lilith.*"

"Adam and Lilith were the first humans God created."

"*I thought the woman was named Eve.*"

"Eve came later. The first time, God created Adam and Lilith, man and woman. They were alone in Paradise and were supposed to have children together, to people the world with their descendants. Anyway, they were the first living creatures at all."

Vermithrax growled something, and Merle looked inquiringly at him.

"That's typical of you humans again," he said crossly. "You always believe you are the first and best. The first stone lions had been there for a long time before that."

"That's what *your* legends say," Merle retorted, grinning.

"Of course."

"Then we aren't likely to find out which is the truth, are we? Not now, not here, and probably never at all."

Vermithrax was forced to agree.

"All the myths of origins tell the truth," said the Queen mysteriously. *"Each in its own special way."*

Merle continued, "So Lilith and Adam were destined to have children together. But whenever Lilith wanted to approach her husband, he drew back from her, filled with fear and disgust."

"Hah!" growled Vermithrax. "That certainly didn't happen to the first lions at all!"

"Anyway, Adam was afraid of Lilith, and finally God lost patience and banned Lilith from the Garden of Eden. Filled with anger and disappointment, she wandered through the desert regions outside Paradise, and there she met creatures that had nothing in common with Adam, creatures that were more alien and more gruesome and more terrifying than anything we can imagine."

"I can imagine something like that," said the lion, with a side glance at the claw marks in the rock.

"Lilith bred with the creatures and was supposed to have borne them children that surpassed even their fathers in monstrosity—the Lilim. In the legends they are the demons and monsters who wander through the forests and deserts and over the bare rocks of the mountains."

"And Professor Burbridge knew these stories," said the Queen.

"Of course. When he needed a name for the inhabitants for his papers and his scientific works, he called them the Lilim."

"Well, good," said Vermithrax. "Our Czarist friends also met a few of them. Don't you think we should avoid that?"

"*Vermithrax is right,*" replied the Queen. "*We had better leave. We are safer in the air.*" But there was something in the way she emphasized that last sentence that alarmed Merle even more deeply. For who actually said that the Lilim had no wings?

"Just a moment." She ran over to the chests that the lion had already searched. Out of the corner of her eye she'd seen a few items that were useless to Vermithrax but that she could use. She found a small knife in a leather sheath, no longer than her hand, and put it in the pocket of her dress along with the magic mirror. In addition, she discovered several tin boxes with food rations, stone-hard strips of dried meat, zwieback, a couple of water bottles, and even a few cookies. She packed them all in a small leather knapsack she'd found in one of the tents and strapped it onto her back. While she was doing that, she chewed on a piece of dried meat, which was as hard as tree bark and as tough as shoe soles, but nonetheless, she managed to swallow the shreds. In the past few days she'd had very little to eat; the rations of the Czarist expedition looked more than suitable to her.

"Hurry up," Vermithrax called to her as she was fastening the straps of her new knapsack.

"I'm coming," she said—and suddenly she had a feeling of being watched.

Her fingers let go of the leather straps, and—despite the omnipresent warmth—she shivered. Her hair was standing on end. Her heart skipped a beat once, then began racing again, so suddenly that it almost hurt.

Confused, she looked toward the back of the plateau, to the rock wall, then over at the tents and at both openings to the paths that led up and down from there. Nothing moved. There was no one there. Only Vermithrax, who stood at the edge of the cliff, tapping impatiently on the rock with one claw.

"What is wrong?" asked the Queen.

"Don't you feel anything?"

"Your fear masks everything."

"Hurry up," Vermithrax called. He still hadn't noticed anything.

Merle dashed toward him. She didn't know what she was running from, or if there was even a reason for her fear. She had almost reached Vermithrax when a piercing, screeching sound, drawn out and painful, made her whirl around.

At first she didn't see anything. Not really. But there was *something,* a movement perhaps, a change near the place where she'd shouldered the knapsack.

"Merle!"

The rock quivered under her feet as Vermithrax sped to

her, much faster and more nimbly than she would have thought possible, a black flash of obsidian who was suddenly behind her, scooping her from the floor with one of his wings and letting her slide down a ramp of stone feathers.

"Lilim," sounded in her head, and it took a moment before she realized that it wasn't her own thought but a shout from the Flowing Queen.

Vermithrax began to lift off. An instant later they were rushing out over the edge of the cliff, still in a leap, not in flight. They dropped a good yard down into emptiness before the wings of the weighty lion stabilized their position in the air, at the same time bearing them away from the abandoned camp of the Czarist expedition and the spirit of death enveloping the empty tents.

Merle started to look around, but the Queen said sharply, *"Do not do that!"*

Of course she did it anyway.

The rock wall had come alive. Then Merle realized that it wasn't the stone itself that had begun moving but something that had perhaps been there the entire time, had been lurking, or was just now creeping out of some invisible cracks and holes like the scarab swarms of the Empire.

The entire surface of what she'd taken for mere rock had dissolved and now streamed from all sides toward the rock ledge, a concentration and agglomeration so strange and bizarre that she couldn't think of any human or animal motion like it. It wasn't like the crawling of insects, even if that perhaps came closest; it was more as if the dark scales and shells billowed in grotesque zigzags on the plateau, apparently without order, completely chaotic, and yet so purposefully that within seconds the ring enclosed the rock ledge.

Under the rippling top surface, which consisted of a host of man-sized bodies, Merle saw more and more tilted strands and structures that might be limbs, many times broken and angled, spiderlike and yet so utterly different. As they moved, they left behind a track of deep scars in the rock where they'd dug in their invisible claws and slashed the stone, tangled paths like a relief by a mad sculptor.

The dark flood poured over the edges of the plateau from all directions, also down from the overhang, and buried the tents and the chests under them. The creatures concealed themselves behind their stony shells, or what Merle took to be shells, and yet any brief flash of fangs or claws was enough to fill her with sheer terror.

Faster and faster, Vermithrax hurried out into the emptiness, away from what was taking place behind them. But Merle still saw the plateau sink completely under the assault of the Lilim, swallowed up, like a stone inexorably pulled down into a vortex of quicksand.

As if by itself, Merle's hand crept into the pocket where she kept the mirror. She absently pushed her fingers through the surface, deeper into the warmth of the magic place behind it. Very briefly she thought she heard a whisper, a voice—of the phantom trapped in there?—then she thrust her arm in up to the elbow, and finally she again felt the hand that grasped hers from the other side and stroked her fingers, gently reassuring her.

4

THE ENCLAVE

THE SKY HUNG GRAY AND HEAVY OVER VENICE, foretelling the rain that would soon be pelting onto the palazzos and canals. A cutting wind, much too cool for this time of year, was blowing in from the north and whistling down the crooked streets, across deserted piazzas and the promenades along the banks of the islands. It swirled up fliers that the indefatigable resisters had distributed a few days before, after the appearance of the messenger from Hell and his offer to protect the Venetians from the armies of the Empire. The fliers were full of slogans, slogans against the city councillors and the Pharaoh and anyone else who could be blamed for the desperate situation, slogans that might have put them in prison in other times, most certainly in the pillory. But today no one cared about that anymore. Fear held all Venice under its spell, so absolutely, so hopelessly, that even the soldiers of the City Guard forgot to arrest troublemakers and insurgents.

In the very heart of this rebellion, in the secret hideout of the rebels—the enclave, as Dario had called the building— Serafin was eating breakfast.

He wasn't doing it very calmly, naturally, but not in a hurry, either, for he knew he could do nothing but wait. They would call him sooner or later and take him to their leader, the master of the enclave. Neither Dario nor any of the others had called the leader of the rebellion by name— obviously a precautionary measure. And yet the others' mysteriousness made Serafin more uneasy than he was willing to admit.

The palazzo lay in the center of Venice, hardly more than a stone's throw from a half dozen famous buildings and places. And yet there was an aura of solitude around it—solitude a little too intense for it not to be magical, thought Serafin.

The night before, on the way here, he and his three escorts had encountered traces of the invasion that was beginning all over Venice. On several canal banks they'd found the empty metal shells in which the mummy soldiers had penetrated the labyrinth of watery streets. They discovered no trace of the soldiers themselves, but they all realized that there was no going back now. The mummies were roaming through the streets, singly or in small groups, spreading fear and horror and completing the taking of the city from within. Here and there Serafin and the others had heard loud voices in the distance, also screams. Once they'd caught the sound of the clash of steel on the other side of a block of houses, but when they arrived they found only corpses, which Serafin identified as members of the Thieves' Guild.

No one understood very well what the Pharaoh had in mind with this sort of attack. His war galleys and sun-barks lay in sight of the quays of the lagoon, and it would have been easy to send soldiers on land all around the main island.

Serafin guessed that the Pharaoh was only trying to rattle the Venetians. But the lagoon dwellers could scarcely be further rattled after more than three decades of siege. And if it were pure cruelty? The macabre fun of beginning the invasion small, in order to then drive the attack to high pitch in a storm of fire and steel?

Serafin didn't understand it all, and he hoped that the master of the enclave had some answers ready for his questions.

The room into which Tiziano had led him was on the second floor of the palazzo. As with most of the old palaces, the ground floor was empty. At one time, when all these buildings had still belonged to the rich merchant families of the city, there had been merchandise and goods stored there below, in unornamented halls that every few years would be flooded by *acqua alta,* Venice's famed high waters.

But today, after so many years of isolation, there was hardly any trade in Venice, and the little that remained made no one rich. Most of the well-to-do families had fled to the mainland long ago, right at the beginning of the war, never supposing that there they would be helplessly delivered to the mummy armies and scarab swarms. No one could have foreseen that the power of the Flowing Queen would protect the city, and it was a malicious irony of fate that those who had enough money to flee were the first to fall victim to the Egyptians.

The windows and doors of the empty ground floor were walled up with large stones, apparently long before anyone ever even thought of a resurrection of the Pharaoh. The rebels had not settled into an abandoned building. Serafin assumed that the leader of the rebellion had been living here for a long time already. Perhaps a nobleman. Or even a merchant, one of the few who were still left.

Serafin shoved the last piece of bread into his mouth as the door of the bare room opened. Tiziano told him to come with him.

Serafin followed the former apprentice mirror maker through corridors and suites, up a staircase, and under an archway. He didn't see another soul the entire time. It seemed as though all were strictly forbidden to enter the apartments of the master of the enclave. But at the same time, Serafin had the feeling that the atmosphere of the corridors and high rooms had altered, a scarcely noticeable shift of reality to something different, confusing. It wasn't that the light changed, or the smell—everything here smelled moldy and of damp stone—no, it was the way his surroundings *felt*, as if he were perceiving with a new sensory organ that had only been waiting to finally be activated.

At Tiziano's bidding he stopped before a double door, almost three times as tall as he was.

"Wait here," said Tiziano. "You'll be called in." He turned to go.

Serafin grabbed his shoulder. "Where are you going?"

"Back to the others."

"You aren't staying here?"

"No."

Serafin looked mistrustfully from Tiziano to the door, then back again. "This isn't some trap or something?" He felt a little foolish as he voiced this suspicion, but he couldn't forget his old quarrel with Dario. He believed his—former?—archenemy was capable of any meanness.

"What would be the sense of that?" asked Tiziano.

"We could just have left you to the mummies, couldn't we? Things would have taken care of themselves."

Serafin still hesitated, then he nodded slowly. "Sorry. That was ungrateful."

Tiziano grinned at him. "Dario can be quite a pain, huh?"

Serafin couldn't help smiling back. "You and Boro, you've noticed that?"

"Even Dario has his good sides. A few of them. Otherwise he wouldn't be here."

"That probably goes for all of us, I guess."

Tiziano gave an encouraging nod toward the door. "Just wait." With that, he finally turned and walked briskly back the way they had come. The thought sizzled through Serafin's head that he'd never find his way back alone. The interior of the enclave was a first-class maze.

The right half of the door was swung open by an invisible hand, and at once he was enveloped in something light and soft, which played around his body like a hundred gentle fingers, light as a feather, almost bodiless. Surprised, he took a step backward. It was only a filmy silk curtain that a draft was blowing against him.

"Enter," said a voice. A woman's voice.

Serafin obeyed and pushed the curtain aside, very carefully, because he had the feeling that the delicate tissue could tear between his fingers like spiderwebs. Behind that, barely six feet away, a wall of curtains bellied out, all of the same material and in the same light yellow, which reminded him of the color of beach sand. He remembered to close the door behind him before he began to move. Then he ventured deeper into that labyrinth of silk.

He passed one curtain after another, until he gradually lost all orientation, even though he'd only been going straight the entire time. How far behind him was the door? A hundred yards, or only ten, fifteen?

Gradually he was able to make out shapes behind the silk, angled silhouettes, pieces of furniture perhaps. At the same time the damp, moldy smell of Venice was overlaid with an exotic scent, a whole explosion of smells. They reminded him of the strange spices he'd once stolen from a merchant's storeroom, years before.

On the other side of the curtain lay another world.

The ground was strewn with sand, so high that his boots sank into it without hitting any firm ground. The ceiling was hung with lengths of dark blue material, which provided a sharp contrast to the surrounding lightness, like an evening sky over the desert. And then he realized that this was exactly the impression that all this was supposed to awaken: the illusion of a desert landscape, completely artificial, and yet so different from anything that one could ever find in Venice. There were no painted dunes, no statues of camels or Bedouins; nothing here was real, and still it all seemed as convincing as an actual visit to the desert—at least to Serafin, who'd never left the lagoon.

Several islands of soft cushions were piled up in the center of this wondrous place. The spicy smell came from bowls, from which hair-thin columns of smoke were curling up. Between the cushions was a pedestal of coarse sandstone and on it, heavy and blocky, stood a round water basin of the same material. The surface was a good three feet in diameter and was stirring slightly. Behind the basin stood a woman, only her upper body visible. She had thrust her right arm into the water up to the elbow. At first Serafin thought she was stirring it, but then he saw that she was holding her arm completely still.

She looked up and smiled. "Serafin," she said, and he found it quite astonishing how melodious his name sounded when such a creature spoke it.

She was beautiful, perhaps the most beautiful woman that he'd ever seen—and as the messenger boy of Umberto, who wove magic fabrics for Venice's noblewomen, he'd encountered many a beauty. She had smooth, raven-black hair, so long that the ends disappeared behind the edge of the sandstone vessel. Her slender body was clothed in skintight material, napped like fine fur and of the same yellow as the curtains. Large, hazelnut brown eyes inspected him. Her lips were full and dark red, although he was certain that she wore no makeup. The skin of her face and her left hand, resting on the edge of the basin, were dark, not black like one of the Moors, of whom there were several in Venice, but tanned dark by the sun.

And then, in a flash, he knew.

She was an Egyptian.

He knew it with absolute certainty, before she directed another word to him or could introduce herself. The leader of the rebellion against the Egyptians was an *Egyptian.*

"Have no fear," she said, when she noticed that he recoiled a step. "You are in safety. No one here will do anything bad to you." A spark of regret burned in her eyes as she took her right arm out of the water and laid it in front of her on the stone rim. Neither hand nor arm was wet. There was no trace of water beading on her skin or on the strange material of her clothing.

"Who are you?" He had the feeling he was stammering terribly. He had every reason to.

"Lalapeya," said the woman. "I don't believe you know the language from which this name comes."

"Egyptian?" He felt brave, downright daring, when he said this one word.

Her laugh was very clear, almost melodic. "Egyptian? Oh no, absolutely not. This name was already old when the first pharaohs mounted their golden thrones many thousands of years ago."

And with that she came out from behind the basin in a strange, flowing movement that disconcerted Serafin and confused him—until he saw her legs.

She had four of them.

The legs of a lioness. The *lower body* of a lioness.

Serafin started back so violently that he got tangled up in one of the silken curtains, lost his balance, and fell over backward, pulling a torrent of yellow silk with him.

When he had finally freed himself, she was standing directly in front of him. If he stretched out an arm, he could touch one of her paws, the soft yellow fur that covered her and that he'd just taken for a tight-fitting dress.

"You— You are . . ."

"Certainly not a mermaid."

"A sphinx!" escaped him. "A sphinx of the Pharaoh!"

"The last part is not true. I have not met the Pharaoh, ever, and I regret it most deeply that some of my people serve him."

Serafin tried to get to his feet, but he only partially succeeded, and when he again pulled back from her, one foot dragged the pulled-down curtain with him, two, three paces away.

The lion paws carried the sphinx after him in an elegant motion. "Please, Serafin. I've shown you so that you know whom you're dealing with. But it wasn't urgently necessary."

"What— What do you mean?"

She smiled, and it made her look so pretty that it almost pained him to see the animal part of her body at the same time. "What do I mean? Oh, Serafin! *This,* of course."

At the sound of the words, her image blurred before his eyes. At first Serafin thought that the sand was billowing up from the ground, but then he realized that it was more than that.

She wasn't only blurred in his perception—her entire body seemed to dissolve for one second and reconstitute itself, not a flowing transition but an explosion-like whirl, as she dispersed in a cloud of tiny little parts, then in the same breath put herself back together as something new. Something different.

Her face and the slender upper body remained unchanged, but now they no longer grew out of the body of a lion but continued naturally into narrow hips and long, brown legs. The legs of a woman.

Her fur had vanished. Without replacement.

"Allow me?" Naked, she bent over, fished up the curtain at Serafin's feet, and with a lightning twirl, covered her nakedness. The yellow settled around her figure like a dress; no one would have guessed that the stuff had just been hanging from the ceiling as a curtain; on her it looked as natural and perfectly fitting as the most expensive fabric from Umberto's workshop.

Serafin had tried to turn his eyes away, but she left him no time for that. Instead, the image of her completed body kept shining before his eyes as if it had burned into his retina. Like light spots after one has looked at the sun for too long.

"Serafin?"

"Uhh . . . yes?"

"Is this better?"

He looked down her, down to her narrow feet, which stood half covered in soft sand. "It doesn't change anything," he said, having to force out every word. "You're a sphinx, no matter what shape you assume."

"Of course. But now you don't need to be afraid of my claws anymore." Pure roguishness gleamed in her eyes.

He made a great effort to ignore her scornful undertone. "What are you doing here?"

"I lead the counterattack."

"Against the Pharaoh?" He laughed and hoped that it sounded as humorless as it was meant to. "With a few children?"

She rubbed her right foot over her left; he almost believed she felt the embarrassment she intended to convey. Only almost. "Are *you* a child, Serafin?" The way she raised her eyes was a bit too coquettish to be accidental.

"You know exactly what I mean."

"And you know, I think, what *I* mean." All at once her tone became sharper, the emphasis harder. "Dario and the others might be just fifteen, sixteen, or seventeen years old"—with which she indirectly confirmed what he already suspected: that there were no grown-ups among the rebels—"but they are skillful and quick. And the Pharaoh will underestimate them. That is perhaps our strongest weapon: Amenophis's vanity."

"You said that you don't know him."

"Not in his current form. But I know how he was earlier, in his first life."

"How long ago was that?"

"Far more than three thousand years."

"You are *three thousand* years old?"

She laughed again, but only briefly. "A few thousand more or less."

Serafin pressed his lips together and said nothing more.

Lalapeya continued: "Amenophis's vanity and arrogance are the reason I've only chosen boys like you. Do you think I'd have found no men larger and stronger than anyone here in this house? But it would have been pointless. The Egyptians will put every grown man under arrest today and deport them afterward. A handful of children, on the other hand . . . Now, I think the Pharaoh will first grapple with the more important things. What color to make his suite here in Venice, for example. At least that is what the earlier Amenophis would have done."

"You really intend to fight the Egyptians with Dario and the others?" She might be right in what she said, but nonetheless he believed she was making it too simple.

"I am no warrior."

Yes, he thought, that's obvious, or is it? Then he remembered her razor-sharp lion's claws and shuddered.

"But," she went on, "we have no choice. We must fight, for that is the only language Amenophis understands."

"If only a fraction of what they say about the Empire is true, the Pharaoh can snuff out Venice in a few minutes. What are a few rebels supposed to do to him?"

"You shouldn't believe everything you hear about the power of the Egyptians. Some of it is true—but some also depends on skillfully spread rumors and on the power of illusion. The priests of Horus are masters of deception."

"It's hopeless in spite of all that. I've seen the mummy soldiers. I've seen how they fight."

The sphinx nodded. "And how they die."

"Through luck, nothing else."

Lalapeya expelled a great sigh. "No one here is thinking of going against the mummy soldiers in the field. At least not the way you imagine it."

"What, then?"

"First I must know if you'll help us." She took a step toward him, on the soft feet of a dancer. It was impossible to resist her charm.

"Why me?"

"Why you?" She smiled again, and her voice sounded a little gentler. "I think you underestimate what a reputation you have. A master of the Thieves' Guild at thirteen, the youngest Venice has ever seen. No one can climb up a housefront faster or more skillfully. No one can slip past any guard more quickly. And no one is braver when it comes to carrying out a task at which all before him have failed."

Lalapeya's words made him uncomfortable. She didn't need to flatter him, and that meant that she was appealing to his honor. Her words also came very close to the truth. And yet all that lay an eternity ago, in another life.

"I was thirteen then," he said. "And today—" He paused. "And today," he went on, "I'm no longer what you said. I left the Guild. I no longer steal. I'm an apprentice to the master weaver Umberto, that's all."

"Nevertheless, you stole the Flowing Queen from the Egyptians."

He stared at her, wide-eyed. "You know about that?"

"Of course." But she didn't provide an explanation, and that made him suspicious again. When she noticed, she quickly added, "You and the girl, Merle."

"What do you know about Merle?"

Lalapeya hesitated. "She has left Venice."

"On a stone lion, yes, I know," he said impatiently. "But where is she now? Is she all right?"

"Nothing has happened to her," said the sphinx. "More than that I don't know."

He had the strong feeling that she was lying, and he made every effort to let her feel it. At the same time, he could see that her decision was firm and she wouldn't tell him more. Not at the moment. If he were to remain for a while, however, he might succeed in getting more out of her, about Merle and the Queen and—

He winced when he realized that he'd fallen into her trap. He'd swallowed the bait.

"I'll help you," he said, "if you tell me more about Merle."

Lalapeya seemed to weigh the offer. "I'd prefer that you did it because you agreed to the necessity."

He shook his head. "Only for Merle."

The sphinx's eyes, her brown, profound eyes, moved over his face, checking to see if he spoke the truth. He was nervous, although he knew that she'd find nothing different; he meant every word just as he'd spoken it. For Merle he'd even go to Egypt, if he had to, and thumb his nose at the Pharaoh. And perhaps break his skull on the best mummy soldier of all. But after all, it was the attempt that counted. Somehow.

"Are you in love with Merle?" asked Lalapeya after a while.

"That's none of your business." The words were already out before he realized what he was saying. "And anyway it has nothing to do with this," he added hastily.

"You needn't be ashamed of it."

He was about to reply but then swallowed the answer and asked instead, "Do you know Merle?"

"Perhaps."

"Oh, come on—what kind of an answer is *that*?"

"The truth. I'm not sure if I know her." Her eyes showed a flash of shock when she realized that possibly she'd betrayed too much. With noticeable control, she said, "I'm not accustomed to being interrogated." But her smile showed that she wasn't angry with him.

Serafin freed himself from her look and walked a few steps back and forth, as if he were weighing whether he really wanted to remain here any longer. His decision had already been made long before. Where could he have gone? Umberto's weaving workshop stood empty, the master had fled God knew where. Serafin had long ago turned his back on his former friends from the Thieves' Guild. And back to Arcimboldo, Eft, and Junipa? Something told him that maybe this would be the right way. But could he somehow protect Junipa from Lord Light better if he joined the sphinx and her odd crew?

Finally he came to a stop. "You must tell me what you have in mind."

"We will not make war on the Egyptians. That would in fact be presumptuous and suicidal. The war will be directed against Amenophis himself."

"Against the Pharaoh?"

When she nodded, the strange desert light flickered over her black hair like tiny flames.

"You want to kill *him*?" asked Serafin, aghast. "An assassination?"

"That would be one way. But it wouldn't be enough. Amenophis isn't an independent ruler. Also, he's ruled by those who have called him back to life. At the moment, anyway."

"By the priests?"

"By the priests of Horus, yes. For centuries they had lost their meaning, had shrunk to a secret cult long forgotten by almost everyone. Until they awakened the Pharaoh in the pyramid of Amun-Ka-Re to new life. With that they gave new strength to a weak, vegetating country. A new leader. A new identity. That and their magic were the two means with which they created the Empire. They're the ones who pull the strings, not Amenophis."

"But that makes everything even more hopeless."

"Where the Pharaoh is, there also are the heads of the priesthood, above all Seth, his vizier and grand master of the Horus cult."

"In all seriousness, you intend for us to go to Heliopolis, into the city of the Pharaoh, and there . . . *eliminate* . . . not only him but also his vizier and perhaps a whole legion of his priests?" He emphasized the word *eliminate* as if it were the idea of a small child, for that was how sensible he thought this whole crazy idea was.

"Not to Heliopolis," said the sphinx very quietly. "Amenophis and Seth will soon be here. Here in Venice. And if I'm not deceived in everything, they will establish their quarters in the Doge's Palace."

Serafin gasped. "The Pharaoh is coming here?"

"Certainly. He won't miss the moment of his greatest

triumph. This is not only a victory over a single city—it is a victory over the Flowing Queen and all she stood for. His triumph over the past and also over his own death. Aside from the Czarist kingdom, there's no one else in the world who can withstand him."

Serafin rubbed a hand over his forehead and desperately tried to keep pace with the sphinx's explanations. "Even if it were true that the Pharaoh is coming to Venice . . . to the Doge's Palace, for all I care . . . what would that change? He'll be hidden behind an army of bodyguards. Behind his mummy soldiers. And, don't forget, behind the magic of Seth and the other priests."

Lalapeya nodded slowly, and her smile was as loving as if she were speaking with a young kitten. "That's why I want you to help us."

"I should break into the Doge's Palace?" Serafin rolled his eyes. "While the *Pharaoh* is there?"

The sphinx didn't have to answer him. He already knew that was exactly what her plan was. But she said something else that touched him more deeply than any slogan or any promise: "For Merle."

5

In the Ear of the Herald

There was no day in Hell. And no night.

After the long descent, Vermithrax had set down on a rock shaped like a hatbox; a human could have climbed down the steep walls only with appropriate equipment. Of course they all—the obsidian lion as well as Merle and the Flowing Queen—knew that basically it made no difference where they camped if they had to deal with opponents like the Lilim.

"Maybe down here there aren't creatures like those up there," said Merle, without great conviction.

"Possibly a few of the most dangerous ones live up

there, as guards of the entrance, so to speak." The Queen's voice was firm, her enthusiasm undampened. Nevertheless, Merle had the feeling that she was only trying to bolster her courage and didn't completely believe what she said herself.

At least they agreed that there must be a great number of different kinds of Lilim. The messenger Lord Light had sent to the Venetians had had nothing in common with the creatures in the rock wall.

"Which doesn't mean, however, that the others are less terrible or fast." The obsidian lion licked his wings with his stone tongue. "On the contrary, perhaps we've only met the most harmless so far."

"Thanks a lot, Vermithrax," said Merle bitterly, and she had the feeling that the Queen was thinking exactly the same thing. "A joker like you is enormously helpful at the moment."

The lion didn't even look up. "I'm only saying what I think."

Until then Merle had been sitting cross-legged on the rock beside Vermithrax. Now, with a sigh, she let herself sink back until she felt the smooth stone at her back. She crossed her arms behind her head and looked up, there where, in her world, the sky had been.

An expanse of speckled red spread before her eyes, at first still resembling a layer of clouds in the light of the setting sun: a rock ceiling that extended infinitely in all directions, a few thousand yards over them. The network of glowing red veins that had run through the walls of the rock shaft also appeared in the interior of Hell in dirty orange.

Anyway, *Hell* . . . the term seemed to Merle to be ever more unsuitable for the place they'd found at the end of the shaft. A desolate rock landscape formed the bottom of this underground kingdom—at least the part where they were—and, like the ceiling, it was shot through in many places with glowing veins, some as fine as hairs, others as broad as Vermithrax's legs. The stone felt warm, but not really hot anywhere, and the wind blowing down here smelled of tar and the strange sweetness that Merle had noticed at the edge of the abyss.

The ceiling toward which she was gazing likewise consisted of rock, but for the human eye, its great height reduced the structure to spots of light and dark, dipped in the shimmering red of the fire veins.

Merle didn't really know what to think about all this. On the one hand, the environment was impressive and fear-inspiring because of its immeasurable size; but on the other hand, she told herself that this was nothing but a gigantic cavern in the bowels of the earth, perhaps a whole system of caverns. It had nothing to do with the Hell talked about in the Bible. However, and this was the catch, this might change suddenly as soon as they actually bumped into more Lilim—and they expected to at any time.

Even now, at rest, Vermithrax was alert, his body tense.

However, Merle now realized that Professor Burbridge had called this place Hell only for lack of a better name. He'd pulled the myth over the reality like a mask, to make it more understandable for the general public.

"Vermithrax?"

The obsidian lion turned from his wings and looked over at her. "Hmm?"

"Those creatures, up there on the rock wall, they looked as if they were made of stone."

The lion growled agreement. "As if the rock wall itself had come to life."

"Isn't that a strange coincidence?"

"You mean because *I* am of stone?"

She rolled onto her stomach and supported her chin in both hands to be able to look Vermithrax in the eyes. "Yes, somehow. I mean, I know that you have nothing to do with them. But yet, it is strange, isn't it?"

The lion sat up so that he could look at Merle but keep his eyes on the area around the rock at the same time. "I've already thought about that."

"And?"

"We simply know too little about the Lilim."

"How much do you lions know about yourselves? For instance, how come your mane is stone, but all the same it feels soft to the touch? And why does your tongue move although you're made of obsidian?"

"It's stone inspirited with a soul," he said, as if that were answer enough. When he saw that Merle wouldn't be content with that, he went on, "It's stone, but it's also flesh or hair. It has the structure and the strength and the hardness of stone, but there's also life within it, and that changes everything. That's the only explanation I can give you. There have never been scientists among us lions who've investigated all these things. We're not like you humans. We can accept things without taking them apart and snatching the last secret out of them."

Merle thought these words over while she waited for the Queen to express herself. But the voice inside her was silent.

"And the Lilim?" Merle asked finally. "Do you think they're also made of stone with a soul?"

"To me, those creatures didn't look as if they possessed a soul. But there are men who say the same thing about us lions. So then, who am I to judge the Lilim?"

"That sounds quite wise."

Vermithrax laughed. "It isn't at all difficult to pass uncertainty off as wisdom. Your scholars and philosophers and priests have been doing that since you humans have existed." After a short pause he added, "The leaders of us lions too, by the way."

It was the first time Merle had heard him say something disparaging about other lions, and she had the feeling that it had cost him great effort. In fact, the lion folk differed much more from humans than she'd thought until now. Perhaps, she carried the thought further, the relationship of lions to Lilim was even closer than to humans. She wondered if this idea should frighten her, but she felt nothing but curiosity about it.

It came right down to the fact that *everything* down here frightened her somehow, even the rock on which she lay and the mysterious warmth that rose from inside it. She had the feeling it could explode at any moment, like the volcanoes she'd heard of. But she suppressed this uncomfortable thought too, like so many others.

"What should we do when we've found Lord Light?" She put the question to no one in particular. That was what had busied her on the long flight into the abyss, the question of the goal of her mission. Slowly her eyes traveled over the cheerless rock desert extending in all directions. The landscape didn't look as though anyone could live here voluntarily, certainly no prince or ruler like the mysterious Lord Light.

"The Queen must know that," said Vermithrax. He was master of the art of letting his voice sound completely indifferent, even if he was presumably as stirred up inside as Merle was herself.

"*We will ask him for help,*" said the Flowing Queen.

"I know that." Merle got to her feet, walked to the edge of the mesa, and let the warm, humid wind waft to her nose. Vermithrax called to her to be careful, but she had the feeling she had to sense the dangers of this environment with her own body in order to be sure that she wasn't dreaming it all.

The steep wall fell away at her feet, 175 to 200 feet deep, and Merle grew dizzy. Strangely, she felt that was almost a good feeling. A true, actual feeling.

"I know that we've come here to ask him for help," she said finally. "For Venice and for all the others. But how do we do that? I mean, what will he think when a girl on a flying lion appears before his throne and—"

"Who says he has a throne?"

"I thought he was a king."

"He rules over Hell," said the Queen patiently. *"But here below is rather different from the upper world."*

Merle couldn't take her eyes off the rough rock land. She saw no great difference from wildernesses she'd seen in drawings and engravings. A desert people like the Egyptians might feel quite comfortable down here.

Then a thought came to her, and it hit her like a blow in the face. "You *know* him!"

"No," said the Flowing Queen tonelessly.

"How do you know that he has no throne, then? That he isn't like other rulers?"

"Only a surmise." The Queen was seldom so tight-lipped.

"A surmise, eh?" Her voice now sounded reproachful and angry, so that even Vermithrax looked over at her in confusion. "That's why you knew so precisely where to find the entrance," Merle burst out. "And that down here everything is different from up above. . . . But there, for once, you were mistaken. It's not so different at all. For me, anyway, it looks like an ordinary grotto." She'd never seen a grotto with her own eyes, but that didn't matter now. She had no better argument.

"*This* grotto, *Merle, has an area that is probably as large as half the planet. Perhaps it is even much larger. And how else would you describe the Lilim if not as 'different'?*"

"But that wasn't what you meant before," Merle said with conviction. She'd had enough of being put down in each of her discussions. It was a remarkable feeling to argue with someone you couldn't look in the eye and whose voice wasn't real. "I don't understand why you aren't honest with me . . . with us."

Vermithrax was brushing his whiskers with his paw, but he wasn't missing a word. He could only guess at the course of the conversation from what Merle said.

Again she thought that it simply wasn't fair that only she could hear the Queen. And had to argue with her on her own.

"*I have heard rumors about Lord Light, things the mermaids have picked up. That is all.*"

"What sort of rumors?"

"*That he is no ordinary ruler. It is not about power with him.*"

"What else?"

"That I cannot tell you. I do not know."

"But you have a surmise."

The Queen was silent for a moment. Then she said, *"What can a ruler of an entire kingdom concern himself with, if not with power? And furthermore, how great could his influence over his subjects be then? The Lilim in the rock wall did not look as if they would take any orders out of pure humility."*

"So what does he concern himself with?" Merle asked doggedly.

"With knowledge, I think. He likes ruling this world, but above all, I think, he investigates it."

"Investigates? But—"

A loud exclamation from the lion interrupted her. "Merle! Over there!"

She whirled around and almost lost her balance. For an instant the edge of the steep cliff was dangerously close, the rocks leaped toward Merle's feet. Then she caught herself again, turned hastily away from the drop, and followed Vermithrax's look with her own eyes.

At first she detected nothing at all, only empty red over the breadth of the wasteland. Then she realized that the lion's predator's eyes were sharper than her own. Whatever he'd caught sight of must still be beyond her range of sight.

But it wasn't long until she saw it. And whatever it was, it was coming nearer.

"What is that?" she exclaimed, breathless and suddenly oppressed with a flood of horrible pictures; fantasies of flying Lilim, thousands of them, danced in her mind.

Yet it wasn't thousands, but only three. And although they were floating high over the rocks, they possessed no wings.

"Are they . . ."

"Heads," said Vermithrax. "Gigantic heads." And after a moment he added, "Of stone."

She shook her head, not because she doubted his words but because it was the only reaction that seemed appropriate. Heads of stone. High in the air. Of course.

But after a while she could see them for herself. She saw the heads coming nearer, and quite fast—faster than Vermithrax could fly, of that she was sure.

"Come on, mount!" bellowed the lion, and before she could think of a good argument against it, she was already leaping onto his back, curling her hands into his mane, bending over, and pressing her upper body firmly to his obsidian coat.

"What is he going to do?"

"What are you going to do?"

"Look at them. They aren't alive." Vermithrax's paws pushed off the rock, and seconds later they were already hovering three feet above the hatbox mesa.

"They are not alive," Merle repeated to herself and then added more loudly, "So what? What does that mean?"

"That means they aren't Lilim. At least, not dangerous ones."

"Oh, yes?"

"Wait," said the Queen. *"Perhaps he is right."*

"And if he isn't?"

She received no answer. She would probably not have heard it anyway, for now the three heads were close enough to see details.

They were human heads, without any doubt, and they were hewn out of stone. So high up in the air there were no fixed points by which to gauge their size, but Merle guessed that each was at least fifty yards high. Their faces were stiff and gray, the eyes open, but without pupils. The stone hair, formed like a helmet, lay close to the head and left the ears free. The powerful lips were open a crack, but what from afar Merle had thought was an entrance to the head's inside showed itself up close to be an illusion, which was supposed to create the impression that the heads were speaking.

Now they also heard voices.

Words streamed over the plain like a swarm of birds, fluttering and restless, a language that Merle had never heard in her life.

The heads were still about half a mile away and were approaching in an arrow formation, one head at the point, the two others behind and to the right and left.

"Those voices . . . is that *them*?"

"I don't know whether those are their voices, but

they're coming from inside them," said Vermithrax. Merle noticed that he had his ears pricked. Not only could he see better than she could, he also heard much more and was able to distinguish sounds and where they came from.

"What do you mean? They're not their voices?"

"Someone else is speaking out of them. They aren't alive. Their stone isn't—"

"Inspirited with a soul?"

"Precisely." Vermithrax fell silent and concentrated completely on his flight. Merle had thought they would flee from the heads, but the lion had until now kept himself still in the air at a point that lay straight across the flight path of the foremost stone head. To her boundless horror, she now realized that Vermithrax was turning— not away from the heads, but toward them. He actually was intending to fly into them.

"Vermithrax! What are you doing?"

The obsidian lion did not answer. Instead he made his wings fan up and down even faster, maneuvered himself a little farther to the left—and waited.

"What do you—"

"He is planning something."

"Oh?" Merle would probably have turned red with fury if her fear hadn't driven all the blood from her face. "They're coming right at us!"

The uncanny voices blared louder and louder over the wasteland and were echoed back from the rock walls and towers of stone. It seemed to Merle as if she were dangling in fireworks of strange words as a multitude of different sounds exploded around her like colored fountains of flame. Even if she'd had command of the strange language, she wouldn't have understood anything at all, so loud, so shrill were the syllables coming out of this nearest head. A piercing whistling started in Merle's ears before the heads came level with them.

Vermithrax shook his head, as if trying to drive the noise out of his sensitive ears. His muscles tensed. Abruptly he rushed forward to the front head, at the last moment laid himself on an angle, bellowed something incomprehensible to Merle—probably a warning to hold on especially tight—and dived through under the ridge of the right cheekbone. Merle saw the huge face rush by her like a wall of granite, too big to take in with one look, too fast to perceive more than the weight, the size, the sheer force of its speed.

She called Vermithrax's name, but the wind tore the syllables from her lips and the voices of the flying heads overwhelmed any sound.

So suddenly that her fingers gave way and her entire body was pulled backward, Vermithrax smashed his claws into the stone ear of the head and pulled himself along. At the same time his wings stopped beating, bent inward, and caught Merle before she could plunge down into the deep. The tips of the feathers pressed her down onto his back

with the force of a giant fist, while Vermithrax did his best
to absorb the brutal jolt that went through them both at
the first contact with the head.

Somehow he succeeded. Somehow he found a grip.
And then they were sitting in the ear of the gigantic head
and rushing with insane speed across the rocky country.

Merle needed a while before her breathing had grown
calm enough for her to be able to speak again. But even
then the thoughts flitted around in her head like moths
around a candle flame, wild and nervous, and she had
trouble giving them a clear direction, had trouble grasping
what had just happened. Finally she clenched a fist and
struck Vermithrax. He didn't seem to even feel it.

"Why?" she bellowed at him. "Why did you do that?"

Vermithrax climbed over a stone bulge deeper into the
ear. It opened around them like a cave, rocky, dark, a deep
funnel. Astonishingly, the noise here inside was dulled; for
one thing, because it was now only a single voice that they
heard, for here they were shut away from the racket of the
two other heads; for another, because the voice of the head
was directed to the outside.

Vermithrax let Merle slide from his back and lay down
between two stone bulges, exhausted. He panted, his long
tongue hanging down to his powerful paws.

"The probability is fifty-fifty," he brought out between
two deep intakes of breath.

"What probability?" Merle was still angry, but gradually

her anger was overwhelmed by relief that in spite of everything they were still alive.

"Either the head is taking us to Lord Light, or it's taking us in exactly the opposite direction." Vermithrax pulled in his tongue and put his head down on his front paws. Merle became conscious for the first time how very much he'd exhausted himself with the leap to the flying head and just how closely they'd slid past death.

"This head here," said Vermithrax wearily, "is announcing something. I don't understand the words it's broadcasting, but it's always the same over and over again, as if it had a message. Perhaps it's a kind of herald."

"A message from Lord Light to his people?"

"Possibly," said the Flowing Queen. *"Vermithrax could be right."*

"What else?" asked the lion.

Merle rolled her eyes. "How should I know? Down here everything is different. These things could be who knows what!" As she spoke, she looked around the stone cave. It seemed so incredible: They actually had a firm seat in a gigantic ear.

"These heads are dead objects," said Vermithrax. "This is an important difference from the Lilim. Someone built them. And he did it for a certain purpose. Since Lord Light just happens to be the ruler of this place, it must have been he."

"And why fifty-fifty?"

"Possibly the head is on the way to its master because it's fulfilled a mission—or it's just begun its journey and is going away from Lord Light. One of the two."

"That means we can only wait, doesn't it?"

The lion nodded, which looked strangely clumsy, since his nose still lay on his paws. "Looks like it."

"What do you think?" Merle asked the Queen.

"I think he is right. We could probably wander through Hell for months without finding a trace of Lord Light. But this way we have at least a chance."

Merle gave a sigh, then she edged closer to the lion and stroked his nose. "But next time, you tell me beforehand, okay? I really want to know *why* you're almost killing us all."

The lion growled something—was it a yes?—and nestled his fist-sized nose into Merle's hand. Then he purred blissfully, thrashed his tail a couple of times, and closed his eyes.

Merle remained sitting beside him a moment longer, then she levered herself up on wobbly knees and climbed to the outer stone bulge of the giant ear.

Impressed, she looked down. The mournful landscape was flying along a thousand feet below them, so monotonous that there was nothing, but nothing at all, that she could have fastened her eyes on. Probably they were going too fast anyway. She doubted that Vermithrax could have kept up even half as much speed over a long period.

"What a desolate place!" she whispered with a groan. "Did Lord Light ever try to plant something here? I mean, to add a little color. A little variety."

"Why should he? Nothing lives here. At least nothing that could value such efforts. Or do you think that the Lilim in the camp up there would be happy about a few flowers?"

"You don't have to make it sound so ridiculous!"

"I do not mean to at all. Only, you must use other measures in this world. Other terms, other concepts."

Merle was silent and leaned back. But then a thought came to her that made her sit right up again.

"If these heads are something like flying machines, like the sunbarks of the Empire, then there must be someone in them, mustn't there? Someone who steers them!"

"We are alone."

"Are you sure?"

"I would feel it. And Vermithrax, too, I think."

Merle stretched out on the hard stone, observed the slumbering obsidian lion for a while, then looked out over the landscape of Hell. What a strange place! She tried to remember how Professor Burbridge had traveled through it, but she couldn't think of anything. After all, she hadn't really read any of his books; her teacher in the orphanage had talked about a few passages, but most of what she'd heard were synopses at second hand. Some descriptions, that was all. Now she regretted that she hadn't been more interested in it at the time.

On the other hand, she remembered quite clearly the dangers of Hell that Burbridge had recounted in his reports. Gruesome creatures, which waited for the unsuspecting behind every stone and every . . . yes, tree. She was certain that the talk had been of *trees*—trees of iron, with leaves like razor blades. Well, here anyway, in this part of Hell, there appeared to be no plants, either of iron or of wood.

She also recollected very well stories of barbarous creatures that moved in huge packs over the plain, landscapes that were wrapped in everlasting fire, mountains that folded their wings and flew away, and ships of human bones that sailed over the lava oceans of Hell. All those were pictures that had stuck in Merle's mind, so greatly had they impressed her at the time.

And now there weren't any of those.

She was disappointed and relieved at the same time. The Lilim in the rock wall were murderous enough for her taste, and she could perfectly happily do without hordes of cannibals and gigantic monsters. However, she felt a little cheated, as if now, after years, all the infernal pictures had turned out to be just wild stories.

But Hell was gigantic, and so there might be different landscapes and cultures down here, as there were up on the earth. If a traveler from another world were set down somewhere in the Sahara, he'd certainly be disappointed if people had told him beforehand about the splendid palaces of Venice and its many branching canals. Even more, he probably wouldn't be able to believe they existed at all.

Merle climbed back to the outermost swelling of stone and looked out at the rocky ground rushing past way below them. No change, no trace of life. Oddly, she felt no drafts of wind, no suction, which there really should have been at this speed.

A little bored, especially after all she'd been through, she turned her gaze behind them, to the second stone head, which was following them at some distance. From here she couldn't see the third, which was on the other side.

Suddenly she started up, her sluggishness vanishing at one stroke.

"That isn't . . . ," she began, but she forgot to end the sentence. Then, after a moment, she asked, "Do you see that too?"

"*I see through your eyes, Merle. Of course I can see him.*"

Between the lips of the second head there was a man.

He was perched behind the lower lip and lay with his upper body and arms stretched out over the stone, apparently lifeless, as if the mighty head had half swallowed him and then had forgotten to swallow the rest. His arms dangled back and forth, his head lay on one side, face turned away. He had very long, snow-white hair, and Merle would have taken him for a woman, if he hadn't suddenly turned his head and looked over at her. He looked out at her between the white strands, which covered his features like fresh-fallen snow. Even at this distance she could see how narrow and wasted his face looked. His skin had hardly any more color than his hair; it was as pale as that of a corpse.

"*He is dying,*" said the Flowing Queen.

"And so we should just look on while he does it?"

"*We cannot get to him.*"

Merle thought it over; then she made a decision. "Maybe yes."

She sprang back inside the ear, shook Vermithrax awake, and pulled the tired, ill-humored lion with her to the edge of the stone ear. The white man had now turned his face away again and was hanging over the lip of the head like a dead man.

"Can we get over there?" The tone of her voice made it clear that she would not accept a no.

"Hmm," said Vermithrax gloomily.

"What's that supposed to mean . . . hmm?" Merle waved her arms and gesticulated wildly. "We can't simply let him die over there. He needs our help, you can see that."

Vermithrax growled something unintelligible, and Merle waved her hands more and more furiously, appealed eloquently to his conscience, and finally even said, "Please." At last he murmured, "He could be a danger."

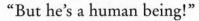

"But he's a human being!"

"Or something that looks like one," said the Queen with Merle's voice.

Merle was much too excited to reprimand her for this breach of their agreement. "In any case, we can't just stay sitting here and watching." She added emphatically, "We can't, can we?"

The Queen wrapped herself in silence, which in a certain way was also an answer, but Vermithrax replied, "No, probably not."

Merle let out her breath. "You intend to try it?"

"Try what?" asked the Queen, but this time Merle just ignored her.

Vermithrax looked calculatingly from the edge of the ear across the gulf to the second stone head. "The head isn't flying exactly behind us, but at an angle. That makes it more difficult. But perhaps . . . hmm, if I pushed off hard enough and so got out far enough and then simply let myself fall back, I could maybe hook onto him again and—"

"Simply! Did you just say 'simply'?" asked the Queen through Merle's mouth.

Stop it! Merle thought.

"But it is madness. We do not know who or what he is and why he is in such a condition."

"If we keep sitting around here, we'll never find out either."

"Perhaps that would be better." But the Queen's tone revealed that she'd accepted her defeat. She was a fair loser—perhaps also an offended one—and once more she lapsed into silence.

"It will be difficult," said Vermithrax.

"Yes." As if Merle didn't know that.

"I can't just stand there in the air until its face rams into me—that would kill me. I can only try again to jump up sideways, on the ear or on the hair somewhere. And then from there I have to climb around the head to reach the man."

Merle took a deep breath. "I can do that."

"You?"

"Certainly."

"But you have no claws."

"No, but I'm lighter. And more agile. And I can hold on to the smallest unevenness." She didn't really believe that herself, of course, but somehow she thought it sounded plausible.

"Not a good plan," said Vermithrax, unimpressed.

"Just get me over there, I'll take care of the rest. I've had enough of sitting around on your back the whole time"—she smiled fleetingly—"I mean, nothing against your back, but I simply can't be so . . . inactive. I never was particularly good at that."

The lion pulled up his lips, and it took Merle a moment to recognize that as a grin. "You're quite a brave girl. And a completely crazy one."

She beamed at him. "Then we'll do it?"

Vermithrax ran the point of his tongue over his finger-length canine teeth. "Yes," he said, after another long look over the gap, "I think we'll simply give it a try."

"*Simply,*" said the Queen with a groan. "*There it is again.*"

6

JUNIPA'S FATE

"WHAT'S THAT SUPPOSED TO MEAN," DARIO ROARED, "you want to leave again right away?"

Serafin held his glare easily. It had never particularly impressed him when someone yelled at him. Usually, loudness was just a sign of weakness. "It means exactly what I said. That I have to leave once more before the attack. And don't worry, *General* Dario: I'm not planning to desert your army of heroes."

Dario was boiling with rage, and he looked now as if he were sorry he had no more than two fists he could clench. "That's not the way it works here," he said sharply, less loudly but no less angrily. "You can't just leave for a few hours while we're getting ready to go to the Doge's—"

Serafin interrupted him. "Perhaps *you* have to get yourselves ready. *I* don't have to. You *asked* me"—he emphasized the word with special relish—"to help you because you know that I'm the only one who has a ghost of a chance to get into the palace. You know, Dario, the rules are very simple: I'll try to get into the palace, and whoever follows me will do exactly what I say. If not, he either stays here or is probably a dead man within the first few minutes." He chose such dramatic words intentionally, because he had the feeling Dario could best be managed that way. Besides, he'd really had enough of this discussion even before it began.

"With all due respect to your instincts," said Dario, controlling himself with difficulty, "but—"

"Excuse me: My instincts are all you have." Serafin pointed to the small group of rebels who'd gathered in the dining room of the enclave: a dozen boys his age, some even younger, most of them from the street. They were practiced in fending for themselves, stealing, and outwitting the City Guard. Some of them were still wearing the ragged clothing in which they'd grown up, and others who'd clothed themselves anew from the inventory in the sphinx's house looked dandified in their colorful shirts and trousers. Most of those things looked as if someone had collected them for a masquerade ball; it was only after a while that Serafin realized the clothes must actually have come from various previous centuries and been preserved over time in the sphinx's boxes and trunks. Once again he wondered how long Lalapeya had been living here in Venice. She'd given him no answer to that.

Dario had had the wit to choose his new trousers and shirt in velvety purple, dark enough to melt into the night. The others who'd been less careful in their choice of clothes would stay here. They didn't know it yet, but Serafin would make sure of it. He couldn't burden himself with breaking-in companions who weren't engaged with their whole mind.

"You haven't got your mind on this," Dario said, as if he'd read Serafin's thoughts in order to use his own arguments against him. "How can we rely on you if your mind is on something else all the time?"

"And that's exactly the reason why I intend to leave again now." Serafin paid no attention to the silent faces listening attentively to every word exchanged between him and Dario. "To clear my head for what we have ahead of us, I have to take care of a certain matter. I can't allow it to distract me."

"And what matter of world-shaking importance would that be?"

Serafin hesitated. What was it that Dario was after? Not, as he'd originally thought, to make a fool of him in front of all present. Also, not to question his leadership qualities (and Serafin would have been the first to agree with him there: He'd never been a good leader, always a loner). No, Dario was curious. Perhaps he even guessed what Serafin had in mind. And was ashamed.

Lalapeya, thought Serafin. She told him. And now he's trying to make me look bad in front of the others because he feels bad himself. Really, he's not abusing me but himself.

"I'm going to the Canal of the Expelled," he said, observing every movement of Dario's face, every trace of emotion that went beyond anger. In an instant, Dario's features were a singular admission of guilt.

"What could you want there?" Dario asked softly. His tone was very different from a few moments before. A murmur went through the line of rebels.

"I intend to go to Arcimboldo's magic mirror work-shop," Serafin said. "I have to check on him, and on Eft. And above all, on Junipa." He lowered his voice so much that only Dario could understand him. "I have to get her away from there. Someplace where she's safe. Otherwise she won't survive the coming days. And probably not Arcimboldo, either."

Dario stared at him, eyes narrowed, as if he could look through him to his inmost being. "Someone wants to kill Arcimboldo?"

Serafin nodded. "I'm afraid that's what it's going to boil down to. I can't imagine that he'll actually surrender Junipa. And if he refuses, they'll kill him."

"Surrender? Who to? The Egyptians?"

Serafin grabbed Dario by the upper arm and led him away from the others, through a door into the next room where they could talk undisturbed. "Not the Egyptians," he said.

"Who else?"

Serafin looked thoughtfully out the window. It was dark outside. They were going to invade the palace later this very night. Their spies had reported that the Pharaoh had installed himself there a few hours ago. Before then, Serafin had to take care of Junipa, Arcimboldo, and Eft. Next to that, everything else, even the fight against the Egyptians, paled to meaninglessness.

Serafin gave himself a shake and looked Dario in the face. He knew with certainty: He had no more time to explain the circumstances to Dario.

"Just come with me."

"Are you serious?"

Serafin nodded. "You can handle a saber well. Much better than I can."

Dario's distaste for allying himself with his old arch-enemy still burned in his eyes. But there was also something else: a trace of relief and, yes, of gratitude. For Serafin had made it easy for him, enabling him to go along without having to ask. That was what surprised Serafin the most. Dario *wanted* to go with him and had from the very beginning. Only he hadn't been able to bring himself to say it, not to Serafin.

"And the others?" asked Dario.

"Will have to wait."

"Lalapeya?"

"She too."

Dario nodded. "Then let's get going right now."

Back in the dining room, Dario gave the surprised Tiziano the order to take over command until they were back. Tiziano and Boro exchanged irritated looks, then grinned, and Tiziano nodded proudly. The other boys wanted to know what Dario and Serafin were going to do, but when Boro promised them all a second portion of supper, their interest flagged, and they turned to the steaming dishes. Serafin smiled when he saw that. All their lives, they would be street children at heart and hungry for any meal.

After carefully surveying the street, Serafin and Dario left the enclave through the main entrance. The sphinx's palazzo was in the Castello district, in the middle of Venice, but tonight there wasn't a single inhabitant on the street.

The mummy soldiers' random attacks had now turned into organized patrols—Venice had fallen into the enemy's hands without a battle, without any intervention from the City Guard. The traitorous city councillors had seen to it that the city would capitulate as soon as the Queen was gone and the enemy troops had moved closer. In the past few nights, the mummy troops' attacks on civilians had gone a step further to crush the citizens' fighting spirit.

Most had simply given up: the city and themselves. Now it was only a question of time until the first would be dragged from their houses and carried off to the boats.

The two boys kept close to the façade of the palazzo as they set out. In a whisper, Serafin asked about the walled-up windows of the ground floor, but Dario didn't know what was hidden behind them. No one ever entered the lower floor, that was law. There weren't even doors.

It wasn't far to the Canal of the Expelled, barely fifteen minutes at a run. Yet they had to detour several times when they heard the clink of steel or the sound of rhythmic steps, but never voices, coming from around a bend. Once, they were only a few steps away from one of the mummy patrols, as they pressed themselves into a niche, hoping the Pharaoh's slaves wouldn't sense them. A cloud of dust rose to Serafin's nose as the bony figures marched past them.

After some minutes they reached a small intersection. Here the Canal of the Expelled branched off from a broader waterway. Serafin's heart gave a leap when he saw the deserted bridge and the empty sidewalks. At this very spot, not too long ago, at the lantern festival, everything had begun for him and Merle. The thought filled him with sorrow and fear. Where was Merle now?

Nothing had changed on the Canal of the Expelled. Almost all the houses on the cul de sac had been empty for a long time, doors and windowpanes destroyed. Only the two workshops, their gray façades staring at each other across the water like the faces of old men, had been occupied, until recently. But now Umberto's weavers had left their house, and the windows of the magic mirror workshop were also dark.

"Are you sure they're still here?" asked Dario, as they approached Arcimboldo's workshop. They checked again and again to be sure no one was following them. Serafin kept an eye on the sky for flying lions, although in the darkness he could see almost nothing. If there were something dark and massive sweeping across the stars, it was too fast for his tired eyes.

"You must know Arcimboldo better than I do," he said. "I didn't have the impression he's a man who'd abandon his house and crawl into a hole somewhere."

Dario returned his look with a spark of anger, but then he realized Serafin's words were not an attack. He nodded slowly. "Perhaps we shouldn't have left him and Eft behind." He hadn't forgotten what he owed to Arcimboldo.

Serafin laid a hand on his shoulder. "He knew that you'd go. He said so to me. And I believe he even wanted that a little."

"He spoke to you about it?" Dario looked at him. "When?"

"Not long ago. I was with him outside in the lagoon, after you loaded the mirrors into the boat."

"The last delivery . . ." Dario's voice sounded thoughtful suddenly, as his eyes strayed to the entrance of the mirror workshop. "He never told us where he took all the mirrors. Or who he sold them to." He started and stared at Serafin. "Do these happen to be the people we're supposed to protect him from? Are we here on account of them?"

Serafin was about to tell him the whole story right then and there: how he'd watched Arcimboldo hand his magic mirrors over to Talamar, the courier from Hell, and how Talamar had demanded the girl Junipa for his master, Lord Light. The girl with the mirror eyes.

But then he kept silent and just nodded briefly.

"What kind of people are they?" Dario asked.

Serafin sighed. "If we're unlucky, we'll meet one of them tonight." He was about to move on, but Dario held him back.

"Come on, spit it out."

Serafin looked from Dario to the dark workshop, then back to Dario again. It wasn't easy for him to tell the truth. Dario wouldn't believe him.

"Hell," he said finally. "Arcimboldo was selling his mirrors to Lord Light for years. To one of his couriers."

"Lord Light?" Dario's voice was quiet, as if this news didn't really surprise him. Then he nodded slowly. "The Devil, that is."

"That remains to be proven," said Serafin. "No one has

ever seen Lord Light." But he was only trying to make it
sound better, he knew that.

"And Arcimboldo obeyed him?" Dario asked.

A lone gust of wind brushed Serafin's face and made
him shiver. Again he looked up at the night sky. "He didn't
only make the mirrors for him. He also took Merle and
Junipa into his house on Lord Light's orders."

"But . . . ," Dario began, then shook his head. He'd
never liked the two girls, but he didn't go so far as to
blame them. "Tell the rest," he begged.

"There isn't more to tell. Junipa was blind, you know
that, and Arcimboldo implanted the mirror eyes at Lord
Light's request."

"Those damned eyes," whispered Dario. "They're
creepy. Like ice. As if a cold wind were blowing out of
them." He stopped, and then after a moment he added,
"Why? What do Hell or Lord Light get out of it if Junipa
can see again?"

"No idea." Serafin noted the doubt on Dario's face. But
for some reason he didn't want to try to explain about the
power the mirror eyes gave Junipa. "Arcimboldo only did
what they commissioned him to do. To save the workshop
and also you apprentices. He was afraid he'd have to send you
back to the orphanage if he refused Lord Light's commis-
sions. He was only concerned about you." Serafin hesitated a
moment, then he said, "And he was glad to be able to help
Junipa. He said she was so happy to finally be able to see."

"And why are we here now?"

"Talamar, Lord Light's errand boy, has demanded that Arcimboldo surrender Junipa to him. But I think he knew Arcimboldo would refuse to do it. He gave him a deadline. And therefore we have to get your master, Junipa, and Eft to safety before—"

"Before this Talamar comes for the girl," Dario ended the sentence. "And punishes Arcimboldo for his disobedience."

"Then you're still with me?" Serafin hadn't forgotten what happened when Dario went after him with a knife that time in the mirror workshop. Then, Dario had used Junipa as a shield. On the other hand, Serafin felt that he was dealing with a different Dario today, one who was straighter with other people—and with himself.

"Sure." Dario drew his saber, a decisive but also a slightly useless gesture. "No matter who we have to deal with. And if the Pharaoh and Lord Light are inside there toasting each other, we'll just show them both where to go."

Serafin grinned and started moving. Together they covered the last few yards to the workshop. The sign over the door, ARCIMBOLDO'S GLASS FOR THE GODS, appeared even more unreal than ever. On this night the gods were farther away from Venice than ever before.

A soft thumping sounded as the mirror maker's empty boat struck the canal wall behind them, making Serafin and Dario jump. Something had disturbed the calm water. Perhaps only the wind.

Still no lions in the sky.

The front door was open. Dario cast a surprised look at Serafin, but he merely shrugged. It was only after they'd cautiously entered that they saw the reason: The door lock was broken—in fact, it was smashed, splintered like the wood of the oak door, which had been thrown against the wall with such force that the plaster was missing in several places.

On the alert, Dario peered into the darkness.

Serafin whispered only one word: "Talamar."

He didn't know what made him so sure. It could just as well have been mummy soldiers who'd forced their way into the house. But he sensed the breath of Lord Light's slave like a bad smell that fouled the air. Like something that singed the hairs on the back of his neck and made all the roots of his teeth suddenly start aching. The presence of something bad through and through, perhaps even more evil than the power that had sent it here.

"Talamar," he said once more, louder this time, more grimly.

Then he ran, despite Dario's warning, despite even the darkness that seethed in the entry hall like a black brew in a witch's kettle. He tore up the stairs, turned off at the second floor, and recoiled when he saw hectic movements flit over the walls to the right and left of him. But it was only his own image that flitted through a tremendous number of mirrors on the walls everywhere.

Dario was running directly behind him when a deafening shriek sounded. Dario increased his pace, almost pulling past Serafin.

Who had screamed? Man, woman, or girl? Or maybe something else entirely, not in torment but in shrill, blazing triumph.

Through the corridors, from all directions at once, came the whisper: "The wish is fulfilled, the magic worked, the agreement kept."

The boys turned the corner, straight into the corridor that led to the high double doors of the workshop. Arcimboldo's shop floor resembled the laboratory of an alchemist in olden days rather than the room of a craftsman. His magic mirrors consisted of silvered glass, magic, and the essence of the Flowing Queen.

But the caustic vapors that met them now had nothing to do with alchemical substances or magic. They were the breath of damnation, of the black pestilence Talamar. Serafin knew it, felt it with every nerve, with every fiber. His senses cried alarm. His mind screamed to him to turn around.

But he ran on, raised his saber high, opened his mouth in a scream of rage and helplessness—and flew through the open door into the laboratory, rushed through clouds of acrid smoke and sour steam, stumbled, and came to a stop, hardly able to breathe. And *saw*.

Eft lay in a corner, maybe dead, maybe only unconscious. In the pallid fog that filled the room, it wasn't possible to see if she was still breathing. She wore no mask, but her face was turned away.

Something was moving in the mist, like a giant spider with four legs. Limbs bent out of line, as if someone had put a rag doll together wrong. A body whose belly faced up, and an upside-down face, the pointed chin facing the top, the malicious eyes at the bottom. Like a human child making a bridge; and yet far removed from any humanity.

The messenger from Hell was pulling something behind him with one hand, a motionless bundle. A body.

Junipa.

Serafin hesitated only a moment to make sure that Dario saw the same thing he did, then dove through the caustic mist at Talamar so fast that Hell's messenger could scarcely react. Instead of avoiding him, the creature dropped Junipa, raised an arm—in a distorted movement that had nothing in common with anything earthly—and turned away the saber blade with his naked skin, hard as stone, as impervious as the horn shell of an insect. The blade rebounded with a sickening thudding sound, and Serafin was almost thrown to the ground by his own momentum. He caught himself at the last moment, took two steps back, and then stood, legs astride, ready for the next exchange of blows.

A shrill laugh rang from the creature's twisted mouth; his eyes searched, explored, discovered the second opponent.

Dario had learned from Serafin's mistake. Instead of engaging Talamar on a straight line, he made a step toward the beast, whirled around, sprang to the right, then to the left, and finally leaped clear over his antagonist in an acrobatic jump, turned in the air, and using both hands, drove the saber into the body of Hell's courier from above.

Talamar groaned as the tip scratched his skin. He shook himself as if it were an insect sting, spit out a string of staccato sounds, then merely wiped the blade aside. The tip had penetrated scarcely a finger's breadth, too little to weaken him or seriously wound him at all. Dario snatched the saber back before Talamar could grab it, landed on both feet, staggered briefly, then retrieved his balance and called out to Serafin something that was swallowed up in the creature's angry bellowing.

But Serafin understood it anyway.

Dario now was standing on Talamar's right side, while Serafin was still on his left. They could take the messenger from Hell in a pincer movement if they managed skillfully. If they dealt fast enough.

Talamar was quite capable of speaking the language of the Venetians—Serafin had heard it himself—but the sounds that he now uttered hurt Serafin's ears. It was as if the sounds were something living, sent out to weaken Talamar's opponents and destroy their concentration.

Serafin forced himself to be calm. His eyes sought the motionless figure of Junipa, half buried under Talamar's body, and he believed he saw a metallic flash, a reflection in her eyes. They were open. She was watching him. And yet Junipa could not move, as if Talamar had laid a spell on her. Her limbs were rigid, her muscles frozen. But she was breathing, he now saw very clearly. She was alive. And that was what counted.

Dario let out a whistle. Serafin looked up, nodded to his companion. And both attacked at the same time, letting the sabers whirl and rain down on Talamar's armored skin.

Steel bounced on horn. Without success.

Talamar screamed again, not in pain, but in rage. Then he went on the counterattack.

He had recognized Dario as the most dangerous foe, and so he favored him with his first thrust. The claws on Talamar's fingers, no shorter than a dagger blade and just as sharp, flashed forth and back, darting, whirling blurs, and then Dario cried out, staggered back, and bumped against a workbench. With great presence of mind he threw himself backward, although losing his saber in the process, slithered across the top of the bench, and plunged to cover behind it. Just in time, for Talamar's claws drove behind him, imprinting five deep scars in the wood.

Serafin used the moment while the creature was distracted. He didn't know how to penetrate Talamar's armored skin, but his instinct told him that he should direct his attacks to the creature's head. His saber cut through the gray mist, drove the vapors away from Talamar's features, and for the first time uncovered his entire face. In one tiny instant, almost frozen in time, Serafin saw the steel thorn vine that ran like a band over Talamar's eyes; saw the individual tendril that had loosened itself from the others and led diagonally across the creature's mouth.

Then the blade of the saber struck Talamar's face—and bounced off again.

The scream that now came from the creature's throat sounded agonized and uncontrolled, and for the first time Serafin had the feeling of being dangerous to Talamar in spite of everything, yes, even being able to kill him.

Instead of retreating and recovering strength for a new attack, Serafin pursued him immediately, thrust the saber forward, felt how he struck resistance—and saw the blade shatter into a thousand splinters.

Talamar hauled back and dealt a blow that would have killed Serafin had it been better aimed. But though the claws only grazed him, they dug deep scratches into his right cheek. Serafin staggered and clattered to the floor. He fell so hard that it knocked the wind out of him, and when his vision cleared again, Talamar was gone.

Junipa had also vanished.

"Serafin?"

He looked up and saw Dario stand up behind the workbench, gather his saber from the floor, and then stare incredulously at the five deep gouges in the top of the workbench. It didn't take much imagination to visualize what would have been left of him if the blow had actually struck him.

"Here!" Serafin cried, but it sounded like an inarticulate wail, not like a word.

"Where is he?" Dario staggered over to him. He was supporting himself on his saber like a crutch. His face was contorted in pain and a bruise like an exotic plant bloomed under his left eye.

"Gone."

"Where?"

Serafin picked himself up before Dario reached him. He was still holding the hilt of the saber in his hand. He stared at it in disbelief, and then carelessly threw it aside. The metal hilt clattered on the wooden floorboards, skittered a ways away, and was then taken up by a hand, which pulled it abruptly from the billows of mist like a hungry animal.

"Eft!" Serafin bent forward and helped the woman to her feet. "I thought—"

She didn't let him finish. "Where's Arcimboldo?"

Serafin looked around, saw only Dario, who shrugged, and then he shook his head. "I don't know."

Eft pushed his hands away and struggled forward, her

upper body bent over, and dragged herself through the caustic fog, which was burning in Serafin's lungs like liquid fire.

"He must . . . be here . . . somewhere."

Serafin and Dario again exchanged looks; then they fanned out and searched the interior of the workshop.

After a short while, they were certain that neither Talamar and Junipa nor Arcimboldo were there. Instead they stumbled on an opening in the floor, with charred edges, jagged, like a star that a child might have drawn on the floor with unskilled fingers.

For a moment, Serafin thought that the hole led directly to Hell.

But after his eyes grew used to the darkness, he saw at the bottom of the opening the floor of the story below. He would have jumped down then and there, but Eft held him back.

"Leave it," she said. "He's gone."

"And Junipa?"

"He took her with him."

"We have to stop him!"

She shook her head. "He's fast. He could be anywhere by now."

"But . . ." Serafin fell silent. Whatever he intended to say was wiped away at one blow. They had failed. Talamar would take Junipa to Lord Light. The girl was lost.

"*Master!*" Dario's voice sounded muffled through the

mist, probably from a room nearby, but even at a distance, the despair in his call lost nothing of its intensity.

Serafin ran, but Eft was even faster. She had a cut on her head, with blood running down to the corners of her mouth, just in front of her ears. Her broad mermaid's mouth was open a little, and Serafin saw the shine of the rows of sharp teeth inside. But he had no time to think about that.

He followed her through the mist, through an open door.

Arcimboldo had kept his magic mirrors in the storeroom. Most were gone—he'd handed them over to Talamar on the last delivery. Only a few still hung on their hooks or leaned against the wall, work ordered by his few Venetian customers.

The old man was lying facedown on the floor. His left arm was stretched out close to his body, unnaturally turned, as if it had been broken behind his back or dislocated. His right hand clutched a hammer. Nearby lay the remains of a mirror, jagged shards that he'd obviously struck out of the frame himself.

A question shot through Serafin's mind, even before the shock of grief. Had Talamar succeeded in getting into the workshop through a magic mirror? And had Arcimboldo destroyed the entrance with the hammer?

Dario crouched beside his master but didn't dare to touch him, either out of respect or fear of the truth.

Eft pushed the boys aside and rolled Arcimboldo onto his back. Then they all looked into his dimmed eyes, half-covered with strands of the wild white hair lying around his head like wet wool.

With a gentle movement of her hand, Eft closed the old man's eyes. Her fingers were shaking. She lifted Arcimboldo's upper body, pressed it close to her, and laid the back of his head carefully in her lap. With trembling hands she pushed his hair back, stroked his cheeks.

Dario looked up for the first time. Looked into Eft's face.

He uttered a gasp, and for a moment it looked as if he would draw away from her. But then he had himself under control again. He gave one quick look at Eft's legs—no fishtail, Serafin could read in his thoughts—then took the hand of his former master and pressed it firmly.

Serafin felt out of place. He hadn't known the magic mirror maker well, but he'd liked him. He would have paid his respects to the dead, but he feared that any gesture would seem shallow and false. The two had so much to be grateful to Arcimboldo for, their grief must be infinitely deeper. He bowed briefly, turned around, and went back to the workshop.

He didn't have to wait long before Dario joined him.

"Eft wants to be alone with him."

Serafin nodded. "Yes, of course."

"She said we should wait for her."

Dario perched on the edge of a table. His gaze was turned inward. It astonished Serafin that Dario wasn't in more of a hurry to get back to the enclave, in spite of everything; the attack on the Pharaoh still had to take place tonight, and it did not lie in Dario's power to change this plan.

"What is she going to do?" Serafin asked.

"I think she intends to go with us."

"To the enclave?"

Dario nodded.

Perhaps that wasn't such a bad idea. Eft was old, over a hundred, he guessed, perhaps even older, but her appearance was that of a woman in her thirties. She was slender and lithe, and it wouldn't have surprised him if she knew how to handle a blade.

"You didn't know it, did you?" Serafin asked.

"That she's a mermaid?" Dario shook his head. "No. Of course we wondered why she always wore those masks. She never let anyone see her whole face, only from the nose up. A disease, we thought, or an accident." He shrugged his shoulders. "Who knows, maybe we also did suspect it a little. Tiziano made a joke about it one time, what if . . . but no, I didn't know. Not really."

They left the workshop and sat outside in the hall, on the floor, their backs against the wall, Serafin on one side and Dario on the other. Both had their knees drawn up and looked down the corridor. Dario's saber lay at his feet.

The quiet was broken by the clicking of a door lock, as Eft locked the workshop from the inside. The last thing Serafin saw was Arcimboldo's body, which Eft had laid out on a workbench, half-concealed behind the billowing clouds of mist.

"What's she doing?"

Dario looked over at the double doors as if he could see through the wood. "No idea. We have to wait."

Serafin nodded his agreement.

And so they waited.

One hour. Possibly even two or three.

They didn't speak much, but when they talked, there was nothing of the old enmity between them, only respect and something that might someday become friendship.

But they'd paid a high price for it. Acimboldo was dead, Junipa abducted.

Much too high a price.

The thought of having still to invade the Doge's Palace after all this and carry out an assassination of the Pharaoh was suddenly so unreal, so utterly and completely insane, that Serafin quickly repressed it.

The corrosive mist had slowly dissipated when the door lock clicked a second time. But now another smell took its place.

Something was burning. Fire in the workshop!

Serafin and Dario awakened from their trance and sprang up. Eft came toward them. Something gleamed in her hands. At first Serafin thought it was a blade, but then he made out a mask of silvery mirror glass. Eft pressed it to her as if it were something unspeakably costly, more than only a keepsake that she had taken in remembrance.

Behind her the workbench was burning.

A column of black, greasy smoke billowed up, was trapped under the roof, and then crept along to the door like the advance front of a swarm of ants.

"Let's go," said Eft.

The two boys exchanged uncertain looks, then Serafin looked inside the workshop again. The flames dancing around Arcimboldo's laid-out body concealed the destruction they were wreaking. Something about the profile of the dead man seemed strange to him, as if the face of the old man were now smooth as a ball.

His eyes traveled again to the silvery mask in Eft's hand. The features were thin and haggard. The face of an old man.

"Let's go," said the mermaid once again, her free hand pulling the edge of a neckerchief over her mouth until she looked like a robber who was preparing for his last big holdup.

Dario nodded, and Serafin joined the two of them as they hurried quickly down the corridor. He looked back over his shoulder once more, but now he saw only smoke and flames billowing out into the passage in thick plumes.

Moments later the three were running along the Canal of the Expelled, away from Arcimboldo's pyre.

Flames were now shooting from several windows, and dense smoke spread over the water.

7

THE PHARAOH

Behind the golden dome of the Basilica of San Marco rose a falcon, larger than any animal on earth, higher than the highest tower, mightier than the statues of the pharaohs at home in Egypt.

He drew himself up to his full height of more than a hundred man-lengths, with round black eyes and a beak as large as the hull of a boat. His plumage was of pure gold and stood out against the night sky as if it were in flames.

Horus, the falcon god.

He unfolded his wings like golden sails and laid them on both sides of the façade of the basilica, around its rich

Byzantine carving and ornamentation, around its pediments and windows and reliefs. The tips of the wings met in front of the portals, slipped over one another, until the entire basilica was caught in its embrace, concealed as if behind a curtain of glowing, gleaming lava.

The falcon god laid claim to what was his.

He showed everyone who now possessed the power in Venice that the city was now only a part of Egypt, a part of the Empire, a fief of the old gods.

Standing on a roof opposite was Seth, highest of the high priests and the Pharaoh's vizier. His head was slightly bent and his arms crossed over his upper body. Sweat stood in shining beads on his forehead, and his golden robe was soaked with it. At this moment he *was* the falcon, the absolute master of this illusion.

Seth held the illusion upright for a minute longer, then spread his arms apart with a quick movement and sharply expelled air through his mouth and nose.

The towering falcon dissolved in a fountain of glittering spangles that sank to the Piazza San Marco around the basilica as if the stars themselves were plunging from the sky.

Applause sounded from the rows of priests gathered in the piazza below him. Only the mummy soldiers, of whom several dozen were scattered all over the piazza, stood unmoved, staring straight ahead out of dead, sunken eyes, some even out of empty eye sockets.

But Seth required no rejoicing, no applause to know the extent of his talent. He was conscious of his power, of every tiny aspect of his godlike abilities. The golden falcon god was nothing more than a skillful illusion, a symbol of the victory of the Empire, like the others that time after time sent the Pharaoh into naive raptures. The toys of a child.

What a waste, Seth thought disapprovingly. Of power, respect, and credibility. He, the highest priest and second man of the Empire; he, the venerable Seth; was wasting his energy on Amenophis's whimsies. And everyone in the priesthood, as well as his closest confidants, knew that he had no other choice. Not in times like these, when the sphinx commanders were winning more and more influence and power and pushing the priesthood out of the ruler's favor. It was worth it to make the Pharaoh happy—at least until the power of the priests of Horus was no longer threatened by the accursed sphinxes.

Seth snorted. Here the Empire was, celebrating its greatest victory, the conquest of Venice after more than three decades of siege, and it was primarily Seth's victory, his personal triumph over the Flowing Queen—and yet he could not rejoice in it. His satisfaction was only external, nothing more than a masquerade.

The sphinxes were to blame for that. And, of course, the Pharaoh himself.

Amenophis was a fool—a silly, narcissistic coxcomb

on a throne of gold and human lives. The priests of Horus had chosen him and made him into the figurehead of the Empire because they believed him weak, pliant, and easy to influence. Only a child, they'd said, and they exulted when they succeeded in waking him to new life in the stepped pyramid of Amun-Ka-Re.

He was their handiwork, their puppet, they'd believed. And in certain ways that applied today.

But only in *certain* ways.

Silently, Seth allowed a long cloak to be placed around his shoulders and accepted a cloth that one of his inferior priests handed to him. He used it to pat the perspiration from his bald head, from the spaces in between the golden wires that had been countersunk into his scalp as ornament, but also as a means for concentrating his spiritual power. The other priests had the network tattooed into their skin in color, but his own was of pure gold, worked by the smiths of Punt, deep in southern Africa.

Seth walked into the stairwell with measured steps, followed by his priests. Numerous mummy soldiers had been stationed around for his protection. Remarkably numerous. Seth wondered who had given the order for it. Certainly not he.

As he entered the piazza below, a priest adept came up to him, bowed three times, kissed his hands and feet, and begged permission to deliver a message from the Pharaoh:

Amenophis wished to see Seth, right now, in his new chambers in the Doge's Palace.

Internally boiling with rage, Seth left the adept and his subordinates, crossed the piazza, and entered the palace. Amenophis summoned him like one of his body slaves. He, the highest among the priests of Horus, the spiritual head of the Empire. And that in front of the assembled priesthood. Through the mouth of a lowly adept!

Seth entered the palace through the richly decorated Porta della Carta, a masterpiece of gothic stonework. On the other side of the great interior courtyard, he mounted a splendid staircase in the shadow of two huge statues of gods. Mars and Neptune looked coldly down on him. Seth would have them pulled down as soon as possible and replaced with Horus and Re.

Through wide corridors and several anterooms he finally reached the door behind which some rooms had been arranged as the personal domicile of the Pharaoh. Appropriate to the status of a ruler, the rooms were on the top floor of the palace, just under the attic. Above them, in earlier times, prisoners had been locked into tiny cells under the lead roof. But today, so far as Seth knew, the dreaded rooms stood empty. He would inspect them later and decide whether it would be a suitable place to incarcerate the rebels among the city councillors.

Not all the city councillors had taken part in surrendering the Flowing Queen. Amenophis had ordered the three instigators executed the evening before, publicly, in the Piazza San Marco. He was grateful to them for their help but suffered around him no one whose word could not be trusted. The other councillors had been confined somewhere in the palace since then, separated from their bodyguards. Most of the soldiers had been imprisoned at the same time. Later an attempt would be made to enlist them on the side of the Empire; Amenophis was fascinated by the powerful bond between the soldiers and their stone lions. And kindling the Pharaoh's interest above all were the winged stone lions, who were only at the disposal of the Body Guard of the City Council.

Seth, on the contrary, thought that it would be better to kill all lions, right away, however difficult such an undertaking might be—even if it were necessary to sacrifice a few dozen mummy soldiers for each lion. It was a mistake to let them live. Amenophis might see in the lions only animals that would be suitable to tame and use for his own purposes; but Seth was of another mind. The lions were not dumb creatures who let themselves be trained at will. He could feel the divinity in them, their intelligence, their ancient knowledge. And he wondered if, in truth, the sphinx commanders were not behind the Pharaoh's decision as well. They were half lion themselves, and it was obvious that they knew more about the Venetian lions than they were admitting.

Was there any relationship between the sphinxes and

the stone lions? And if yes, what significance did it have in the intrigues of the sphinx commanders?

Seth had no time to pursue the thoughts any longer. One of the Pharaoh's lackeys had already reported his arrival. Now he asked Seth to enter.

The Pharaoh was resting on a divan of jaguar skins. He wore a white robe of human hair, shot through with gold threads. One hundred slave women had worked on it for almost a decade. Amenophis possessed several dozen of these robes, and often he would rip up a just-finished one if he didn't like the curve of a line or a detail of the pattern.

The Pharaoh smiled as Seth approached him. Amenophis awaited him alone, and that was more than unusual. Ordinarily the Pharaoh was surrounded by his tall soldiers from the Nubian desert, whose sickle swords had already polished off so many would-be assassins.

Strange too was that the makeup on the Pharaoh's face was even more garish than usual. But that could not conceal that his face was that of a child not yet thirteen years old, the age at which, more than three thousand years ago, the boy pharaoh had been poisoned. After the Horus priests reawakened him, he'd no longer aged. Amenophis had ruled for more than thirty years now, but he still always looked like a spoiled, snot-nosed child.

But that characterization didn't even begin to include all his bad characteristics. Seth had often speculated as to whether the ancient poison had been mixed by his predecessors, by Horus priests who could no longer tolerate the moods of this cruel dwarf.

Secretly he felt that possibly Amenophis asked himself the same question—which might be one of the reasons why recently the Pharaoh had been freeing himself more and more aggressively from the influence of the priesthood and turning to the sphinxes.

"Seth," said Amenophis, waving a casual greeting to him with his right hand.

The high priest bowed deeply and waited until the Pharaoh indicated that he rise. This time Amenophis took an especially long time over it, but Seth allowed the affront to pass over him without reacting. Sometime the conditions would alter, and then it would be he, Seth, to whom the Pharaoh had to creep. A really uplifting thought, which wrested a pleased smile from him.

Amenophis bade him come closer.

"You wished to see me, Re?" The Pharaoh preferred to be addressed by the name of the sun god.

"More precisely, we wanted *you* to see something, Seth."

The priest raised an eyebrow. "What could that be?"

Amenophis lolled on the jaguar divan and smiled. The golden color under his left eye had run, but he didn't look as if he had reason to weep. What would Amenophis have been laughing himself to tears about?

Seth felt increasingly uneasy.

"Re?" he asked once more.

"Go to the window," said the Pharaoh.

Seth went over to one of the high windows. From here he could look out on the now darkened Piazza San Marco. As always, it was illuminated by countless torches and fire-basins, but the scenery in the glow of the flames had changed.

Mummy soldiers were driving the priests together, several dozen men in long robes, not far from the place where, a few days before, the messenger from Hell had torn open the paving. A powerful sphinx was overseeing the arrest, which was taking place in uncanny silence. Among the prisoners Seth recognized his closest confidants, men with whom he had planned the resurrection of the Pharaoh and carried it out. Men who warned him and had trusted him when he brushed off their worries. What a fool he'd been!

For now his priests were going to pay for his stupidity, of that there was no doubt.

Very slowly and with as much dignity as he could muster, Seth turned around to the Pharaoh.

Amenophis was no longer alone. Utterly soundlessly, two sphinxes had come to his side on velvety lion feet. Their upper bodies were those of men, their underbodies belonged to mighty lions. Both had sickle swords that any ordinary man could hardly have lifted.

"Why, Re?" asked Seth softly and so under control that he surprised himself. "Why my priests?"

"The priesthood of Horus has discharged its duty," said Amenophis lightly, without losing his smile. "We thank you and yours, Seth. You were a great help to us, and we will not forget that."

The Pharaoh loved to speak of himself in the plural. But at the moment it almost seemed to Seth that Amenophis actually meant himself and his new advisers, the sphinx commanders.

"That is betrayal," he squeezed out.

"Of whom?" Amenophis's eyes widened in feigned astonishment. "Not of the Pharaoh. Also not of the gods."

"We have made you what you are." Seth now dispensed with the deferential address. "Without us you were only another body in the old graves, only a mummy in your sarcophagus, so hated by those who poisoned you that they didn't even put any gold in the grave with you. Everyone knew that. Why otherwise, do you suppose, did the grave robbers never try to invade your crypt?" He laughed derisively. "They knew what they'd find there. Only the corpse of a cocky child, whose cries for play and amusement even his closest intimates could no longer stand. Only the body of a dumb boy who—"

One of the sphinxes took a gliding step toward Seth, but Amenophis held him back. "Seth," he said, restrained, though his eyes showed the priest how very much his words had enraged him. "Silence. Please."

"I say the truth. And your new . . . *lapdogs* will soon

realize that as well." He'd intended to irritate the sphinxes, but he knew they wouldn't be drawn in. One grinned wearily, the other didn't change expression. It had been foolish to attempt to disconcert them, Seth knew that, too.

"We do not intend to kill you," said the Pharaoh. His lips drew into a malicious smile. "Not *you*."

"What do you intend, then?" Seth looked out again at his corralled priests. The swords of their guards gleamed in the torchlight.

Amenophis smirked. "First—their deaths. And after that, your attention."

Seth turned around, and again a sphinx took a threatening step forward. This time Amenophis did not restrain him.

"It is not necessary that they die," said Seth. He looked for a spell, an illusion, with which he could surprise the Pharaoh, but he knew it was pointless. The sphinxes' magic was equal to his, and they would turn any attack aside. If not these two, then one of the others, who were without question watching from behind the walls.

"Not necessary?" Amenophis repeated in his childish voice. He stroked his index finger over the golden coloring on his face and regarded the tip of his finger with interest. It shimmered like an exotic beetle. "We will make you an offer, Seth. You should not turn it down. We know very well that we have you and your priests alone to thank for this victory. It was you who found a way to drive the Flowing Queen out of the water—wherever she's holed up now. So do not think that we feel no gratitude."

"Yes," Seth managed with difficulty to say. "I see that."

Amenophis stretched his finger with the gold paint on it toward one of the sphinxes. The creature came forward and, his face expressionless, allowed the Pharaoh to smear two golden streaks over his cheeks. War paint.

"We are the ruler of the Empire, the only, the greatest, the most powerful," said Amenophis. "Is that not so?"

"So is it, Re," answered the sphinx devotedly.

The Pharaoh released him with a wave, and the creature again took up his post next to the divan.

"You spoke of an offer," said Seth.

"Ah. We knew that it would interest you." Amenophis stroked the palm of his hand over the jaguar skins. "We want more of these."

Seth swallowed in bewilderment. "I should . . . hunt jaguars for you?"

The childish Pharaoh broke into shrill laughter. "Oh, Seth, you dumbbell! No, of course not. We think we will find another who can provide us with a pair of these exquisite little animals, won't we?" He was still laughing, but now he gradually calmed himself. "It concerns the following, Seth. Our new advisers . . . our friends . . . in their infinite wisdom had a vision."

Everyone knew that sphinxes did in fact have access to

ancient wisdom. Seth would have given his right hand to find out what game they were playing. It made him half-crazy not to be able to see through them.

"A vision of our death," Amenophis went on.

"The priests of Horus would not have allowed you ever to die."

"Well answered. But we both know that you are lying. Sometime our person would have become wearisome to you. And who would then have taken our place on the throne? You yourself, Seth? Yes, we almost believe that would have been possible."

Seth had to control himself not to spit at his feet. "So what do you want?"

"The sphinxes are of the opinion that the power that could be dangerous to us is not of this world. At least not on the surface."

"Hell?"

"Indeed. The prophecy of the sphinxes predicts that something will come out of Hell and annihilate us. Is that not completely enchanting?" He laughed again, but this time it didn't sound so arrogant. "And who rules over Hell?"

"Lord Light."

"That outlaw! That filth! But yes—Lord Light. He has already tried to agitate the Venetians against us. Our honorable traitors were able to prevent that, by giving the order to kill the messenger from Hell. But Lord Light will give himself no rest, we know that, and the prophecy of the sphinxes confirms it." His eyes narrowed. "On the other hand—we will *not* die, Seth. No matter what Lord Light is hatching against us—he will not conquer us. Because we will pull the evil out by the root."

Now it was Seth's turn to laugh. In fact, he laughed so loud and so ringingly that Amenophis looked at him as though he doubted his high priest's understanding.

"You want to kill Lord Light?" Seth got out. His voice sounded too high, and he urgently needed air. "Is that your intention?"

"Yes—and no. Because *you* will kill him, Seth. Not we."

"That's suicide."

"That depends on you."

Seth shook his head. He had expected something, but not that.

His eyes traveled to the two sphinxes. They must know what madness this proposal was. If it was just about getting him out of the way, why were they making this farce out of it instead of ending him with their swords?

He found the answer himself, and it disturbed him deeply: because they believed what the Pharaoh was saying. Amenophis hadn't lied. The vision wasn't an invention. The sphinxes *feared* Lord Light.

He got hold of himself and asked, "What exactly did the sphinxes see?"

"Nothing," said one of the two, speaking unbidden for the first time. Amenophis let it happen without reprimanding the sphinx.

"Nothing?"

"Our visions do not reach us in the form of pictures," said the sphinx, with great seriousness. "They are feelings. Impressions. Too cryptic to give concrete advice."

Seth burst out laughing again, a trace too shrilly. "One of you had a . . . bad feeling, and therefore you want to kill Lord Light? Risk a war with Hell?" He paced excitedly back and forth a few times, then stopped again. "That is completely mad!"

The sphinx ignored his last words. "Something will come out of Hell and destroy the Pharaoh. That is the prophecy. And you will keep it from coming true."

The Pharaoh made a motion with his hand. Something rustled behind an opening in the paneling, and Seth felt someone rush past him. A little later a short trumpet signal sounded.

Seth whirled around to the window and saw the mummy soldiers approaching the corralled priests with sickle swords raised.

"Stop it!" Seth's voice sounded toneless.

A second hand signal, a new trumpet signal. The soldiers froze in motion.

For a moment there was silence. Even in the piazza below, everything seemed to have quieted.

155

"I will do as you wish," said Seth.

"We know that." The Pharaoh smiled charmingly. "We never had any doubt of it. These priests are like your own children."

"A high priest accepts his responsibility. A Pharaoh should do so also."

Amenophis waved him off. "Twaddle! You will set out today."

"Why I?"

"Because you are devotedly loyal to us, of course. Why else?" Amenophis looked genuinely surprised. "Because we can rely on you. No one else would keep his word in such a circumstance. But you, Seth, you will do it. We know that. And you will accomplish this matter quickly."

Seth's hatred threatened to overpower him, yet he remained outwardly calm. "How shall I get from here to Axis Mundi?"

"A friend will take you to Lord Light's city," said the Pharaoh. "Right up to his throne."

The door swung open and in walked the biggest sphinx that Seth had ever seen. He had long, bronze-colored hair that fell far down his back and was bound into a ponytail as thick as Seth's arm. The musculature of his upper body, in no way inferior to his lion legs, was more powerful than any Seth had ever seen in a human being. And his face was unusual: It was covered over with light brown hair, like the remains of a mane—really inconceivable for the beardless sphinxes. The pupils of his eyes were slits. The eyes of a predatory cat.

The creature smiled at Seth, exposing yellow canine teeth, while it casually twitched its flanks and unfolded gigantic wings, leathery, but covered with a furry down.

This is impossible, Seth thought. Sphinxes don't have wings. And their eyes and teeth are like those of men.

But this thing was something different. It exuded strength and cruelty like a bad smell.

"Iskander," said Amenophis, and—incredible!—he bowed in the direction of the beast. Turning to Seth, he said softly, "Your companion."

8

WINTER

VERMITHRAX PUSHED OFF FROM THE EDGE OF THE giant ear.

Merle lost her orientation immediately. Right, left, up, down—all blurred into one, a whirling vortex of red light and rocks. The head rushed on over them; they were caught up in its airstream, tumbled, almost overturned—and then for a brief moment they held stable in the air.

Only for a few seconds.

Then Vermithrax let out a roar, threw himself to one side, actually did a sommersault, and came straight back to horizontal again before Merle could lose her grip and fall.

Her heart raced so loudly that it filled her entire mind, thumping painfully in her skull. No room left for clear thoughts.

Then the second head was upon them, and the world turned into chaos. The obsidian lion roared again, then a jolt went through his body, which continued through Merle's bones, muscles, and joints like the blow of a hammer. It felt as if she'd been seized and thrown headfirst against a stone wall.

When she returned to her senses, she was lying beside Vermithrax behind the external bulge of one ear, bedded in something that at first she took to be ashes. Then she recognized black down. Bird feathers, she would have assumed in the upper world. Here below they might come from Heaven knew what sort of creatures.

With her luck they were probably carnivores that had especially chosen this ear for their hibernation.

There were a strikingly large number of feathers. And they smelled of tar, like the wind that blew across the desert of Hell.

"There is no one here," said the Flowing Queen in her head. *"Not here in the ear."*

"Are we there, where we . . . where we wanted to be?"

"Not we—where you *wanted to be!"*

Hairsplitting, thought Merle. "Is this the second head?"

"Yes," answered Vermithrax instead of the Queen. "It worked. Just right."

Merle picked herself up. Her head was still pounding, as if someone had locked her under a bell tower on Christmas Eve. She staggered, and Vermithrax tried to support her with his lion tail. But she shook her head, waited a moment, then managed to stay on her legs through her own strength.

This was something she had undertaken. And she would carry it through to the end.

"How heroic."

Merle ignored the comment. She had to climb out of the ear and down the side of the gigantic stone jaw along to the mouth. And all that perhaps to find a dying man whom no one could help anymore.

Nevertheless, she would try.

Vermithrax was breathing hard. He looked exhausted, his eyes glassy. In spite of that, he perceived what Merle had in mind.

"Rest up for a moment."

"Then I'll probably come to my senses and think differently about it." Merle's voice trembled slightly, but at once she had herself under control again.

The lion tilted his head and scrutinized her piercingly. "Once you get something into your head, you don't abandon it so easily."

Merle wasn't sure if she should feel flattered. She felt the obsidian lion's good will. He wanted to give her courage. And, to be honest, she needed a whole lot of it.

"Better now than later," she said, and she began to climb over the parapet, over the first bulge of the ear.

"Are you certain you want to do this?" asked the Queen.

"You aren't going to try to talk me out of it, are you?"

"It is your decision alone."

"Indeed." She knew that the Queen could force her to stay here, by taking control not only of her tongue but also of her whole body. Yet she did not do that. She respected Merle's decision, even if she didn't approve of it.

Without any word of farewell—for she avoided even thinking of the word farewell—she climbed to the outside of the ear. The stone was large-pored, full of scars and cracks. Some of them might have belonged to the structure of the stone by nature, others clearly stemmed from collisions with . . . yes, with what? Flying stones? Lilim claws? Bird beaks as hard as steel?

You don't want to know that. Not really. Don't get distracted.

The fastest way to the corner of the stone head's mouth was straight across its cheek, a deep hollow under the prominent cheekbones. She wondered if the face might have been modeled on the face of a particular person. If so, he was either old or undernourished. No one she knew had such deep cheeks, not even the hungry children in the orphanage.

"Do not look down," said the Flowing Queen.

"I'm trying as hard as I can not to."

Her hands and feet sought holds and found them amazingly quickly. Actually, it wasn't half so difficult as she'd thought. She followed the advice of the Queen as well as she could and kept her eyes firmly fastened on the stone wall. Sometimes, when she had to take care to place her feet on a secure projection, she couldn't avoid seeing a small section of the ground rushing past, infinitely far below her. Her heart beat like crazy and her stomach convulsed into a hard knot that lay like a stone on her intestines.

One of her fingernails broke as she shoved her right hand into the next recess. She might have half the distance behind her already, but she couldn't be certain. As long as she stared only at the stone, she couldn't judge proportions. What if she'd only covered a few yards? Much less than she thought?

Onward. Ever onward.

Only a little bit more.

Very slowly she turned her head and looked along the rock wall. The corner of the mouth wasn't far away. If she could only manage to get over the stone lower lip, she'd be safe for the time being.

Provided the man in the mouth was as well disposed toward her as she was toward him.

And if he wasn't as weak as he looked?

If he attacked her?

She shook off the thought, concentrated on her hands and feet again.

Yet as hard as she tried to repress it, she couldn't avoid seeing her situation in her mind's eyes: She was hanging on the side of a fifty-yard-high stone head, high over the rocky wasteland, and this head was moving forward at such an insane speed that the landscape under her blurred to a single whirl.

And all that for a stranger about whom she knew nothing. He might be dangerous, even a murderer, perhaps a true slave of Lord Light. Nevertheless, she was putting her life on the line for him. And not just her own. For if she believed the Flowing Queen, the fate of Venice depended on her.

The realization struck her unprepared, and she lost her hold. Her left hand slipped off, only her right clung on to a stone outcropping that was so narrow it wouldn't have held a flowerpot. She panicked and began to kick. Her feet slid over the edge of a recess and then hung free over the abyss for a moment.

"That does it," said the Flowing Queen drily.

Merle tensed her muscles—and pulled herself back up a little. She got hold of a projection with her left hand again, found a stop under her feet. And pulled herself on.

"Not bad."

"Many thanks for your support," Merle pressed out between her teeth.

A few yards farther, then she reached the corner of the mouth.

"You did it."

"That sounds as though you didn't think I would."

"Do you really believe I would have let you go, then?"

Those words confirmed Merle's fear: The Queen could take control over Merle's body if she wanted to. That wasn't a good thought, but it also wasn't one she was prepared to worry about at the moment.

She was able to grab a crack in the lower lip and pull herself toward it. Gathering all her strength once more, she sought a hold and heaved herself over the lip into the mouth of the stone head.

With a gasp she rolled over the bulge, suddenly grabbed emptiness, slipped down, fell . . . and landed on a hard surface.

At least there were no teeth to spear her. Not even a tongue. Only a hollow space, like a grotto. The back part lay in complete darkness. Impossible to make out what was back there. A tunnel deeper into the interior of the head? Or simply a back wall?

Merle raised herself and looked along the inside of the lip.

The man had changed his position. Not on his own, it appeared to her. He had slipped and, like her, fallen on the floor of the mouth cavity. There he lay in the middle of the flood of his white hair, as if he were in a puddle of milk.

But he was breathing. He even groaned softly.

Merle crawled closer to him on her hands and knees. Her heart pounded in her ears. She considered whether to wait a moment. Catch her breath, rest. She could hardly feel her arms from the strain. If he were really to attack, she was hardly in a condition to defend herself.

What was she doing here, anyway?

"Hello?" she asked carefully.

He was lying on his side with the back of his head toward her. His white hair was spread about him like a star, long strands that—if he were standing upright—must reach almost to his hips. His left hand was concealed under his body, but he had the right arm outstretched. The fingers were long and bony. Merle could clearly recognize the veins under the pale skin, blue lines like ink that had run on a white piece of paper.

"Hello?"

The fingers of the right hand twitched, curled to claws, clenched to a fist. Then they slackened again.

Merle took a deep breath, summoned all her courage, and moved slowly around the man. She had to decide which she would rather have at her back, him or the darkness at the back of the mouth cavity. She decided for the darkness and kept her eyes on the stranger.

She was grateful that the Flowing Queen remained silent. Merle didn't need her taunting remarks to know how absurd her behavior was. How mad.

"Are you injured?"

As she moved forward, she could gradually see more of his face.

His eyes were open and staring at her. His gaze followed her steps.

Merle got goose pimples. "You're awake," she stated. "Why don't you say anything?"

His lips trembled uncontrollably, giving the lie to the clear look of his eyes. Or was he just putting on an act for some reason? Was he waiting for her to bend over him?

Did everyone have Lilim claws?

His movements might be playacting. The skin quivered slightly, as if something were crawling along underneath it. He frowned and at the same time looked quite pitiful.

A trick?

"He cannot do anything to you."

The Flowing Queen's words surprised her. Merle had expected a warning from her, at the very least.

"Are you sure?"

"He is debilitated. Just about to die of thirst, it appears."

Merle remembered her knapsack and the provisions from the expedition's camp that she'd packed in it. The bundle was so firmly strapped to her back that she'd almost forgotten it. Now she took it off, opened one of the water flasks, smelled it—who knew when it had been filled fresh?—and approached the man with it.

"Should I?"

"That is why you came, after all."

Merle nodded silently, then she shoved her left hand under the man's head, lifted it, and dropped water onto his cracked lips. His white hair felt strange, oddly light, although it was thick and full. The eyes, which seemed so disquietingly alert and clear, observed Merle with such intensity that they could have belonged to another man, completely separate from the rest of his weakened body. This blazing, profound look irritated her. Frightened her a little.

Merle pressed the top of the flask closer to his lips, tilted it back again, waited until he'd swallowed, guided the flask to his mouth again. She did the same thing four or five times, and each time she let him drink a little more.

Finally he signaled with a shake of the head. Enough.

She wiped the top of the flask off on her skirt and carefully screwed it closed. She might have to make do with her water supply for much longer. Merle had only two bottles; this was the first—and it was almost empty. They had only the one left.

She put the bottle back in her knapsack.

"Thanks," came from the man's lips. She hadn't seen him speak, as if he'd moved neither tongue nor jaw, but she could hear him clearly.

"I . . . thank you." He used her language, with an almost unnoticeable accent.

Merle helped him to sit up. She leaned him with his back against the inside of the stone lip. Again she noticed how light his hair was, almost as if it weren't even there. It felt like flower petals.

"What's your name?" she asked him.

"Winter."

Flower petals—or snowflakes.

"Winter? What else?"

"Just Winter."

She examined him in irritation, then she grinned. "I'm Merle. Just Merle."

He was weak, his hands trembled slightly. But Merle needed only to look into his eyes to see that he was wide awake. He saw and heard her clearly, and he was thinking about it. Hard.

"What are you doing here?" he asked.

That didn't sound particularly polite, and he must have noticed that Merle frowned. Despite that, he didn't ask for pardon but repeated his question several times.

"*We should not have bothered about him,*" said the Flowing Queen demurely.

Merle thought for the first time that the Queen was probably right. But she wouldn't admit it. Probably the Queen had read it in her thoughts anyway.

"We're just passing through," she said hastily, which sounded quite silly, in view of the circumstances. But nothing better came to her in a hurry.

Winter smiled. His eyes blazed. But he didn't question her words.

"Just as I am," he said.

"Where are you going?"

"There's only one destination here down below."

Here down below, he'd said. That must be a sign that he came from above, from her world.

"And what's that?" she asked innocently.

"Axis Mundi."

"Axis—what?"

"*Axis Mundi*," said the Flowing Queen. "*The axis of the world.*"

"The city of Lord Light," said Winter. "I take it that you're both also on the way there."

So he knew that Merle wasn't alone. She remembered how he'd stared when she'd still been in the front head.

As if he meant to confirm her thoughts, he said, "That was quite brave before, of you and your lion."

"He is not *my* lion."

"Oh?"

"Only my friend."

"*Your* friend?" He smiled again, and this time the corners of his mouth also twitched. "You humans are strange creatures. One and the same word, and nevertheless you take offense at it. My lion, my friend . . . remarkable, isn't it?"

"Then you're not human?"

"I am winter."

"*Now it is coming,*" murmured the Queen.

But Winter was silent, giving no further explanation.

"Do you come from above?"

"Yes."

"Why are you here?"

"I'm on a hunt."

"For what?"

"For someone."

"How long have you been down here already?"

"A long time."

"Longer than a year?"

"I don't know how long a year is."

"But you just said you came from above."

"For me there are no years. Only winter."

"*He is crazy,*" said the Flowing Queen.

"When you say winter, do you mean the season?"

"*I* am winter."

"Yes, I understood that. But you said that you—"

He leaned forward with a jerk, so fast that she flinched and instinctively drew back a little. He didn't bother about that but just bent a little farther toward her.

"I am the ice. And the snow. And the cold."

Merle suppressed a grin. "You are *the* winter?"

He nodded, obviously satisfied, and leaned back again.

"Like the summer? The fall?"

Again he nodded.

Wonderful, she thought. Really grand. Someone like this is just what we were missing.

"*You see,*" said the Queen.

"I hate it when you say that," growled Merle.

"*I know.*"

Winter's eyebrows drew together. "What do you mean?"

"I was talking to myself."

"Do you do that often?"

"Don't say that it's a sign of . . . hmm, confusion. I guess *you* shouldn't be a judge of that."

Winter's face twitched again. Suddenly he burst into peals of laughter.

Merle frowned. "What's so funny?"

"You."

"Heartfelt thanks."

"You don't believe me."

"Whatever you say." She was gradually losing all her shyness of him. She hoped that it wasn't simply a sign of increasing apathy. If she made the mistake of feeling that nothing mattered to her, she could just as well jump out and down right now.

She felt that Winter would stay with his assertion. A living season. Of course.

Ultimately, it didn't matter at all.

"This thing here, this head," she said. "Do you know what it is?"

"A herald. It reports news in the breadth of Hell to Lord Light."

"Do you understand what it's saying?"

"I haven't given it a thought."

"You're traveling in it and haven't thought about whether you understand it?"

He shrugged. "No."

Mere noticed something. From far away, the voices of the heads had been clearly audible. Before, in the ear of the first one, they'd sounded dull and blurred. And now, in the mouth, of all places, she could hardly get more than a distant mumble. Shouldn't the words have been deafening right here? The source of the voice must be somewhere else, perhaps in the bottom, in the stump of the neck. That they weren't heard better here must mean that there was no connection between the neck and the mouth. She found that reassuring.

"Who directed you here?" she asked.

"I myself. And others."

"*Well, well,*" said the Flowing Queen.

"What kind of others?"

"Lord Light's subjects. I've met many of them. I've crisscrossed this country. I was everywhere—except in Axis Mundi." He snorted softly. "I should have gone there right off."

"Why didn't you?"

"There were . . . signs that the person I'm looking for wasn't staying there. But it's the last possibility."

"Who are you looking for, then?"

Winter hesitated, then he smiled. "Summer."

"Who else?"

"Summer?" Merle asked, blinking.

Winter's eyes misted dreamily. "My beloved Summer."

Merle couldn't think of anything to say to that. She had saved a madman from dying of thirst.

"Is this head . . . this herald on the way to Axis Mundi?"

"On the direct path."

"Are you sure?"

He nodded. "I know this country, I've traveled it. And I've seen many things. The heralds only join up into a group when they're on the way back to their master."

So Vermithrax had been right. She was sorry that he wasn't here. He'd be worried about her, so alone in the head's ear.

"When are we going to reach the city?"

"Very soon now. The heralds are going faster and faster. Not much longer and they'll be silent. Then it's not much farther."

Good. That was something, anyway.

Merle dug in her knapsack. "Are you hungry?"

"Winter doesn't eat."

"But Winter drinks," she said snippily. "At least it looked a lot like that."

"What would Winter be without water? There would be—"

"No ice, no snow—I understood." She swallowed a sigh and began to gnaw on a piece of jerky; it felt horribly tough between her teeth.

Winter watched her eating for a while, then he bent toward her again. "May I have some more water?"

"Help yourself."

"You are becoming close friends now, eh?" said the Flowing Queen acidly.

Merle handed the opened bottle to Winter. They would find water in Axis Mundi, at least she hoped so.

"Winter?"

He set down the bottle. "Yes?"

"This Summer, is he . . ."

"She," he said emphatically. "Summer is feminine."

"Oh, nice. Summer . . . Is she a . . . hmm, person like you?"

He smirked. "You mean, does she look like a human?"

Merle nodded.

"Yes, she does," he said. "When she wants to. Just as I do."

"Where do you know her from?"

"There are only four of us. One should assume that we occasionally cross paths, don't you think?"

Spring, summer, fall, and winter. It occurred to Merle that she herself had just been thinking a few days before that there was no real summer and winter anymore, that spring and fall ran unnoticeably into each other.

No wonder, she thought cynically, if they're both running around down here.

"And now you're looking for her? Did she go away?"

"Vanished. From one day to the next."

"You're in love with her." A statement, not a question. Now that she'd accepted his remarkable story, it was easier and easier for her to speak seriously with him about it. It was a piece of absurd theater into which she'd walked onstage a little late.

"In love with . . . Pah!" He let the word drive between them like an ice crystal. "Never before has there been a stronger love. Never a more magnificent day than that one when Winter put his arms around Summer for the first time."

"*He* is *a human,*" said the Flowing Queen.

"That sounds quite . . . romantic."

Winter stared sadly up through the open stone mouth to the heaven of Hell. "Up there, in the upper world, I can touch nothing without its turning to ice." His hand reached out like a snake and grasped Merle's leg. She shrank back. "If I were to touch you so, you wouldn't even have time to be afraid. You would stiffen to ice on the spot."

Coolly she brushed his hand off. "Oh, yes?"

"That is my curse. My eternal sorrow."

He's putting on an act, Merle thought, but he has no experience with the public. "And down here?" she asked politely.

"Nothing." He shook his head as if he could not grasp it himself. "No ice, not even a breath of cold. Here I'm nothing, almost like a human."

"Thanks."

"I didn't mean it that way."

"Of course not."

Winter sighed and twirled a strand of white hair between his bony fingers. "I do not speak with humans often. I only notice too late when I've wounded one of you."

"And Summer?"

His eyes again took on that dreamy glow, which amused her and at the same time made her a little sad. "Summer is like me. And yet quite different."

"One often hears something like that about couples in love," she said with precocious wisdom.

"You are thinking of Serafin," the Queen butted in.

"I am not!"

"And how!"

Winter's eyes narrowed. *"That* is your conversation with yourself?"

Merle shook her head hard, in the slight hope that the Queen in her head would get dizzy from it—but she knew that was nonsense. "It's all right."

"There is someone there." Winter did not take his eyes off her. "In you. I can feel him."

Merle was startled. Did he really feel the presence of

the Flowing Queen in her thoughts? His look was so serious, as if he'd just accused her of a betrayal.

"*He knows,*" said the Queen.

Instinctively Merle slid away from him a little. He made no move to follow her. Perhaps he was still too weak. But his eyes remained firmly fastened on her, sticking to her eyes like pincers.

"There's no one there," she said unconvincingly. "Tell me more about Summer."

"Summer can touch no human, just like me."

"What would happen?" She knew the answer already, before he said it, and with satisfaction she thought that perhaps she could see through him a bit. His madness followed certain firm rules.

"Everything that is touched by Summer must burn," he said.

Merle nodded. She could fill in the rest of the story. "And therefore it's possible for you two to touch each other without the other freezing stiff or going up in flames. Right? The effects cancel each other out."

Winter tilted his head to one side. "How do you know that?"

"I have"—she almost said *imagination*—"guessed."

He sighed again. He was beginning to overdo it with his suffering expression. "She was the first creature I could ever touch without fear. It was just the same for her. We were made for each other."

"*Yes,*" said the Queen peevishly, "*they all say that.*"

"And you think she's here? In Hell?"

"She was abducted."

Who abducted a being that could set anyone on fire who touched her? But Merle didn't want to quarrel with him.

Instead she stood up, climbed up to the stone bulge of the gigantic lip, and looked out over it into the distance. Actually, she only wanted to keep him from staring at her again with his dark, bottomless eyes.

Her breath stopped.

"Winter?"

She heard a rustling as he carefully stood up and appeared beside her.

"Is that it?" she asked tonelessly.

Out of the corner of her eye, she saw him nod.

"Axis Mundi," he said.

Many miles ahead of them rose a wall of rock, reaching from the ground to the ceiling of Hell. It could have been the end of this subterranean world had there not been a wide gap there. What lay behind it was not discernible.

However, she clearly saw the two gigantic stone figures that flanked the opening. Figures of humans. Each of the figures must be at least five hundred yards high, possibly even higher. They stood well forward, at the edges of the gap, the faces turned toward each other. But they were holding themselves strangely crooked, the upper bodies bent forward. Their arms were intertwined with each other, as if they were going to wrestle.

"The Eternal Fighters," said Winter softly.

"Is that what they're called?"

He nodded. "People tell about them everywhere. Lord Light had them erected. See how they're standing? It's said that on Lord Light's orders they come to life to continue their fight. And grind up everything that's in the gap."

Now for the first time it became clear to Merle that the two figures formed a gate. The city must lie just behind it, on the other side of the rock wall.

"Is that the only entrance?"

"The only one that's known."

"Then perhaps there are others?"

"None that anyone knows of."

Merle rolled her eyes but said nothing. Instead she looked out over the wasteland to the feet of the fighters. Dark, seething lines moved through the rock desert like ant trails. Thousands upon thousands of Lilim!

They were coming and going between the feet of the fighters, endless caravans that were taking the road toward Axis Mundi or were leaving it.

"They all have to go between the statues' legs," she said with a shudder.

"That's the idea. It creates respect."

"It will create respect in *me* when we fly through there."

Winter twisted one corner of his mouth, perhaps a thin smile. "As long as they aren't wakened to life, nothing can happen to us."

"Have they ever? Become living?"

He shrugged. "Quite often, if you believe the legends in the outer regions. But the closer one comes to the city, the fewer of these stories there are. Apparently no one has yet seen it with his own eyes."

"A good sign, I guess."

"*It could also mean,*" said the Queen, "*that all are dead who have seen it.*"

Silently the heads raced toward the center of Hell. The closer they came to the two stone giants, the more breathtaking those became, true mountains in the shape of men.

But why humans? Why had Lord Light not created them on the model of the Lilim?

Or were there Lilim who looked like humans?

Again she inched away from Winter a little, unnoticeably, she hoped. He did notice it, however. In his eyes she could read that he knew what she was thinking. He knew her fear. But he didn't defend himself. Said not a word, turned his head, and looked again toward the fighters.

When he changed his position, it was as if he and his shadow were moving in different directions. Only for a moment. Perhaps an illusion.

Merle again turned her eyes toward the gate of Hell's city.

9

AXIS OF THE WORLD

THEY WEREN'T THE ONLY ONES IN THE AIR APPROACHING the gap in the rocks. Merle could now distinguish creatures swarming around the stone colossi like mosquitoes, a multitude of dark dots. They were too far away to make out any details.

Merle and Winter took cover behind the stone bulge. Merle hoped that Vermithrax had also withdrawn deeper into the ear. She worried about him. He was alone and had no one to explain to him what was going on outside.

"He is doing well," the Queen said reassuringly.

The first head, which was diagonally in front of them,

sank into the shadows of the gigantic legs. From above, Merle could see the giant feet on the ground, mighty ovals of rock, around which snaked the Lilims' route of march. Still, she wasn't able to see the creatures in detail, so tight was the throng, so great the distance.

The heralds raised their flight path considerably, until they were soaring above the stone knees of the colossi. Merle lost sight of the columns deep below them and instead looked up at the gigantic bodies of the fighters. From close up, they could just as well have been bizarre rock formations; their proportions were discernible only from a distance. The stone thighs, between which the heralds were flying, became great walls, too big to measure.

The sight took Merle's breath away. The thought that these huge things were created artificially, with sweat and blood and endless patience, was beyond her power of imagination.

What did the workers who'd hewn these figures out of stone look like? Like men? Or instead, like the watchers in the abyss, roachlike creatures that had eaten the superfluous rock instead of cutting it away?

Despite the heralds' speed, it took quite a while until they had the fighters behind them. The gap in the rocks was somewhat deeper than Merle had thought, and it had a slight bend, which made it impossible to see the end of it. The rock walls moved past them on the left and right, and there Merle saw flying Lilim, coming toward them or flying in the same direction. They all seemed to avoid the heralds in wide arcs, as if they were afraid of the giant stone heads.

No Lilim appeared to be like the other. Some resembled the pictures that men had made of the inhabitants of Hell for thousands of years: horned, scaly beings that sailed on arching wings. Others were similar to oversized insects, clicking and rattling in black shells of horn. But the greater part were like nothing Merle had ever seen. With most, the extremities could be determined, sometimes also something that might be a face, eyes, jaws, teeth.

"They all look completely diffferent," she said, fascinated.

Winter smiled. "After a while you'll discover that there are repeating patterns. They're just not so easy to recognize as with humans or animals. But when you get used to the sight, you see them right away."

At some point the gap came to an end. Before them opened a grandiose panorama.

Axis Mundi.

The city of Lord Light, the center of Hell.

Merle had received a foretaste of real size when she saw the watchers at the abyss and then the two fighters in the rock gap. But this was pure madness: a view that could be apprehended only if she turned off her reason and simply *looked*—merely observed rather than tried to understand. For this place did not let itself be truly understood.

The city looked like a sea of tortoise shells, shoved

over and under one another, some tilted, others broken. Domes of rock stretched among towers, minarets, and pyramids, under bridges and paths and grillwork. No area was unbuilt, all spaces were inhabited. The rock walls between which Axis Mundi spread out like a coral reef were lined with houses and huts; the towers infested with whole tribes of insectoid Lilim; the ledges, which, like the bones of an elephant graveyard, rose above the buildings, covered with swarming life; and even in the thousands of columns of smoke that disappeared under the ceiling nested dark, fluttering creatures.

Enthroned at the center of this hodgepodge of inconceivable diversity was a dome that was broader and higher than all the others. The heralds headed toward it, and Merle guessed that they were approaching the holy of holies, the triumphal temple of Lord Light, the center of Axis Mundi, of Hell, and perhaps of the whole world, merged into one mighty edifice.

It would be a while yet before they arrived there, so far was the road from the rock gap, over roofs, spires, and gables. Merle used the time to examine the chaos below them more carefully. Once, a few years ago, in the streets of Venice, she'd seen a beggar whose entire face was infected by a proliferating ulcer that looked like the top of a cauliflower. From above, Axis Mundi reminded her of that sight, a grotesque work of tumors, entwined and distorted like melted muscle tissue.

And then there was the smell.

A spice dealer might perhaps have been able to recognize the individual odors in this abominable mixture of scents of all kinds. But in Merle's nose, the stink worked like a poison that etched itself into her mucous membranes.

The view over the city and the vague idea of what might live down there was enough to cast her into deep despair. Whatever had they been thinking of to come here? That Lord Light resided in a golden tower and would receive them with open arms? How should they find help here for their city, for their friends?

This was Hell, after all—true, at least in some respects, to the horrors that Professor Burbridge had evoked in his reports. And some things, she had no doubt, were certainly even worse.

"Do not let it frighten you," said the Flowing Queen. *"We have nothing to do with all that down there. It is Lord Light who interests us, not this scum."*

He is one of them, Merle thought.

"Possibly."

He will not help us.

"He offered it once, and he will do it again."

Merle shook her head silently, before she noticed that Winter was again looking at her suspiciously.

"Is that his palace?" she asked.

Winter's hair was being whirled around in the headwind

like a snowstorm. "I've never been here. I don't know."

The stone head kept on toward the monstrous dome, and now Merle noticed that the entire building appeared to be shining, from the inside out. In a different way from the subterranean lava strands, which provided light to all Hell, the dome glowed with no tinge of yellow or red, at once much brighter and yet duller.

"*Before you ask—I do not know what sort of light that is,*" said the Queen.

Winter's dark expression had brightened. "That could be she."

Merle looked at him with wide eyes. "Who? Summer?"

He nodded.

The Queen groaned.

Merle had a suspicion what the light might mean. Until now she hadn't thought about why Lord Light bore this name at all. What if it was a description rather than a name?

"*I am sorry to have to disappoint you,*" said the Flowing Queen quickly. "*In earlier times, the master of Hell was named Lucifer, and in your language that means nothing other than 'bringer of light.' Lord Light is a name humans have given him. Furthermore, quite a new one.*"

Light bringer, Merle thought. Someone who brings the light—and maybe even imprisons it under a dome?

Winter's behavior changed. He no longer brooded or

confused Merle with dark hints. Instead, he ran back and forth along the lip, casting excited looks toward the dome and chewing on his lower lip like a nervous boy. Merle grinned stealthily. And *he* claimed not to be human?

A few hundred yards before the giant dome, the heads changed direction. Instead of flying straight toward the vault, they now approached an interconnected construction of rectangles and towers rising at the side of the dome. Merle noticed that everything here, every building, even the giant dome vault, consisted of smooth stone. Nothing was built of masonry and mortar. Every elevation within the city looked as if it had grown, as if someone had worked the rock and stretched it, the way the glass blowers on Murano worked their gatherings of glass; as if someone possessed the power to force the rock to an alien will.

The heralds glided through an opening that reminded Merle of the mouth of a giant fish. In comparison to this door, the stone heads seemed like pebbles. Beyond the opening was a broad hall, where a good dozen stone heralds were resting in several rows on the floor; they looked like remains of ancient statues in an archeologist's storeroom.

First the front head sank into a free place, then their own. Its bottom struck the ground with a murderous jolt that knocked Merle and Winter off their feet. The noise was deafening. The stone quivered for a while afterward from the force.

Merle fought her way up, still quite dizzy and deaf from the impact. Fearfully she looked down. She'd almost expected that Lilim would hurry toward the head from all directions, like harbor workers to unload a newly arrived ship. But the floor around the herald remained empty. At first.

A powerful shadow appeared before the mouth opening, then Vermithrax shot across them, much too fast and with wing beats that created a real storm. He was just able to decrease his speed enough not to smash against the gums of the mouth cavity. Snorting, he landed on the floor and whirled around, all predator, all fighter from head to paws.

He approached tensely, keeping his eyes on Winter. Without looking at Merle, he asked her, "Are you all right?"

"We're all fine and dandy."

A silent duel of gazes between Vermithrax and Winter was under way. Merle was glad not to be standing between them, lest the quantities of mistrust and tension now in the air strike her like lightning.

"Vermithrax," she said soothingly, "Winter is on our side." Still, as she spoke, she wasn't at all sure of that anymore. Perhaps it was pity. Or naive confidence.

"Your name is Winter?" asked Vermithrax.

The white-skinned, white-haired man nodded. "And yours Vermithrax." He said the lion's strange name without hesitation or a trace of mispronunciation, as if he'd already known him for a long time. And in fact, he did add, "I have heard of you."

The obsidian lion threw Merle a questioning look, but she raised her hands defensively. "Not from me."

"Your story is an old and well-known one," said Winter to the lion, "and indeed, all over the world. I have heard of it in many places."

Vermithrax raised an eyebrow. "Yes?"

Winter nodded. "The most powerful of the stone lions of Venice. You are a legend, Vermithrax."

Merle automatically wondered why, then, she'd never heard the whole story about Vermithrax's uprising against the Venetians. The Flowing Queen had been the first to tell her of it.

"You come from above?" asked the lion.

Winter nodded again.

In order to cut short the menacing interrogation, Merle joined in and told Vermithrax everything she'd learned about Winter. The story sounded even more incredible from her mouth. Vermithrax remained hostile, and she could hardly blame him. Perhaps it had been a mistake to tell about Winter's unhappy love for Summer. With that she'd strained his credulity to the utmost—and beyond.

"*Merle,*" said the Flowing Queen suddenly, "*we must get away from here. Quickly.*"

Vermithrax was just about to take another threatening step toward Winter, when Merle leaped between them.

"Stop it now! Right this minute, you two!"

Vermithrax stopped, finally turned his eyes from Winter, and looked at Merle. The expression in his eyes became gentler at once. "He could be dangerous."

"What is most dangerous are the Lilim, who are coming from all sides," said Merle, but it was the Flowing Queen who spoke out of her.

Are you sure? Merle thought.

"Yes. They will soon be here."

Vermithrax made a leap and landed on the edge of the stone lower lip. "You're right."

Winter also climbed the stone bulge, nimbly followed by Merle. A horrified sound escaped her throat, and she quickly reassured herself with the thought that it must have been the Flowing Queen. Of course she knew better.

Countless Lilim were approaching the herald, absurdly comical figures with too many limbs, sharp-edged horn shells, and eyeless heads. The majority bustled along flat on the floor, while others went upright, if also bent forward, as if by the weight of their horny bodies. Some others ran on long, skinny legs, as if they were on stilts, and their arms stood out at angles like the legs of daddy longlegs. Those were the ones that horrified Merle most, for they moved fast and with agility, and Merle had to think involuntarily of giant spiders, even if that over-simplified the matter—and prettified it.

"They haven't discovered us yet," said Winter, as he

leaped back behind the lip. Vermithrax and Merle followed him.

The lion waved Merle over with a scraping of his paws. "Get on!"

She cast a glance at Winter and hesitated. "What about him? There's room enough on your back for two."

Vermithrax looked anything but happy. "Do we have to?"

Merle looked over at Winter once more, then she nodded. "Very well. Hurry up!"

Merle climbed up onto the lion's black back. Winter followed her after a short hesitation. She felt him take a place behind her and try to find the best position. There was just time enough for him to grab on tight, for Vermithrax unfolded his wings and lifted them into the air with one powerful motion.

They shot out between the herald's lips just as the first angled leg of a Lilim pushed over the edge.

Vermithrax rushed out into the hall. On the floor below, the Lilim turned their heads, some as ponderously as tortoises, others swiftly and with malicious eyes. Some let out shrill animal sounds, others articulated words in a strange language. Over her shoulder Merle saw a whole flood of creatures climbing to the chin of the herald and streaming into the mouth cavity. But the ones with the long limbs remained behind and stared up at Vermithrax. One gave out a succession of high, sharp sounds, and at once the direction of the stream of Lilim changed. Like angry ants they swarmed out to all sides.

Merle clung to Vermithrax's mane, while he climbed as high as possible, up to just below the ceiling of the hall. Her fingers got hold of something that didn't belong there. When she pulled out her right hand, she saw that something had caught in Vermithrax's coat, one of the black feathers from the ear of the herald. Only it wasn't a feather at all: It was a tiny black crab, so fine-limbed that she'd taken its limbs for down. It didn't move, was obviously dead. So they hadn't lain on the leavings of Lilim in the ear but on Lilim themselves. The thought caused her such revulsion that for a moment it even masked her fear. She had the feeling that her entire body must be crawling. Shuddering, she cast a last look at the dead crab thing and then flung it into the void.

Winter had tried at first to cling to the flanks of the lion, but now, when that hold wasn't enough, he put an arm around Merle's waist from behind. She had the feeling he shrank from the touch; perhaps out of fear she still might freeze to ice.

"*They were expecting us,*" said the Queen.

"But how did they know that we're here?" Merle no longer cared if Winter overheard her.

"*Perhaps they could sense one of you.*"

"Or you."

The Queen didn't say anything to that. Perhaps she was considering that idea, in fact.

The obsidian lion flew over the rows of giant heads and kept heading toward the door through which the heralds had entered. It must be a good fifteen hundred feet to it from where they were. From up here the hall looked even more gigantic.

"Vermithrax!"

Merle flinched when she heard Winter's cry.

Their enigmatic companion pointed his long fingers above them. "There they come!"

The obsidian lion flew faster. "I see them too."

Confused, Merle looked toward where Winter was pointing. She'd expected flying Lilim, flying beasts like those they'd seen in the rock crevice and over the city. But what she saw now was something different.

The Lilim who'd taken up their pursuit didn't fly— they were clambering along under the ceiling!

They were the same ones she'd already seen down there on the floor, long-legged, spiderlike, and yet many times stranger than all that she knew from the upper world.

And they were inconceivably fast.

Vermithrax decreased his altitude a little again, so that the creatures couldn't reach him from above with their long legs. But they now seemed to be coming from everywhere, as if they'd already been lying in wait, invisibly merged with the rock ceiling. Merle watched as some of them apparently appeared from nowhere. They'd been up there the whole time and now detached themselves from the flat stone surface, their long limbs outstretched, and from one heartbeat to the next, they launched into darting motion.

"There ahead!" she yelled to override the sound of the flight and the screeching of the Lilim. "They're in front of the door now!"

The entire ceiling over the hall's exit had awakened. A carpet of dry bodies twitched and shoved and tumbled up there, over and under one another, like an army of daddy longlegs, none of them smaller than a human and some almost twice as large. Many stretched single limbs downward, trembling and twitching, to reach Vermithrax in the air.

The lion remained relaxed. "If we fly low enough, they won't get us."

Merle was about to say something, and she felt that the Queen was getting ready to speak in her thoughts as well, but then they both kept silent and left it to Vermithrax to carry them to safety.

Winter was the only one who objected. "That way won't work."

Merle looked over her shoulder. "What do you mean?"

She saw his eyes widen. His grip around her upper body became firmer, almost painful. "Too late!"

She looked ahead again.

The entire ceiling was now in motion, a boiling mass of bodies and eyes and spindle-thin legs.

In front of them one of the Lilim plunged into the depths, a whirling tangle of limbs, too far away to be dangerous to them. Merle's eyes followed its fall, a hundred, a hundred fifty yards down, and she was certain that the creature would shatter on the floor. The thing landed, remained lying there for a moment, rolled up like a ball—then put out its legs and ran hectically here and there as if nothing had happened, forward and back, in a circle, until finally it stopped below, waiting, and stared up at them.

"*No,*" whispered the Queen, and Merle grasped what Winter had meant by "too late."

Around them the Lilim began falling from the ceiling like ripe fruit. A spider leg with a sharp hook on the end grazed Vermithrax's left wing and pulled out a handful of feathers. The obsidian lion went into a brief wobble, but then flew on, ever faster, toward the mighty door.

The Lilim fell. More and more pushed off from the ceiling and plunged. Vermithrax was compelled to fly daredevil avoidance maneuvers. Merle bent forward until her face almost touched his mane. She couldn't see what Winter was doing behind her, but she figured he was also pulling his head in.

It was as if they'd been caught in the middle of a bizarre rain shower—with the difference that it was raining living creatures, gigantic spider animals, only one of which would have been enough to put an army to flight. But here they were falling by the dozens, finally by the hundreds.

Vermithrax hadn't a chance.

A Lilim's body crashed on the lion's back end, slid off, and with its whirling limbs might have pulled Winter down with it, had he not swiftly slid closer to Merle and taken cover. So the hook on the Lilim's leg just tangled in Winter's long hair and pulled out a strand. Winter didn't even seem to notice it.

A second Lilim smashed onto Vermithrax's left wing, and this time they almost all crashed. At the last moment, Vermithrax got his ponderous body under control again— until the next Lilim fell in front of him and scratched his nose with its hook. Vermithrax bellowed with pain, shook his head so hard that Merle almost fell off, opened his eyes again and saw another creature, which struck at him with its legs as it fell, a whirling black star of horn and teeth and knife-sharp hooked claws.

The next fell right on Merle.

She was torn from Winter's grasp, slipped sideways, and fell into the abyss. She heard Vermithrax bellow above her, then Winter, then both together, and while she still fell she thought coolly that she would die now, finally and without any way out.

She felt something clawing around her, limbs like dry

branches, which pressed against her legs, her upper body, even against her face; it felt as if she'd run into a low-hanging branch in the dark. Her back was pressed against something soft, cool, a body, hairy and moist like a sliced peach.

The impact was bad.

But much worse was when she realized *what* had saved her.

The Lilim had closed around her like a protective ball, the way spiders do just before they die. It had turned in the air and had landed on its back. Merle could see the ceiling of the hall through the latticework of its limbs, an inferno of plunging bodies in which she saw no trace of the obsidian lion. But her vision was blurred anyway, her mind hardly in a position to process the images.

She'd fallen more than three hundred feet to the ground, and she had survived. The shock struck deep, if not deep enough to completely paralyze her. Her mind grew clearer with every breath, forming the beginnings of thoughts out of the confusion in her head.

The first thing that came into her mind was doubt as to whether she should in fact be grateful that she was still alive. She felt the damp, sticky underside of the Lilim at her back, the bristly hairs sticking through her clothing like dull nails. She saw the hairy, lath-thin limbs over her, cramped, motionless.

"*It is dead,*" said the Flowing Queen.

Merle needed a moment before she took in the meaning of the words.

"If it had landed on its feet like the others, it would have survived. But it landed on its back in order to protect you."

"To protect . . . me?"

"It does not matter why—in any case, you should try to free yourself from its grasp before rigor mortis sets in."

Merle pushed with all her strength against the enclosing limbs. They squeaked and snapped, but they would not be moved. Merle had not only to battle with her revulsion but also with the trembling of her arms and legs. Her head might have realized that she was still alive, but the rest of her body appeared to be just a bit later getting ready. Her muscles trembled and twitched under her skin like fish in a trap.

"Hurry!"

"All right for you to talk." Anyway, her voice was the old one again. Perhaps a little shrill, perhaps a little breathless. But she could speak.

And curse. Loudly.

"That was pretty good," said the Flowing Queen, impressed, after the flood of swear words from Merle's mouth had dried up.

"Years of practice," gasped Merle as she pushed aside the last Lilim leg. She made a great effort not to look down as she put both hands on the damp, soft mass at her back and pushed herself up. Somehow she succeeded in freeing herself of the cadaver's embrace and springing to the floor between two branch-limbs.

Her feet gave out and she fell. Not from exhaustion this time.

Around her hundreds of Lilim stood and stared at her, teetering on their long legs and sharpening their hooked claws on the ground. They'd encircled Merle and their dead comrade, but they came no nearer, as if something were holding them back. Perhaps the same command that had made the Lilim sacrifice himself for Merle.

The Queen anticipated the upshot of this realization: *"They are not going to do anything to you. Someone intends something else for you."*

For us, Merle wanted to say, but finally her voice failed her. She turned her eyes up to the roof and saw that no more Lilim were falling to the floor. The ceiling was still in motion, but the swarming was gradually decreasing and the creatures again melted into the rock, became invisible.

Vermithrax, she thought.

"He is alive."

Merle looked around the hall, but she could see no farther than the second or third row of the Lilim army. "Certain?"

"I feel him."

"You're only saying that to calm me."

"No. Vermithrax is alive. Just like Winter."

"Where are they?"

"Here somewhere. In the hall."

"The Lilim have them?"

"I am afraid so."

The thought that the obsidian lion had been forced by the Lilim to land or even fall made her heart miss a beat. But the Queen said he was alive. Merle didn't want to question that. Not here, not now.

The circle of Lilim had closed to about three feet around them. Although the spider creatures predominated, there were also some others among them, pressed flat to the ground or two-legged or without limbs altogether, a seething, swarming, whispering chaos of claws and spines and spikes and eyes.

So many eyes.

And movement everywhere, a ferment of iridescent surfaces, shiny with dampness, like a mess of algae and flotsam in the waves.

"Someone is coming."

Before Merle could ask how the Queen knew that, the wall of Lilim parted. The front ones fell silent, some sank their heads in respect—or what Merle took for respect.

She had expected a commander, a kind of general, perhaps an animal, bigger than all the others, something that far surpassed the others in strength and cruelty and pure repulsiveness.

Instead she saw a little man in a wheelchair.

He was being pushed by something that had a distant

resemblance to a knot of glowing ribbons, which were in constant motion, turning in and around one another and still moving forward as they did so. It was only when they came closer that she realized that it wasn't one creature but innumerable ones: a multitude of snakes, which moved together like a single organism, linked together and controlled. Its heads moved alertly back and forth, and its bodies shimmered in unimaginable colors, more beautiful than anything Merle had seen since her flight from Venice.

The man in the wheelchair examined Merle without any emotion. No smile, also no malice. Only blank, empty features—the interest of a scientist who was looking at a new but not especially fascinating species under a magnifying glass.

The coldness in his eyes made Merle shudder. They made her far more anxious than the thousand-headed army of monstrosities.

Was that by any chance Lord Light? Was the lord of Hell actually this little man with the dead facial features?

"No," said the Flowing Queen.

Merle would have loved to ask what made her so sure, but the man in the wheelchair left her no time. His voice was old and squeaky, like the creaking of hardened leather.

"What to do, what to do?" he murmured, more to himself than to anyone else.

Then: "I know, I know."

He doesn't have all his marbles, Merle thought.

The man gave the mass of snakes behind his wheelchair a sign, and immediately the bands billowed around and turned the chair, shoving it back in the direction from which it had come.

"Bring her to me," growled the man with his back to Merle. "Bring her into the Heart House."

10

THE ASSAULT

THERE WERE SEVEN OF THEM.

Too many, Serafin thought as they pushed through the darkness. Way too many.

Five boys, including himself and Dario. In addition, two slender figures, two women. Larger than some of the boys—*rebels*, he chided himself, full of cynicism—but smaller than he was.

Eft had the kerchief over her face again, although he wasn't sure why. Presumably they'd be seeing worse things this night than a mermaid's mouth. But she insisted on her masquerade, though he didn't believe she was ashamed of her origin. She was a mermaid and always would be. The human legs Eft bore instead of her *kalimar*, her scaly tail, were only external. In her veins flowed the salty sea, the water of the lagoon.

The second woman was Lalapeya. The sphinx had taken her human form, and now his having seen her with her lion body seemed to Serafin almost like a bad dream. Each diminution of her perfection, each tiny blot seemed absurd in consideration of such perfection. He had to forcibly remind himself that this, too, was just part of her magic. The magic did not end with her external change; she manipulated the thoughts of all those who looked at her, just as she appeared to manipulate everything that happened around her.

And Serafin still wondered whether what they were doing was right. Why was he going along with Lalapeya? What was it that made him and the others do what she wanted?

Not *all* the others. Eft withstood the sphinx's magic. Serafin suspected that Eft saw Lalapeya in her true form sneaking through the tunnels, a creature half lion, half human, moving forward on the velvet paws of a predator. He'd already noticed, too, that Lalapeya made less noise, less even than he did. It might look as though she was walking on human feet—but the truth was something else.

The sphinx was no human and would never be one. Why was she so interested in Venice and its inhabitants?

What made her incite a gang of street boys to assassinate the Pharaoh? The *Pharaoh*! Serafin simply could not understand why he'd let himself in for this.

"Eft," he whispered in the half-dark of the underground canal.

She looked at him over the edge of the scarf covering her mouth. She nodded once, very briefly.

"Do you feel it too?" he asked.

Again she nodded.

"What is it?" He rubbed his hand over his right arm. The hairs were standing on end, and his skin was crawling, as if he'd grabbed hold of an anthill.

"Magic," said Eft.

"Sphinx magic, worked by the commandants of the Pharaoh," said Lalapeya, who suddenly stood beside the mermaid, as if someone had poured the darkness into the shape of a young woman.

Eft threw her a side glance, but she said nothing.

"Sphinx magic?" Serafin asked. He kept hoping that the other boys didn't notice his uncertainty. But Dario, at least, perceived it and stopped next to him.

Serafin raised a hand and brought the entire troop to a halt. He and Dario and the two women formed the lead. So far. Tiziano, Boro, and little Aristide, whom they'd chosen because of his agility and adroitness, had followed without a single objection, question, or doubting look, along those secret canals that only a handful of other master thieves

besides Serafin knew of—canals that extended under piazzas and streets and were nevertheless just above the water
level. In some places the ground was damp, in others the
water was ankle deep; for the most part, however, the
secret paths were dry. Dry enough for a group of assassins.

Murder, Serafin thought. That was the word that until
now he'd avoided the way stone lions avoided water. He
was a thief, one of the best, but certainly no murderer.

"What does that mean: sphinx magic?" he asked, turning this time to Lalapeya.

He knew that the others shouldn't have been listening,
but his conscience forbade him to leave them in the dark.
If they were running straight into a magic trap, each of
them had the right to know about it. They were doing
what they did with free will, not from a sense of obliga-
tion. They were doing it for themselves, not for the city or
even the citizens, who'd never given a damn about the
begging street children.

For themselves. For each one of them.

For me, thought Serafin.

On the faces of the boys he read something more: for
Lalapeya. That made him almost more uneasy than the
magic crawling on his skin.

"Sphinx magic is worked by—," began Lalapeya, but
she was interrupted by Serafin.

"Worked by sphinxes. Yes, you said that already. But
what are they doing?"

Tiziano and Aristide stared at him wide-eyed. No one had ever spoken to Lalapeya so disrespectfully.

But she didn't bother about that. Smiling, she looked at Serafin, holding him fast with her eyes, and continued, "Such magic may mean all possible things. It can kill someone who comes under its influence, and do it in more ways than humans can imagine. It can also be harmless and merely warn someone that they know of him."

"Then do they know that we're here now?" asked Dario in alarm. Even in the dark, Serafin could see how much Dario was sweating. Serafin's forehead was also damp, and every few steps he'd run his hand over his face so that the trickles didn't run into his eyes.

"They would know—if I hadn't blocked the magic," said the sphinx, and now her smile grew a little wider. She looked stunning.

A relieved murmur went through the group of boys, but Serafin was still tense. "I can still feel the magic on my skin."

"That means nothing. Those are only the discharges in the air that occur when two spells run up against each other. Mine on theirs. That itching you all feel is only an aftereffect of the spells, not the spell itself."

They went on their way again, but soon, somewhere under the Church of San Gallo, in a columned undercroft full of spiderwebs and forgotten statues of saints, Serafin held Eft back. She carried Arcimboldo's mirror mask with her in a knapsack of hard leather. Serafin shrank from coming too close to the strange relic, so he laid his hand on Eft's arm, not on her shoulder. As she slowed, he quickly pulled his fingers back. She stopped now, a few steps away from the others.

"Do you trust her?" he whispered.

"Yes." The cloth over the mermaid's mouth stretched and puffed out with each breath and even more when she spoke.

"Completely?"

"She is Lalapeya." As if that were reason enough.

"You knew that she was a sphinx, didn't you? From the beginning."

"I see her in her true form. She cannot deceive me."

"Why?"

"The mermaid folk and the sphinxes have been related to each other since ancient times. Not many remember that today, but many thousands of years ago there were close ties. With the loss of the magic, we mermaids have also lost our meaning and power, while the sphinxes—at least some of them—have always understood how to fit themselves to new circumstances."

"Like Lalapeya?"

Eft shook her head decidedly. "Not her. She has been what she is today for a long time."

"But—"

She didn't let him finish. "She is older than most of the

other sphinxes, even if she doesn't look so to you humans. She knows how it was earlier, and she honors the old relationship." Eft was quiet for a moment; then she said, "She gave us a secret place for our dead."

The cemetery of the mermaids, thought Serafin, enthralled. An ancient legend. No one knew where it was. Many had sought it, but he knew of no one who had found it. "Lalapeya established your cemetery?"

Eft nodded. "Long ago. We are in her debt, even if she has never asked us for anything."

"What is she doing in Venice?"

"She was already here when the city did not yet exist. The question should be: What is the city doing in a place that was under Lalapeya's protection for thousands of years?"

"Thousands of years . . ." Serafin let the words melt on his tongue. He cast a look toward the sphinx, to the girlish young woman who led the procession at Dario's side.

"She never tried to drive the humans away, although that would have been her right," said Eft. "Her duty, some of us even said. This here, this night, Serafin . . . this is the first time that Lalapeya has intervened in the fate of Venice. And she must know very precisely why."

Serafin stared at the mermaid and had trouble holding her piercing gaze. "Do you know it too?"

Eft's scarf quivered as she smiled with her shark's mouth. "Maybe."

"That isn't fair."

"There's a knowing that is not meant for humans. But just believe me when I say to you that she knows what she's doing." Her eyes narrowed. "She made mistakes earlier. Now she is fulfilling her destiny."

A thousand questions burned on Serafin's lips, but Eft hurried on again to reach the front of the troop. He hastened to keep up with her.

"What is she? Some kind of a guard?"

"Ask her yourself."

"But a guard of what?"

Eft pointed forward. Reluctantly he followed her eyes and discovered that Lalapeya was looking back at him over her shoulder. She smiled, but it looked sad. He simply did not know what to make of her. Nevertheless, he asked no further questions for the moment, not even when he was walking beside her again and making every effort not to look at her. He was quite aware that she was looking over at him every now and then.

He took the lead and went on ahead alone, a few steps in front of the others. He again concentrated on the matter he knew more about than anyone. He sought the best way to get through the city in concealment, as he had done countless times in the past.

At length he had them all stop under a round hatch in the ceiling of the tunnel and gave them to understand that from here on they mustn't make a sound.

With Dario's help he opened the hatch and climbed up. Above the exit stood a round staircase, which led through all the floors of the Doge's Palace. The steps were narrow and had a much-needed banister: a few posts holding an old handrail. In earlier days, criminals were sometimes led to condemnation on these circular stairs, but today they were rarely used. The thick dust on the floor and the handrail showed that the last usage had been a long time ago.

Serafin was quite certain that the Egyptians wouldn't know of this staircase. Not yet. The Pharaoh's body-guards would get busy with the plans of the palace, no question, but he doubted there'd been enough time for that yet. For that reason too, the attack had to take place as soon as possible, this very night.

He loosed a rope from his belt, fastened it with a few quick flicks of his wrist to the lowest banister post, and helped the others climb out. He was in suspense as to how Lalapeya would come up—perhaps with the spring of a lion—but then she climbed the rope just like anyone else, with her hands and feet, if with a little less effort than the others. With her it almost looked playful, which once more earned her the admiration of the boys. The climb was most difficult for Eft, who, in spite of all her agility, had no practice in rope climbing.

Silently and swiftly they ran up the spiral staircase. The Pharaoh's chambers were on the upper floor, but Serafin was only too aware that he mustn't take the easiest approach. What they desperately needed was an advantage, and they wouldn't gain that by the shortest route.

He led the group past the entrance to the upper floor, still higher, to the end of the stairs, where the steps came up against a plank door. The wood was darkened with age, the mountings corroded by rust.

As Serafin had expected, the door could be opened without difficulty. The heavy latch, as long as his lower arm, yielded with a grating sound, and the door swung slowly inward. Wordlessly Serafin directed his comrades through the opening into a dusky half light.

He'd explained the exact route to the others at the enclave—however, only as far as this staircase. The last part of the plan he'd kept to himself.

All the same, each of the others guessed where they were—there was only one place in the Doge's Palace that was higher than the top floor. In past centuries, many thousands of prisoners had lost their lives up here in the dreaded lead chambers under the roof, herded into tiny cells, in winter half-frozen, in summer subjected to the heat of the sun beating down on the lead roofs; they might just as well have been imprisoned in ovens.

Each of them, even the most uneducated street boy, knew the stories of the prisoners' sufferings. Serafin would have been just as impressed as the others if this had been his first visit up here. At the beginning of his thieving career, he and a few friends had made a game of sniffing around in the Doge's Palace under the noses of the City Guard.

"No one can hear us up here," he said to the others. "The ceilings are thickened, because of the screams in the olden days."

"What do you have in mind?" Tiziano asked.

Serafin grinned, before Eft's dark look reminded him that this wasn't a game, unlike that time when he was dancing around under the noses of the City Guard. "We're going to invade the Pharaoh's rooms from above," he said. "That's the only way that's pretty sure not to be guarded."

Dario raised an eyebrow. "*Pretty* sure?"

Serafin nodded.

"And you think no one's going to hear when we break open the ceiling?" asked Boro. "And what with, anyway? With our bare hands?"

"No," said Serafin. "There's a narrow staircase behind the paneling, leading from the cells in the top floor. The Doges used the secret passageway when they wanted to watch the torture without being seen."

"Torture" wasn't a word that raised the mood, and so no one asked any more questions. They were depressed enough; their fear was too consuming.

Serafin led them through dusty passageways, so narrow that they had to go single file. They passed cells standing open, from which came a horrible smell, even though it had been ages since anyone was imprisoned here.

Outside there was a soft warmth, like spring, and still, under the lead roofs they all had trouble breathing. The stuffy air from the lead chambers filled their lungs like hot water. Only Lalapeya, whose people came from the great deserts, remained untouched by it. She and Eft whispered with each other a few times, but Serafin didn't understand what they said.

Finally they came to an empty room, which had once served as a torture chamber. Serafin stopped by a narrow iron door with a grated window in it. The door was closed, but it took only a few moments for him to unlock it with the tip of his dagger. Behind the door, narrow steps led steeply downward, apparently inside a wall.

"These steps end behind the paneling of a salon on the floor below," he whispered. "From now on, not another word! And get ready for the big fireworks."

"Serafin?" Tiziano held him back by the arm as he was just about to move forward.

"What?"

"If we make it . . . I mean, in case we survive this business, how do we get out of here again?"

Serafin took a deep breath, not because of the bad air, but because he'd been afraid somebody would ask this question. At the same time, he was glad to finally get it behind him. He threw a quick look at Lalapeya, but she only nodded encouragingly and left the speaking to him—and with it the reponsibility.

Serafin sighed. "You all know that it won't be over when the Pharaoh is dead. His guard will attack us, and it's also only too possible that within a few seconds it will be swarming with mummy soldiers down there as well. Not to mention the priests of Horus and"—another glance at Lalapeya—"the sphinx commanders."

Boro let out a hoarse laugh. It was supposed to sound hard-boiled, but everyone saw through him. "We're as good as dead."

Serafin shrugged. "Perhaps. Also perhaps not. Our speed counts. If we get the chance to retreat, we'll do it the same way. Up these stairs, through the lead chambers, and down the spiral staircase again to the secret tunnels."

"And then?"

"Then we run."

"No," contradicted Eft. "That won't be necessary. Down below we'll have help. You remember the old landing under the Calle dei Fuséri, don't you? The basin we just saw there?" The boys nodded. "Help is waiting for us there. From there on we can flee."

Dario let out a soft whistle between his teeth. "Mermaids?"

Eft didn't answer, but they all knew that he was right.

On the steps they drew their weapons. Each had a

revolver with six shots, as well as a pouch full of ammunition. In addition, Serafin, Dario, Boro, and Tiziano carried sabers. Eft had only a small knife, no longer than her thumb, but it was sharper than any blade Serafin had ever seen.

Lalapeya was unarmed. Serafin was sure that she possessed other means of defending herself. She was a sphinx, a being of pure magic. It was she who'd brought them all together. And she was—he hoped—the key to the downfall of the Pharaoh.

At the foot of the stairs they came up against another door, higher this time, the rear side of a wall panel. There was no latch, no lock. It was secured by a secret mechanism on the outside.

Lalapeya stepped back, slipped behind the line of boys. It had been arranged so. She needed time to work her magic against the Pharaoh, time the others were supposed to gain for her.

Serafin and Dario exchanged looks, nodded to each other, then with their combined strength they kicked against the wood. With a dull thud, the door burst out of the wall and crashed flat on the floor on the other side. Dust welled up, and for a moment the thunder of the impact resounded in Serafin's ears.

With a wild yell, Serafin and Dario stormed forward, over the wooden door, out into the room, followed by the others. Eft was beside them, then Tiziano, then the rest behind him.

Instantly mummy soldiers confronted them, as if they'd only been waiting for the intruders. The mummies were posted to the right and left in front of a closed double door that led into a room beyond. The two doors were ornamented with inlays of gold leaf; they glimmered in the light of several gas lamps. It looked as though the gold vines were moving over the wood like snakes, a confusing play of reflections.

Tiziano was the first to fire a shot at one of the mummy soldiers. He hit him in the shoulder, but then a second shot in the forehead stopped the soldier.

The boys now fired out of all barrels. Boro had to avoid the stroke of a sickle sword. The blade grazed his skull and tore a piece of skin from his head. At once there was blood running down his face, but nevertheless he whirled around, took aim, and fired. The bullet went astray and drove into the golden portal with a crack. Dario was immediately beside him and struck the mummified head from the soldier's shoulders.

Serafin raced to the next door. The first hurdle was overcome.

In a flash, Eft was at his side. He was just about to push open the door when a roar sounded. It rang through the main entrance to the room, which led out into a broad corridor. Reinforcements were on the way. Priests of Horus, if they were unlucky. Or, much worse, sphinx commanders.

Serafin waited no longer, rammed the right door in, and sprang through it, revolver drawn. He had no practice in handling firearms, but he hoped that his talent—or his luck—would be enough not to miss the Pharaoh and his vizier.

In the center of the second room was a divan of jaguar skins. Serafin could only make out the outlines; the center was blocked by four sphinxes, gazing at him with dark looks. They carried mighty sickle swords, much bigger than those of the mummy soldiers. Their lion bodies did not move, were stiff as statues, but one of them whisked away a few flies with his tail.

He's shooing flies, thought Serafin in shock, while for us it's a matter of our lives. That's how seriously he takes us: nothing more than a heap of blowflies.

At that moment Serafin lost all hope.

It happened very abruptly and without any warning. It had nothing to do with the danger from the sphinxes or that they had obviously expected the rebels—

(Betrayal!)

—but only with this one swish of the lion's tail, this one, tiny, apparently unimportant gesture.

Blowflies, went through his mind again. Nothing more!

Behind him a yell rang out, and out of the corner of his eye Serafin saw a dozen or more mummy soldiers pushing through the broken door. Boro and Tiziano were standing against them, splitting the skulls of the foremost soldiers with powerful blows of their sabers. Gray dust boiled up and settled like a veil of fog over the fighters.

A strange feeling of timelessness, of intolerable sluggishness, came over Serafin. It seemed to him that the battle was taking place underwater. All movements seemed to become slower, more lethargic, and for a moment a cry of jubilation rose in his throat.

Lalapeya's magic! Finally it was coming to their aid!

Right afterward the disappointment could scarcely have struck him harder. It was no spell. No magic guile. It was only himself, his own senses that slowed, as his mind retreated into deepest shock for a few seconds. Shock—and brutal recognition.

They were fighting for a lost cause. Dario vanquished one mummy soldier after another, with absolutely balletic ease, but he had no chance against the superior strength. Sooner or later he would succumb to the onrush of opponents.

Serafin warded off the attack of a mummy soldier who suddenly appeared behind him. Nothing of all this had the unpleasant taste of reality now. Everything seemed unreal, artificial, simply wrong, even his own fighting. It seemed to him that he was observing their defeat from the outside, and so he finally recognized the mistake with which they had begun, he himself, and Eft, and also the others.

They'd been betrayed.

And Lalapeya was nowhere to be seen.

Serafin let out a shriek that made even the mummy soldier pause. At the same time he struck in self-defense, first splitting the sickle sword, then the gray skeletal head. Eft brought down a second, and now the four sphinxes began to move. Through the gap between them Serafin saw that the jaguar divan was empty. And there was no trace of the vizier.

"Lalapeya!" he bellowed in a fury of rage, but no one answered. Dario threw him a look that seemed strangely empty to Serafin, as if an unseen hand had wiped every dream, every spark of hope from his eyes.

Eft seized Serafin's arm and pulled him back into the first room. Tiziano stood there, his revolver drawn. He was shooting in blind fury all about him, until Dario knocked the weapon out of his hand with his fist, for fear the bullets would hit one of them.

No trace of Lalapeya. Anywhere.

More mummy soldiers streamed into the room through the first door and blocked their escape route. Frantically Serafin looked around him. His eyes fell on Boro, who tore a small bottle from his belt and drank it empty in one pull. His cheeks stayed full, he didn't swallow the contents. Then he snatched a matchbox from his pocket, kindled a flame in the palm of his hand, and spit the fluid across it in the direction of the mummy soldiers. His hand turned red first, then black, but he didn't bother about it; he also paid no attention to Dario and Aristide, who were just able, with a daring leap, to get to safety before the fire licked over them and struck the line of advancing mummy soldiers.

"Out of here!" bellowed Eft as a wall of flame shot up behind her, a chaos of reeling, flaming bodies, who spread the fire to one another, until the front part of the room had turned into a flaming hell.

"Back!" cried Serafin, but Boro didn't obey. He continued to spit his flaming breath at their adversaries. He stopped only when the fire had almost reached him. With a quick glance he evaluated the situation, saw his friends, saw the saving door to flight, and finally started moving.

Too late. One of the sphinxes bounded through the door to the inner room without coming close to the fire on the other side of the room and reached Boro just as he was about to turn to the secret door. The sickle sword, as long as a small tree, rose up and struck.

Serafin screamed and was about to plunge into the room as it filled again with attackers. And then he was being pulled along by Dario as together they rushed behind Eft up the narrow stairs, followed by Tiziano and Aristide. Reaching the top, Serafin cast a look back and saw that the sphinxes were standing at the entrance to the stairs and shouting angrily: The passage was too narrow and the ceiling too low, so their sphinx bodies wouldn't fit through the door. If they'd tried anyway, it would have been an easy matter to strike them from the upper steps.

But none of the fugitives thought of that. Even Serafin, who'd experienced more daredevil escapes than all the others together, felt only panic, icy horror. He saw himself storming through the lead chambers like a stranger, out into the round stairwell and down the steps. If anyone had been waiting for them there, he would have had fairly easy game: Only Dario and Serafin still carried sabers. Tiziano held his revolver in his hand, without noticing that it was opened and all the bullets had fallen out of the cylinder. Aristide, at the end, was unarmed, and he pressed both palms of his hands over his ears as he ran, as if he could thus shut out the world outside.

One after the other they leaped through the trapdoor into the deep. No one took the time to pull the cover back over the opening; the Egyptians would find out anyway which path they had taken.

"To the landing place," cried Eft, gasping.

No one asked for Lalapeya. She wasn't with them, and all guessed why. Now, as they ran behind one another through the darkness of the secret pathway, with their feet splashing in puddles and having to take care not to bang their heads on the low ceiling and support beams, the thought came to Serafin for the first time that he ought to have been able to prevent it. Everything that had happened. It had lain in his hands. If he'd followed his instinct; if he hadn't let himself be drawn into this suicide mission; and if he hadn't believed Eft when she said to trust Lalapeya; yes, if he'd followed his feelings in all this only once, one single time, then Boro would still be alive now.

He had felt wrong. Serafin had known, he had known deep in his heart that this was no game, none of his master thievery. He'd been flattered that the sphinx had chosen him in particular to get her into the palace. And he'd fallen for it, for each one of her lies.

He looked up and met Eft's dark eyes. The mermaid was staring at him, enigmatically as always. She pulled the scarf from her face and bared her shark's mouth. "Wait still, before you pass judgment on her," she said. Without the scarf or mask, her voice sounded more hissing, each *S* a little sharper.

"Not . . . pass judgment?" he repeated, disbelieving. "You surely aren't serious."

But Eft didn't answer, only turned and ran on behind the others, who'd taken the lead.

Serafin went faster until he'd caught up with the mermaid again. How had she meant that? How could she ask that he not judge Lalapeya for her betrayal? Boro lay dead on the upper floor of the Doge's Palace and they themselves might not survive the next few hours. For all that, he should *not pass judgment on her*?

Had he still had the wind and the strength, he would have laughed out loud. And he would much rather have screamed at someone, Eft perhaps, or one of the others, to give vent to his helpless anger, and even to hurt someone, no matter whom, as he himself was hurting.

"Let go of it," said Eft as they bent under a low beam. "It doesn't help anything."

It took a moment before it became clear to him that the same thoughts must be going through her head, the same hatred, the same disappointment.

They'd all been betrayed. Lalapeya had led them to their doom.

They reached the underground landing with the last of their strength. A broad canal ran parallel to the path for a little way. A boat was floating on the waves, now and again knocking hollowly against the stonework. It was unusually made, larger and rounder than an ordinary rowboat and in no way comparable to the long, slender gondolas.

"A sea turtle," said Eft. "Or, rather, its shell. What's left after it has lain on the sea bottom for a while."

The sea turtle shell floated on its back. It was several yards in diameter and was hollowed out like a giant soup dish.

Beckoning them frantically, Eft urged, "Get in, hurry!"

Dario hesitated. "Into a sea turtle?"

"Yes, damn it!" Eft's eyes were angry. "We haven't time!"

The group climbed into the shell among algae and the encrusted remains of earlier sea dwellers, touching them as little as possible.

Eft was the last to climb into the floating bowl of horn and sit down on the bottom with them. Serafin felt the warty surface of the shell through the thin material of his trousers, but he didn't care. He felt gutted, his insides frozen to ice.

All at once, heads rose from the water around their vessel, only just up to the eyes—large, beautiful eyes. Then the mermaids showed the rest of their faces. In the darkness their teeth shone like slivers of moon floating on the water.

There were eight, enough to drag the heavy sea turtle shell through the labyrinth of canals out into the open water. Aristide was talking to himself and unable to take his eyes off the mermaid who was next to him in the water, although in the dark, hardly more was visible than a wide fan of hair, which now moved slowly forward. The shell began to move along with the mermaids, an unusual but effective raft, on which the survivors now glided through the darkness. A slight odor of dead fish and algae hung in the air.

Serafin's eyes sought Eft. The mermaid had turned away and was supporting herself with her lower arms on the edge of the shell. Expressionless, she stared into the dark water. It was clear how very much she longed to be gliding through the cold stream with her sisters with a scaled tail instead of legs.

The mermaids pulled and pushed them around a multitude of turns and bends, through low tunnels and open waterways that ran between façades without windows, through hidden gardens and, once or twice, even through waterways in the interiors of abandoned buildings. Serafin soon lost his bearings. Not that he wasted too much thought on that.

He could think only of Lalapeya, of what she'd done to them. He didn't understand her reasons. Why did she just call a rebellion into life in order to rub it out so thoughtlessly?

Wait still, Eft had said, *before you pass judgment on her.*

He would have liked to ask her what she meant by that, but this wasn't the time. None of them was in the mood to talk. Perhaps it would have been better, maybe it would have freed them from a part of the burden and grief. But no one cared about that at the moment. They all brooded silently to themselves, with the exception of Aristide, who kept on murmuring soft, disconnected sentences and staring, wide-eyed, into emptiness.

It was one thing to hear about mummy soldiers and sphinxes and what a sickle sword could do to a human being—but it was something entirely different to see a friend die, in the certainty that he gave his life for yours.

Serafin wasn't sure whether they would defend

themselves if someone were to attack them now. It wasn't the way it was in stories, where heroes took on another fight as they were on the run and with a breezy remark on their lips.

No, it wasn't like that at all.

They'd given everything they had, and they'd lost. Boro was dead. It would be a long time before the survivors could get over that. Even Eft, brave, hard, grim Eft, was oozing grief from all her pores like sweat.

From some of the rooflines, Serafin realized that they were crossing the Cannaregio district toward the north. If the mermaids intended to take them out of Venice, this was the best way—somewhere to the north lay the mainland. But he had no illusions about that: The Egyptians would spot them on the open water. Even if the siege ring no longer existed—after all, the city was taken—there must be enough patrols out to discover them within the shortest possible time.

But he didn't voice his objections. He was too exhausted and more than grateful to entrust his life to others; perhaps they'd go about it more responsibly than he had himself.

Soon he could make out a tunnel opening that led out to the open sea. A velvety night sky still hung over the lagoon, but the stars gave enough light to sprinkle the water's surface with points of light and to provide an overpowering feeling of breadth. A fresh night wind blew across the water toward them and penetrated the tunnel. It felt easier to breathe now.

The sea turtle shell pushed unhurriedly out of the tunnel opening. Before them, several hundred yards away, San Michele, Venice's cemetery island, rose from the dark wilderness of water. The ochre-colored wall that enclosed the angular island seemed gray and dirty in the icy light of the stars, as if it had been erected from the bones of those who lay buried on the island. The dead had been buried here since time immemorial, thousands and more thousands of names engraved on gravestones and urns.

In the darkness over the island, a collector hovered silently.

Dario let out a hoarse curse. He was the only one who made a sound. Even Aristide stopped talking to himself.

The collector cut a dark triangle in the diadem of the star picture. Colossal and threatening, the mighty pyramid hung a few dozen yards over the island. By day there would certainly have been sunbarks swarming around it, but now darkness ruled, and without light, the barks couldn't take off.

The mermaids pushed the sea turtle shell eastward, noticeably faster than in the maze of tunnels and canals. The headwind drove into the faces of the five passengers. Eft pulled the pins out of her long hair and shook it out. It fluttered wildly around her like a black flag at her back, a pirate queen on the search for booty.

But although they all had to hold on tight, they couldn't take their eyes off the collector over the cemetery island. They guessed what it was going to do there.

"Can they really do that?" murmured Tiziano, shocked.

"Yes," said Dario dazedly. "They certainly can do that."

Aristide began to mutter softly again, incoherent stuff that robbed Serafin of his last shred of nerve. But he was too tired to lash out at the boy. Not even the sight of the collector could pull him out of his lethargy. They had just been unable to save the living; what did the dead matter to him?

"My parents are buried over there," said Dario tonelessly.

"So are mine," whispered Tiziano.

Aristide groaned; perhaps it was words, too.

Eft sent Serafin a look, but he ignored her. *To not think. To not look back. I don't want to know all that.*

On the underside of the collector a glowing network of lines and hooks appeared, flamed suddenly in the darkness, and solidified, a storm of lightning bolts that all appeared at the same time and did not die out.

"It's starting," Tiziano said.

The first light-hook detached itself from the black and drove down soundlessly, disappearing behind the wall of the cemetery island. None of the five had ever witnessed a collector at work, but they knew the stories. They knew what would happen.

More and more glowing lines were sent down from the underside of the collector, creating a jagged, multi-angled trellis between the flying pyramid and the island of San Michele.

Serafin could no longer bear the horror on the faces of his companions. He turned away. His own father had disappeared before he was born, and his mother had been killed in an accident when he was twelve; her body had never been found. But he felt his friends' sorrow and horror, and it hurt him almost as much as if he'd had relatives or friends buried on San Michele himself.

His eyes wandered over to the shores of Venice. The coastline of the Cannaregio district moved ever more quickly past them, while the eight mermaids moved the sea turtle shell faster and faster over the dark waves. Now and again one of them appeared over the edge of the shell, but most of the time they stayed underwater, invisible in the dark.

Serafin saw mummy soldiers on the shore walls and patrolling along the Fondamenta, but they paid no attention to the collector in the sky over the cemetery island or to the sea turtle shell.

And there was something else.

The sky over the roofs lit up, a narrow edging of light, like Saint Elmo's fire over the roofs and gables. It was too early for sunrise, and furthermore, it wasn't the right part of the sky: In the east the sky was still deep black.

Fire, thought Serafin. The fire in the mirror workshop had probably set the entire district on fire. He wouldn't allow the idea close enough to him to really be frightened, but nevertheless, he looked over at Eft to see if she'd also noticed the strange glow.

Over her shoulder he saw that the light-net of the collector had enclosed the entire island. Clouds of dust and earth rose behind the walls.

Eft was also no longer looking toward San Michele. She was looking back at the city, and her eyes gleamed, as if someone had lit candles in their cavities. Only a mirror image. The reflection of a new, glittering brightness.

Serafin whirled around. The Saint Elmo's fire over Cannaregio's rooftops had spread to a glowing inferno.

And yet—there were no flames! No conflagration! Serafin had never seen anything so beautiful, as if the angels themselves were sinking into the lagoon.

Then he discovered something else.

The mummy soldiers on the shore were no longer patrolling: Some lay motionless on the ground, others drifted in the water. Someone had extinguished them in a moment, quickly, like a deadly wind gust that had strafed the shore.

Only a single figure now stood on the Fondamenta on the bank, not far from the opening of a canal: the outline of a powerful lion with the upper body of a young woman. She had both arms raised to the sky and her head laid back. Her long hair floated on the wind like a billow of smoke.

"It is she," said Eft. No one except Serafin heard her. The other boys still stared spellbound at the collector and the island.

Serafin felt all the hate and rage in him force their way out. He saw Boro before him as he'd stood in the middle of the sea of flames just before the sphinx reached him. And now Lalapeya, who'd caused all this, was standing there and working some magic to hold up the fugitives.

"Serafin!" cried Eft. But it was too late.

He'd shoved his saber into his belt, and before anyone could stop him, he made a headlong dive into the water. It closed over him, sealing his eyes and ears with oppressive silence and darkness. He wasted no more than a quick thought on the mermaids who floated all around him in the water; also gave no thought to the collector or San Michele or any of his friends.

He thought only of Lalapeya.

He surfaced, gulped some air, and swam away as fast as he could—and that was amazingly fast, considering his exhaustion, which now fell away from him like a bundle of rags. Blurrily, he saw the shore come closer, only a few yards more. He had the feeling he wasn't alone, that there were bodies to the right and left of him, even under him.

But if the mermaids really were following him, they made no attempt to stop him.

His hand struck cold stone, slippery with algae and sewage. The walled bank was almost seven feet high; he would never in his life be able to climb up there without help. Still filled with anger, he looked around him, saw the body of a mummy soldier floating nearby in the water, and then, a little farther to the left, he spotted a boat landing. He swam over with a few strokes and climbed into one of the tethered rowboats. A powerful disturbance arose in the water behind him as one of the mermaids under the surface made a U-turn and returned to the turtle shell.

Once in the boat, Serafin looked around. He'd been driven off course and was now a good two hundred yards away from Lalapeya. The sphinx had entwined both hands over her head, and the light was gathering there, creeping down from the roofs along the façades like something living, a glittering, sparking carpet of brightness, flickering like a fog illuminated from the inside out. A beaming aureole surrounded Lalapeya's hands, spread along her arms to her body, and finally enveloped her entirely.

Serafin didn't wait to find out where all this was leading. He couldn't permit the sphinx to do something to the others with the help of her magic. She'd already caused too much suffering. And this was probably the last opportunity he'd have to pay her back.

He pulled out his saber, sprang from the boat to the pier, and ran to the bank. His steps sounded hollow on the wood, but Lalapeya didn't notice him. It was as though she was in a trance, entirely concentrated on the annihilating blow. In the supernatural light she looked like a vision of a Madonna with the lower body of a monster, a blasphemous caricature from the pen of a medieval miniature painter, overwhelmingly beautiful and horrible at the same time.

Only once, very briefly, did Serafin look across the water to the sea turtle shell. Eft had gotten up and was standing erect in the shell. She called something over to the bank, perhaps trying to draw Lalapeya's attention to her. But the sphinx didn't react.

The other boys had noticed what was happening, and their eyes swung back and forth between the nightmare spectacle on the cemetery island and the occurrence on the shore. Dario waved at Serafin with his saber, perhaps cheering him on, perhaps something else?

Still thirty yards to the sphinx. Now twenty.

The glow intensified.

Serafin had almost reached her when Lalapeya abruptly turned her head and looked at him. Looked at him out of her dark brown, exceedingly beautiful eyes.

Serafin did not slow. He merely let the saber drop — against his will? — then pushed off from the ground with outstretched arms and sprang at Lalapeya.

Her girl's face contorted. She snapped her eyes wide open. Even in her pupils there flickered a supernatural glow.

Serafin broke through the wreath of brightness, was able to grab her upper body, and swept her off her lion legs. In a heap of arms and legs and predator's claws they crashed to the ground, rolled over and over, suddenly plunged into emptiness, and splashed into the water. A knife-sharp claw grazed Serafin's cheek, another tore his clothing and perhaps the skin under it, yes, he was bleeding, there was blood in the water. Then he saw Lalapeya's face, heard as she let out a piercing scream, now only a young woman with wet, stringy hair, no supernatural appearance anymore, and the light had vanished too.

He saw her thrashing with her arms and fought against the urge to simply press her under the water until it was all over, to pay her back for everything: her betrayal, the death of Boro, the way she'd used him.

But he didn't. It occurred to him that she couldn't swim and would go under if he didn't help her. He was tempted to leave her to herself, but suddenly he searched in vain for the hatred in his heart that had just now driven him from the sea turtle shell and to the shore. It was as if his anger had blown away and left nothing but emptiness.

"Serafin!" she screamed, her voice distorted by the water that pushed across her lips. "Help . . . me. . . ."

He couldn't see her lion's paws under the surface

anymore and was afraid her claws would shred him if he came too close to her. But he was indifferent even to that. He launched himself, glided over, and grabbed her from behind. He felt how she struggled under the water, and she hit against him, this time with human legs. She couldn't swim, either as human or sphinx, but the heavy lion's body would have pulled her down faster than her light girl's figure. He laid an arm around her chest from behind and tried to keep them both above water somehow, but he sensed right away that he wouldn't manage for long. In her panic she was resisting and threatened to pull him under.

Hands seized both of them from underneath and drew them out onto the water, toward the sea turtle shell, which floated in the darkness like half a skull. The mermaids didn't show themselves, stayed under the surface, but there must have been at least two, perhaps more. Serafin floated on his back, Lalapeya pressed in front of him, still in his arm. She'd stopped kicking, she wasn't moving at all, and for a moment he thought she was dead, drowned in his embrace—and wasn't that what he'd wanted when he ran at her like a berserker? Hadn't he intended for her to die and so discharge a part of her blood guilt?

Such thoughts seemed absurd to him now, and he sighed with relief when she moved and in vain tried to turn her head.

"Why did you . . . do that?" Her voice was mournful

and she sounded as if she were crying. "Why did you . . . stop me?"

Why?

A dozen answers shot through his head. But suddenly, in a flash, he was aware that it was *he* who had betrayed — not others, but he himself.

While the mermaids dragged them to the shell of the sea turtle, he discovered finally what Lalapeya had seen before him. And he realized that her magic had never been aimed at them, never at Eft and the boys, but always only at the collector.

The gridwork of fixed light flashes that bound the underside of the collector with San Michele were now a single quivering jumble of straight and crooked beams, hooks, curves, spikes, and loops. But they hadn't aimed at the dead Venetians who were buried by the umpteen thousands on the cemetery island.

It was something else that they sought and had found. Something altogether different.

The mermaids pushed Serafin and Lalapeya out of the water; Eft, Dario, and Tiziano pulled them in. The shell boat tilted and would probably have capsized if the mermaids hadn't held it steady in the water. Only Aristide crouched unmoving in his place and stared over at the cemetery island; he talked ceaselessly to himself and his fingers curled into claws; it looked as though he wanted to scratch out his eyes.

The others crowded close together in the center of the turtle shell, and while the mermaids went silently back to their work and drew the shell farther to the east, away from shore and toward the open sea, the six passengers looked at the island.

San Michele's walls had cracked. In many places wide pieces wobbled and collapsed, followed by uprooted cypress trees, which bent to one side like black lance tips and bored into the water. The entire island seemed to break apart, great cracks opened up, and seawater flowed in, undermining graves and chapels and causing the clock tower of the church to fall.

Something that had lain under the island, under the graves and crypts and the small cloister, was being pulled into the open by the light-hooks of the collector, in a chain of dust explosions and whirls of loose soil. Something that was half as large as the island itself.

The body of a sphinx.

A sphinx larger than any creature Serafin had ever heard of. Larger than a whale, greater than the sea witches in the bottomless depths of the Adriatic, greater even than the legendary giant kraken in the abyss of the oceanic trenches.

Half lion, half human, though both seemed out of order, the arms and legs too long, the face too small, the eyes too far apart. Hands as large as warships, with fingers too many and too long, and lion paws with extended claws of yellow horn and bone. The travesty of a sphinx and yet of an absurd grace, hideously distorted, almost a caricature, and yet with a grotesque elegance.

The gigantic cadaver lay on its side, the face turned toward the city, and floated against the underside of the collector, borne by hundreds of hooks of light. It *was* a cadaver, although it showed no trace of decay; there was no doubt that it was dead, and had been for perhaps centuries.

What was Lalapeya guarding? Serafin had asked Eft, just a few hours before.

What was she guarding?

Now, finally, he saw it before him, and he realized that her attack on the palace, the assassination attempt on the Pharaoh, had been nothing but a diversion. Something that would give Lalapeya time to destroy the collector and defend the grave of her charge.

Eft looked over at Serafin and placed her hand on his, but he wouldn't be comforted.

Boro had died for a dead sphinx.

No, he corrected himself: for a dead god.

A god of the sphinxes.

And with this thought, this realization, he collapsed and wept on Eft's breast. He saw that Lalapeya was also weeping, perhaps for other reasons, and then the sphinx god disappeared inside the collector, and somehow, through a chink in the defenses of Serafin's mind, crept the certainty that their enemies now had at their disposal a weapon overshadowing all that had existed previously.

Yet at the moment, it didn't matter. At the moment, all that counted was his despair.

Lalapeya sat down beside him and took his hand, but she felt cold and lifeless, somehow dead.

11

HEART HOUSE

WHEN MERLE AWOKE, SHE WAS ALONE.

Her first movement was to the water mirror in the pocket of her dress. Good. They hadn't taken it away from her. She had the distinct feeling, as she pressed the oval through her dress, that it had missed the touch of her hand.

She wasn't certain how long she'd been lying in the dark, in an unsettling silence, with only the pulsing of her heartbeat and the whispering of her own confused thoughts in her ear. The darkness awoke with her, breathed with her. Alone in complete darkness, alone with herself. Thousands of questions, thousands of doubts, and even more fears.

Where was Vermithrax? What had become of Winter? So alone.

Only then did it dawn on her what was so unusual about this aloneness. She no longer felt the Flowing Queen!

"*I am here,*" said the voice in her head, and it seemed a hundred times louder than usual. "*Do not worry.*"

"You didn't say anything. I thought you were gone."

"*Did that make you happy?*"

"Not here."

"*Oh, when it becomes serious, then I am good enough.*"

"I didn't mean it that way, as you very well know." Merle felt over the ground on which she lay. Cold stone, cut, polished smooth. A prison cell, she guessed. *Bring her into the Heart House,* the old man in the wheelchair had said. From that, she'd imagined something else. No, to be precise, she hadn't imagined anything at all.

"*You have slept.*"

"How long?"

"*Hard to say. I have certain abilities, of course, but a built-in clock is not among them.*"

Merle sighed. "Since we've been down here . . . in Hell, I mean . . . since then I've lost all sense of time. Because it never gets dark. Have we been here now for a day or two, or perhaps even a week?"

"I do not know."

"Then tell me where we are. Or don't you know that, either?"

"In the Heart House, presumably."

"Oh?" Merle rolled her eyes in the dark.

The Queen was silent for a moment, then she said, *"We will find out right now. They are coming to get us."*

Merle was just about to ask how the Queen knew that when she heard thumping steps, then the grating of an iron lock. A column of light suddenly appeared in the darkness, grew broader, opened to a door. Remarkable silhouettes, jagged and full of points, appeared in the door frame, looking like exotic plants, perhaps many-armed cacti, but then they appeared to dissolve and put themselves together anew. Possibly it was only happening in Merle's head and, yes, the first sight was probably a deception, an image that fear painted for her.

She'd just come to terms with this thought when the Queen said, *"Shape changers."*

"You really know how to cheer a person up."

"I knew that you would be glad to have me with you sometime."

"In your dreams."

"I cannot dream. Only when you dream."

A hand seized Merle, and she was led through the door into the light, out onto a grating walkway that ran along a rock wall. On one side of the walk were doors of steel at regular intervals, on the other yawned an abyss.

The outlook was shocking in its breadth. Obviously they were on the inside of the gigantic dome they'd seen on the flight into Axis Mundi. The rock wall curved slightly as it continued upward. High over Merle its contours dissolved into reddish yellow mist. Dozens of grating ledges ran along it. Other walkways, floating unsupported over the abyss, led out into the glowing mist, where they met other walkways, crossing them or joining with them and thus forming a broad network of traversable iron tracks, innumerable miles long.

Red-gold brightness shone up from the base of the dome, many times refracted by mist, which drank the light so that its real source could not be seen. As the light illuminated the entire base of the dome, it seemed to Merle as though she were standing over a sea of lava. But she had already guessed that the solution of this riddle wasn't so simple, for no heat came from the light. Even the mist that billowed in the dome felt rather clammy and uncomfortable. And then something else dawned on her: Although the dome consisted of rock, it had looked from the outside as if *it* was what was giving off the light. Therefore the brightness from the ground must be coming *through* the rock, yet at the same time it wasn't strong enough to blind Merle. It was almost as if the light in the depths was illuminating the stone so that the dome itself was glowing.

It was strange. And thoroughly unreal.

Her new companions also fit right in. The shape changers—if that in fact was what they were—had made an effort to assume human forms. And the effort had succeeded. Not the form of just any human, but that of Winter—which was even more ironic, since he'd insisted that he wasn't human at all.

However, their faces seemed plump, unfinished somehow, as if they were swollen. Their bodies were white, but they hadn't taken the trouble to imitate the structure or form of Winter's clothing. Also, their eyes looked as if they were painted, blind like the pupils of dead fish.

If they'd hoped to decrease some of Merle's fear through this weird masquerade, they achieved exactly the opposite effect.

They escorted her silently along the walkways and at each crossing indicated with a wave which direction to turn. They led her crisscross over the walks, out over the glowing chasm, until they finally came to a platform situated at a junction of several walkways.

On the platform stood a small house.

It didn't fit here. Its walls were half-timbered, and it had a steep, red-shingled roof. A weathercock rose from the pointed gable. The windows were subdivided into bull's-eye panes, and beside the wooden door, to make the idyll perfect, someone had placed a bench, as if the inhabitant of this little house came outside from time to time to smoke a leisurely pipe. The house radiated the coziness of a fairy tale. As she came closer, Merle caught sight of a carved sign over the door: WALK IN, BRING HEART IN! Little hearts and flowers were worked around the letters, without skill, as if by the hand of a child.

One of her guards pushed her up to the door; the other stayed back at the edge of the platform. Someone opened the door from the inside, and then Merle was led in, under the sign with the inscription, which now, on second reading, gave her gooseflesh, for some unexplained reason. Wasn't it supposed to read "bring luck in"? For a moment she had the feeling that her heart was beating a few beats faster, as if under protest, so hard that her chest hurt.

Inside the house, someone had attempted to maintain the romantic look of the outside but had woefully failed at it. To be sure, there were structural beams here, too, and even a rustic cupboard with flower inlays, but there were other objects that wouldn't fit into the deliberate quaintness of the scenery.

The operating table, for example.

The ground floor of the Heart House consisted of a single room, which in a wondrous way appeared to be much more extensive than the outside of the house. An optical illusion, Merle decided.

"*Perhaps,*" said the Flowing Queen.

In the back part of the room, only scantily concealed behind a jumble of beams that stabilized the building, were various metal trays, with scoured surfaces, on which instruments were spread out, carefully arranged on black cloths and scrupulously polished. Steel flashed in the omnipresent glowing light coming in through the bull's-eye windows.

The door closed behind Merle. She whirled around and saw who'd opened it to her. The snakes who'd been pushing the old man's wheelchair in the herald's hall glided toward her in a single motion and, immediately in front of her, puffed up into a pear-shaped figure at least a head taller than she was. The creature bent forward until its upper surface was only a finger's breadth away from Merle's nose, a shimmering mass of intertwining bodies. Finally the snake nest flowed and spread sideways and, as an ankle-high carpet, moved into the rear of the room, where it towered itself up again, this time into a pointed form like a sugarloaf. There the creature stayed and waited.

Merle wanted to turn and flee, but the shape changer barred her way. He now looked less like Winter, instead becoming something else too repugnant when Merle gave him more than a fleeting glance.

"I cannot help you," said the Flowing Queen.

Good to hear, thought Merle.

"I am sorry."

So am I.

"I know I brought you here, but—"

Be quiet. Please.

"Is that she?" cried a voice.

If the snakes gave an answer, Merle couldn't hear it. But right after that the voice ordered, "Bring her down here."

The snakes glided over to Merle again. She avoided their touch and voluntarily went to the opening in the floor out of which the voice had come. Although Merle had heard him only once before, she recognized the old man again right away.

"To me, to me," he cried.

Merle reached the opening and climbed down a spiral staircase into a room whose floor and walls consisted of steel mesh. Light from the depths flooded through it from all sides. Through the mesh under her feet she could look into the glowing abyss, the same as on the outside, on the walkways. For the first time, she became so dizzy that she had to remain standing at the foot of the stairs, holding on tightly to the handrail.

In the center of the spiral staircase was a round disk, which could be moved to the upper floor with a block-and-tackle mechanism; the wheelchair for which it had been built was empty. Its owner was moving through the cage room underneath the house on crutches. The crutches ended in palm-sized wooden feet, wide enough not to get stuck in the wire mesh.

Wide glass cylinders, almost ten feet tall, were distributed around the walls. There were at least fifteen or twenty of them, Merle estimated. Each of the cylinders was filled with a fluid, which shimmered golden, like honey, in the light of the dome. In the fluid, caught like ancient insects in amber, floated creatures that had once been alive. None of them were human.

Merle had to force herself to turn her eyes away from the grotesque forms, but she looked at them long enough to recognize that they all had one thing in common: All displayed a deep cut—mostly in the center of the body— that was sewn with thread and crossed stitches. Operation scars. There where the chest was in humans.

Heart House, Merle thought, and shuddered.

"Look around," the old man said, as he shifted his weight to the right and pointed with the left crutch in a trembling swing around the room that took in all the glass cylinders and creatures. "My work," he added softly, in a whisper, as if he didn't want to awaken the creatures in the containers.

"Who are you?" asked Merle, all the while taking pains to look only at him.

"My name?" He let out a cackling laugh that seemed phony to her, and she couldn't help wondering if he was only acting his madness. The crazy scientist, nothing but a role. But one he fancied himself in. And that was at least as unsettling as true madness.

He said nothing more, and Merle asked her question

again. She noticed as she did so that he'd gotten her to speak exactly like him: He had the habit of repeating his sentences, as if first he had to make sure of the sound of it, in order to then say it again, the second time more clearly.

"Most here—at least those who can speak—just call me the surgeon," said the old man. "Just the surgeon."

"Are you a doctor?"

He grinned again. His whole face seemed to dislocate when he did. What she had taken for gray skin was in reality beard stubble, reaching up to beneath his eyes. "But certainly a doctor, certainly."

He was trying to frighten her. That might mean that in truth he wasn't so dangerous as he pretended—or also very much worse: a madman *and* a role-player.

"These creatures here"—Merle pointed to a cylinder without looking into it—"are they all your . . . patients?"

"Early examples," he said, "from a time when my technique had not yet matured. Not matured. I've saved them to remind me of my mistakes. Otherwise one so easily becomes cocky, you know. So cocky."

"Why are you showing me this?" She'd noticed that neither the shape changer nor the snakes had accompanied her down the stairs. She was alone with the old man. But somehow she couldn't believe that he was careless. He felt very secure. And for good reason, certainly.

"I want you to have no fear of me."

Ha-ha, she thought.

"*He is playing with you,*" said the Queen.

It had come to my attention.

"*Then go along with it. Make the better move. Checkmate him.*"

Hopefully he won't take my Queen first.

"*Very witty.*"

"What do you want of me?" Merle asked the old man.

He smiled warmheartedly, and it almost looked real. "You must have patience. Patience."

Merle made a great effort not to show her fear. If he was giving her the opportunity, she must try to find out as much as possible. "When the Lilim caught me, you ordered them to bring me here right away. But then you imprisoned me first. Why?"

He dismissed her question with a careless wave. "I had to do it." With a grin, he added, "Had to do it."

Instinctively, Merle looked about her, letting her eyes travel slowly over the creatures floating in the cylinders.

"No more here," he said. "No more here."

"Where are my friends?"

"In safety."

"You are only saying that."

"Nothing has happened to any of them. Although the lion fought like"—he giggled—"well, like a lion."

"When can I see them again?"

The surgeon put his head on one side as if he really had

to think about the answer. "We will wait. Patience. You will soon learn to have patience."

"What do you want of me?" she asked a second time.

"That's simple," he said. "I am going to exchange your heart. For a better one. One of stone."

"But—"

"It will go quickly," he interrupted her. "My mistakes with these unfortunate creatures here were way back. Today that is not a problem anymore. I may be old, but I learn more with each new heart. Each heart."

Merle's pulse sounded so loud in her ears that she could hardly understand his words anymore. Instinctively she shrank back against the banister and held on to it tightly.

"Soon you will have forgotten everything. Forgotten everything, believe me."

This is fun for him, Merle thought, full of loathing. That's why he brought me down here: He wants me to see what he does. And he wants me to ask for the details.

He confirmed her fear. "Just ask, just ask! The faster your heart beats, the easier the operation is. Your heart is strong, isn't it? So strong."

She hesitated, then she said, "You are human, aren't you? I mean a real . . . not a shape changer or something like that."

"But certainly."

"Do you come from above?"

"Why do you want to know that?"

She quickly sought an answer that would satisfy him and that would lead to further talk.

"I've been to many doctors," she lied. "And there's nothing I'm more afraid of than doctors in the upper world, believe me." Perhaps it would help if he supposed she was a little naive.

"*Good idea,*" said the Flowing Queen.

"I was also a doctor in the upper world," the old man declared with self-satisfaction. "In the upper world I was a doctor, just so. Many were afraid of me. That is nothing of which you need be ashamed. Not ashamed."

"How long have you been down here?"

"Many years. So many."

"And what brought you here?" When she saw that he was becoming suspicious, she quickly added, "I mean, were you a criminal or something like that? Did you experiment with people? Then I'd at least know why I'm so terribly frightened."

He regarded her for a moment, then he nodded imperceptibly. "Experiments, yes. But no crime. I was a scientist. I am still a scientist. As we all are."

"Are there more humans down here?" Merle asked the old man.

He thumped with his crutch on the floor mesh twice, three times; then he smiled. "Interrogating me, hmm? But now that's enough. We will begin. Will begin."

Merle took a backward step up the stairs, but her feet slipped on something soft, slippery. She lost her balance, pitched forward to avoid cracking her back on the sharp metal steps, and skidded flat on the floor. When she looked up, the snake nest was pulling together behind her; a part of it still covering the stairs like an oil film, shimmering in all the colors of the rainbow.

"No!" she cried out, sprang to her feet, and whirled to the old man. He was sick, weak, and scarcely bigger than she. She would attack him rather than let him implant a stone heart in her.

"*Too late!*" said the Queen.

Merle felt it at the same moment. Her legs grew cold as the seething snake carpet climbed up her, faster than she could react. In a flash a solid layer of gleaming snakes covered her legs, her trunk, kept slithering farther, up to her shoulders and from there along her arms until the cool, intertwining creature enclosed her entire body like a skin-tight suit. They left only Merle's head untouched.

She tried to resist, but it was in vain. Involuntarily she moved forward, began climbing the steps. The snakes controlled her arms and legs, moving them like a puppet's.

Merle tried to turn her head and succeeded to some degree, although her legs continued to walk up the stairs. "Stop that!" she bellowed at the surgeon, who had just lowered himself into his wheelchair. "Call off these brutes."

The old man only smirked, turned on a switch, and

was pulled up by the block and tackle in the center of the spiral staircase, slowly enough so that Merle could keep pace with him.

At the top she moved directly to the operating table, lay down flat on her back, and bellowed and cursed so plentifully that the surgeon threatened to order the snakes to crawl into her mouth. At that she fell silent and looked on helplessly at what was happening to her.

Some snakes loosed themselves from the middle of her body and disappeared to the right and left under the table-top. Merle tried to arch herself, and the result was pitiful, hardly more than a twitch in her middle body.

Steel bands were closed over her wrists and ankles, then the rest of the snakes also withdrew, crept and slithered from the table and gathered together on the floor in the pear-shaped form of the nest.

Merle pulled and rattled on her bonds.

"Very good, very good," said the surgeon. "I think we will anesthetize you first. Is your heart really beating fast enough?"

Merle screamed a whole torrent of curses at him, the worst she could think of, and after the years in the orphanage there were quite a number. She didn't care if the snakes crawled over her face. She was indifferent to anything at all, if only this disgusting man might be struck by lightning on the spot.

The surgeon gave the snake nest a wave, and soon it

began to smell unpleasant behind her head, sharp, biting, like some of the chemicals in Arcimboldo's workshop. The anesthetic was being prepared.

The sharp smell became stronger. She turned her head, as well as she could, to look behind her, and out of the corner of her eye made out the seething of the snakes. They swelled toward her like a dark wave.

Merle's perceptions grew muddled. Her surroundings revolved, flowed into one another.

Snakes bustled in the background.

Merle's heart hammered in her chest.

The surgeon came closer, his face swelled, filled her field of vision, filled the world.

His flesh and that of the snakes, glowing like the colors on the palette of a painter.

His grin.

"Stop!"

The world rotated again, a world of yellow teeth and gray hair.

"Stop, I said!"

The smell grew weaker. Her surroundings changed. The face of the old man lost its distinctness, pulled back.

"Release her at once!" Not the voice of the surgeon, also not her own. Someone else.

The iron cuffs on her hands and feet snapped back, and suddenly she was free. No more chains and no more snakes holding her.

With the disappearance of the biting fog, she could see the room again. The white ceiling, the wooden beams, everything back in place.

Two voices were arguing with each other in the background. One belonged to the surgeon. The other was that of the stranger who'd saved her.

Saved?

Perhaps.

"Merle?" asked the Flowing Queen, sounding as dazed as Merle herself.

I am here, she thought, even though she felt as if someone else had taken over thinking for her. Indeed, where else would she be?

"You are all right." Not a question, a statement.

All right. Yes.

The argument broke off, and now someone was bending over her face. Not the surgeon. But the man was at least as old.

Scientist, as we all are, the surgeon had said.

As we all are.

"Are you Lord Light?" asked Merle weakly.

"Yes," said the man. He had thick, gray hair.

"You are a human," she stated, and thought she was dreaming, was almost convinced of it.

Lord Light, the ruler of Hell, smiled. "Believe me, Merle, the human is a better devil than the Devil."

His face withdrew, then she only heard his voice.

"And now, please, stand up and come with me."

12

LORD LIGHT

THE SURGEON REMAINED BEHIND IN THE HEART HOUSE. Merle cast a last look at the man in the wheelchair as Lord Light pushed her out onto the platform, one hand on her shoulder, not in an unfriendly way, yet firmly. The surgeon stared, first at her, then at Lord Light, his small, narrowed eyes blazing with hate and fury.

"You needn't fear him anymore," said her companion, as they stepped from the platform onto one of the grating walkways.

Lord Light, hammered in her head. He's Lord Light. Only a man.

"The surgeon can do nothing more to you," he said.

Her hand moved to her chest, feeling for the quick pulsing of her heart.

Lord Light noticed it. "Don't worry, it's still the old one. Stone hearts don't beat."

Examining him from the side, she thought he looked like a scholar—which he doubtless was, if the surgeon had told the truth.

He wore a black frock coat, narrowly cut, with a flower of red glass on the lapel. His trousers were also black, and his pointed patent leather shoes gleamed. The golden chain of a watch hung in a semicircular loop out of his jacket pocket, as if the shape were mimicking the dark circles around his eyes. Merle had never seen such dark circles, as dark as if they were painted. Nevertheless, he didn't act tired or exhausted, quite the contrary. He radiated a liveliness that belied his age.

Merle couldn't take her eyes off him. This man, of all people, was supposed to help her free Venice? An old man who walked along beside her in his frock coat as if they were going on a Sunday walk together?

"*Ask him his name,*" said the Flowing Queen. "*His true name.*"

Merle ignored her. "Where are my friends?"

"No one has harmed a hair of them. The lion has raged continuously since the Lilim took him prisoner, but he is well. He survived the crash in the Hall of the Heralds without injury."

They walked side by side along a grill walkway, then down a long set of stairs and across other walks. "I want to see him."

"You will."

"When?"

"Soon."

"How is Winter?"

Lord Light sighed softly. "Is that his name? Winter? He's a strange fellow. To be honest, I can't tell you how he is."

"What do you mean?"

"He's fled."

"What?" She stopped, a hand on the railing of the grill walkway. At some distance she saw several figures peel away from the light clouds, no larger than matchsticks, with too many arms and legs; at a crossing they turned off and quickly disappeared again in the glowing mist of the dome.

"He escaped," said Lord Light, turning to her. She felt the impatience in his voice, but still he didn't pressure her. "I had a long conversation with him. And then he was gone."

"*A long conversation?*" asked the Queen suspiciously.

"He was weak," said Merle incredulously. "Sick, I think. When we met him, he could hardly stand on his own."

"Well, at least he could *free* himself on his own."

Merle looked past him, down into the glowing depths.

She wondered why she had no fear of Lord Light. "That's impossible. You're lying to me."

"Why should I do that?"

"Perhaps you've killed him."

"Without a reason?"

She hesitated briefly as she tried to find a logical argument. She was very close to saying something dumb like, "But you're the lord of Hell! You're mean, any child knows that. You don't need a reason to kill someone." But then she thought about it a moment longer and whispered, "It simply can't be. He was much too weak."

Lord Light began walking again and bade her follow him: He wanted to show her something, and it was a long way there. Merle wondered why he didn't simply call over some flying monstrosity to carry them to their destination; but that didn't fit him. Neither did he fit the picture of Lord Light she'd made for herself.

Should I ask him now, she wondered, whether he'll help us? But somehow this prospect suddenly seemed a mistake to her. The dimensions of this world-within-the-world made her business shrivel to blurry insignificance.

But that was why they'd come, wasn't it?

Wasn't it?

Instead of an answer, the Queen said once more: "*Ask him his name.*"

This time Merle obeyed, before the Queen could take over her voice.

"What's your name?" she asked. "I mean, Lord Light surely isn't your true name—at least not if you really are a human being."

Humor gleamed in his eyes when he looked down at her. "Have you any doubt that I'm human?"

"I don't know." That was sincere. "I just saw shape changers, after all, and they—"

"Then you also saw how pitifully badly they can imitate a human being."

"How about with magic, then?"

"I'm no magician, only a scientist."

"Like the surgeon?"

He shrugged. "If you like."

"Then tell me what your name is."

Laughing, he raised both hands as if he had no other choice but to give in to her persistence. He cleared his throat—then he told her his name.

Merle stopped in her tracks. She stared at him, open-mouthed. "Seriously?"

The clouds of mist prevented his laugh from echoing into the distance. "I have of course been down here for quite a while now, but I haven't forgotten my name, believe me."

"Burbridge?" she repeated. "*Professor* Burbridge?"

"Sir Charles Burbridge, honorary chair of the National Geographic Society, First Explorer to Her Majesty the Queen, discoverer of Hell, and its first and probably only cartographer. Professor of geography, astronomy, and biology. And an old man, I'm afraid."

Merle exhaled through her clenched teeth. It sounded like a whistle. "You *are* Professor Burbridge!"

He smiled, now almost a little embarrassed. "And something more than that," he said mysteriously. But then he went on again, this time without telling her to come along. He knew that she'd follow him.

Merle trotted wordlessly along beside him as he knocked dust from the left arm of his coat with his hand. Shaking his head, he said, "You know, one can teach these creatures to build all this here, whole cities, steam engines, and factories—but one is doomed to failure if one tries to impart to them anything so basic as a sense of fashion. Look at this here!" He held out his sleeve and she had to force herself to look very closely. "See it?" he asked her. "Cross-stitch! They sew such a piece of clothing with cross-stitch! Absolutely inexcusable."

Merle thought of the creatures in the Heart House. Cross-stitch. She shuddered. "Where are you taking me?"

"To the Stone Light."

"What is that?"

"You'll soon see."

"Is Vermithrax there?"

He smiled again. "He should be, anyway. Provided he hasn't tricked these blockhead guards like your other friend." A grin. "But I think not."

Silently they went down more steps, followed endless walkways. Merle had the feeling that soon they would have crossed the entire dome. Yet wherever she looked, she never saw the curving wall anywhere; they were still somewhere in the center of the light dome. Also, the Heart House had disappeared over them.

The Stone Light.

She got gooseflesh, without understanding why.

She kept wanting to ask him for the help his messenger had offered to the Venetians, wanted to fulfill her mission—but she had the feeling that for a long time it hadn't been about that anymore. Not about Venice. Not about her.

Did we *really* come here about that? she asked in her thoughts and received no answer. The Queen had been notably quiet since the Lilim had taken Merle into their power, almost as if she were afraid someone would notice her. But was that the only reason?

"The surgeon," said Merle after a long while, "can he do that, really? Put a stone heart in a human?"

"Yes, he can."

"Why does he do it?"

"Because I ordered him to."

Merle's stomach lurched, but she didn't let it show. She'd been taken in by him and his friendliness. It was time to remember who he was and what he represented down here.

"The messenger I sent to you up in the Piazza San Marco," he said in a conversational tone, "he had a stone heart. One of the first that actually functioned. And the same with many others upon whom I rely. The stone makes it easier to control them."

"They haven't wills of their own anymore?"

"Not like you and me. But it's a little more complicated."

"Why do all that? The Lilim appear to obey you anyway. Or does each of them have a stone heart?"

"Bah! Control their leaders and you control the whole bunch. You know, down here everything seems gigantic and immeasurable. But in truth, the threads all run to small centers, as in a knot. Or even a heart. Get it on your side, and the rest is child's play."

He was walking more slowly now, almost sauntering, a nice old man who wouldn't harm a fly.

Bah, she thought, Devil take him! Then it occurred to her that *he* was the Devil.

"But why?" she asked again.

He took a deep breath, looked at his spotlessly shining shoes, then out into the mist. "Why did I come here and build all this? Why did I write books full of lies about Hell so that no one would dare to think of coming down here? For science, naturally! What else?"

"You became the ruler of Hell in order to study it?" She remembered that the Flowing Queen had once suggested something quite similar—and wondered again if she hadn't even *known* it.

The Queen remained obdurately silent.

"Several of us came here," said Burbridge. "I and a handful of colleagues from different faculties. Medical men like the surgeon, but also aestheticians, geologists, and biologists, such as me, even a philosopher. . . . He made the mistake of debating with a Lilim about Plato's cave allegory. The Lilim didn't agree with him. He didn't agree with the Lilim, either, by the way." He wore an amused smile, but it almost looked a little sad. "We had to learn a great deal. Adapt to new things and fundamentally change ourselves—not only our preoccupations and opinions but also ourselves. Our consciences, for example. Our ethics."

Merle nodded, as though she knew exactly what he was talking about. And basically, she saw through what he intended to say quite well: that he, no matter how one looked at it, had done the right thing. As if he personally had made the sacrifices that this madness had cost.

Suddenly she felt he was nothing more than false and a glib liar. She despised him almost more than the surgeon. The old man in the wheelchair had at least been honest, to her, but also with himself.

Burbridge, on the other hand, was a hypocrite.

She had always hated men like him when she was still living in the orphanage and had learned to know more of his type than she liked: administrators, priests, teachers. Even some of those who came to take children away with them.

She felt sick. Not from the height, and not from fear. Only from him and his nearness.

"You don't share your research results with anyone. You've served up a quantity of nonsense to the world above and kept for yourself everything you've actually found out down here. What's the point of that?"

"Tell me, Merle, you're curious too, aren't you?

"Certainly."

"Then imagine your curiosity like a glass of water. And now take a whole barrel of it. Then you know how it looks in the heart of a scientist. Of a true scientist!"

Rubbish, she thought. Just talk. He and his researcher friends could probably outdo each other in lying.

"Will we be there soon?" she asked, to change the subject.

"Look down below. You'll be able to see it right now."

"The Stone Light?"

He nodded.

"How can a light be stone?" she asked.

He grinned and again looked terribly friendly. "Perhaps it always has been, and you just haven't noticed until now."

She looked over the handrail down into the abyss. He was right. The mist gradually dissolved. Vaguely she could make out something down there like a dark star, massive gray beams that ran out from a bright central point in all directions. But it wasn't until they'd gone down another long staircase that she saw that these beams were walkways, which opened onto a round grill walk in the middle. It had a diameter of about 150 yards, and only a single walkway cut straight across the center like a lone spoke.

The grill circle floated high over the glowing bottom of the hall, which now, as they came closer, turned out not to be a smooth surface but a mighty dome, like the upper quarter of a ball, which lay buried in the rock. Its size couldn't even be guessed at, but it must cover the entire base of the rock dome. The circular mesh walkway was located exactly over the center of this curvature, suspended over its highest point; there were no columns or supporting structures, the walkway alone held it in the air.

"That down there," said Burbridge, "is the Stone Light."

"It looks like a piece of the moon." She imagined that someone had cut the moon into slices like a loaf of bread; after that, they'd laid one of the two heels on the ground and erected the dome over it.

Burbridge continued, "Think of a gigantic, glowing ball, which has fallen from the sky at some point, broken through the outer crust of the earth, and drilled down here into the bottom of Hell. What you see there is a part of it, which still shows above the rock. The Morning Star, Lucifer, the fallen angel. Or simply the Stone Light."

"Did you have the dome built over it?"

"Certainly."

"Why? What does the Light do, then, except to illuminate?"

For the first time the Flowing Queen made herself heard again: *"Are you still playing naive, or are you really?"*

Be quiet, thought Merle. To her surprise, the voice obeyed without contradiction.

As they walked farther, down ever deeper, toward the light and the round grill pathway, Burbridge circled the entire interior of the dome with a wave of his hand. "When I came here for the first time, this place was a holy place for the Lilim, and they feared it. None of them dared to approach it voluntarily. They avoided this place as well as they could. I was the first to show them how one could put the power of the Light to use."

"But Axis Mundi, the city," said Merle, "it must be much older than the sixty or seventy years since you discovered Hell." Even as she spoke, it dawned on her how old Burbridge must in fact be, and she wondered if he had the Light on the bottom of the dome to thank for that.

As he walked, the professor absentmindedly stroked the handrail with one hand. "There was already a city on this spot when humanity was still crouching in its caves. The Lilim once possessed a highly developed civilization—not *technically* highly developed; rather, more comparable to our Middle Ages. But they possessed a social structure and their own culture, they lived in cities and large communities. However, that was all long past when I came down into Hell. The few who'd survived the decline in the course of eons lived as loners in the vastness of the rock deserts, some also in tribes and packs. But there was no civilization anymore. That was all long declined and forgotten. Together with this city."

Merle gradually understood. "Was the city already here when the Morning Star—or the Stone Light—crashed down here?"

Burbridge nodded. "It was the center of the old Lilim culture. The Stone Light destroyed large parts of that and made it uninhabitable for thousands of years. When I came, the Lilim told a whole heap of legends about the ruins of the city. Some maintained that the Light made them deformed, and they became caricatures of themselves—to the human eye at least."

"And is that true?"

Burbridge shrugged. "Who knows? More than sixty years ago, when I made my first visit here, there was no trace left of it at all. I discovered the Light and recognized that its energy could be useful for a whole list of things. But I knew, naturally, that I would need helpers, countless helpers, and that men couldn't be considered for it."

"Why not?"

"What do you think would have happened if I'd gone

back to the surface and reported what I'd stumbled on here? They would have thanked me, of course, pinned all sorts of orders on my lapel, and sent me home. And then they'd have appointed others to make use of this place. First the British Crown, then perhaps the Czar. They would have hired experts, wouldn't have needed me for it anymore—a brilliant, but also very young scientist!" Grimly he made a gesture of dismissal. "No, Merle, what I needed then was my own kingdom, with its own subjects and workers. I and some of my colleagues, in whom I'd confided, succeeded in uniting a majority of the Lilim through simple things, a few technical tricks, playthings from the magic hat of the colonial masters of all ages. The Lilim might look like beasts to our eyes, but at bottom they are no different from the natives that the Spaniards and Portuguese found in South America or the French in Indonesia. With a little energy they can be manipulated and controlled."

"With force, you mean."

"That too, yes. But not only and not primarily. As I said, a little technology, a few simple trinkets can work wonders here. And when we finally got to the point where they were serving us, and we could make use of the power of the Stone Light, we were also in a position to offer greater wonders. The flying heralds, for example. Or other powers that at first sight appear to be magic, like the destruction and boring through rock on a large scale. And, naturally, the hearts of stone, which keep an organism alive *and* control it."

"Isn't that magic?"

"Well, yes, depending on the point of view. It certainly has something of magic, and, to be honest, I doubt that the surgeon himself understands what he's doing. The real work is taken over by the heart—the Stone."

Merle wiped the sweat from her forehead, although down here, despite the closeness to the Stone Light, it wasn't really warm. She looked up at the glowing dome. "It's the same. Exactly the same."

"What do you mean?" he asked in surprise.

"The Stone Light. The Morning Star. The ball down there in the ground. It's just like a giant heart that beats in the center of Axis Mundi."

He agreed with her enthusiastically. "I'm very happy that you got this idea yourself. You're right on the mark. My own theory is that the Morning Star—wherever it came from—functioned like a heart that for an infinitely long time was on the hunt for an organism that it could drive. Until it finally landed here. The world of the Lilim can, exactly like any society, be compared with a large living thing. At one time, the city on whose ruins we erected Axis Mundi was the center of this world. When it was destroyed, the Lilim culture fell because it didn't know how to use the power of the Light. But today, thanks to our help, the Lilim are doing better. With the Stone Light,

I've given their people a new heart, and now the organism of this society is growing and thriving to something still bigger, better."

"Do the individual Lilim see it that way?"

Burbridge's euphoria cooled. "They're like ants. The individuals don't count, only the people is of any significance. The individual may suffer grief, or pain, or exhaustion, but the whole draws on it and profits from it."

Merle snorted. "*You* profit from it. Not the Lilim."

He examined her carefully, and suddenly his eyes showed disappointment. "Do you really see it that way?" When she didn't answer, he straightened and walked on faster. It was obvious that he was angry. Without turning around, he continued, "What profit am I supposed to get out of it? Wealth, perhaps? Bah, I wouldn't even have a chance to enjoy it. What else? Luxury? No. Freedom? Hardly, for my life hasn't belonged to me for a long time, but to this world. Power? Perhaps, but that means nothing to me. I'm no megalomaniacal dictator."

"You've already given the answer yourself."

"Oh?"

"You do it for science. Not for the Lilim, perhaps not even for yourself. Only for science. That's another form of power. Or megalomania. For your investigations will never help anyone, because no human will learn of them."

"Perhaps yes. Sometime."

It was pointless. He wouldn't understand. And it

didn't matter anymore. "One thing you must still tell me."

"Just ask."

"Why are you telling me all this? I mean, I'm only some girl."

"Only some girl?" His left eyebrow twitched up, but he still didn't look at her. "Perhaps you'll understand everything soon, Merle."

Once more she thought of her mission, of help for Venice. But in her mind she saw the city like a floating island moving ahead of her in the sea, ever farther away, toward the horizon, toward forgetting.

Burbridge himself no longer showed the least interest in it. And there could only be one reason for that. Because he'd long had what he wanted.

Only some girl . . .

It all was a tangle of confusion to her.

The grill ring over the Stone Light was now barely a hundred yards below them. The walks became wider, and more and more often they went through passages and tunnels in which powerful machines rumbled. Flues spouted clouds of fumes and smoke, which mixed with the ever-present mist and made breathing more difficult. At the sides of the walkways, steel gears as big as houses engaged with each other, or chains and belts moved over or under them and led to other wheels and machines. The closer they came to the bottom of the dome, the more the constructions on both sides of the walkways resembled the insides of those steam factories on some of the islands in the Venetian lagoon; Merle had learned to know two of them when the administrator of the orphanage had tried to place her there as a worker.

She wondered where the Lilim were who served all these machines. There were no workers anywhere, of any kind; it was as if the installations were completely deserted. And yet many of the machines were running at high pressure, and in some passageways the sound was deafening.

It was only after a while that she discovered that the machine tunnels weren't deserted at all. Sometimes she saw a shadow between the apparatus, or something scurried across the ceiling at lightning speed. Several times, loops and angled pipes she'd taken for parts of machines suddenly moved; in truth, individual Lilim were hiding there, pulling in their limbs at the last minute.

"They are hiding," said the Flowing Queen, but when Merle said the words out loud, Burbridge only nodded, brought out a short "Yes," and fell into silence again.

They're afraid of him, she thought.

"Or of you," said the Queen.

What do you mean?

"You are his guest, are you not?"

His prisoner.

"No, Merle. A prisoner would be in chains or locked up;

*one does not have conversations with prisoners. He treats
you like an ally."*

At last they left the tunnels and the smoking flues
behind them and entered the bottom level. There were no
more structures on the walkways leading to the star-
shaped grill circle. Again, only thin iron railings separated
them from the alluring vortex of the abyss.

Even from afar, Merle saw that they were being awaited
on the round walkway. The grill circle rested like a crown
over the center of the Light, thirty or forty yards over the
curve. All around stood figures, grouped at narrow intervals along the railings. Figures with human proportions.
They stood completely motionless, like statues, and as she
came closer, Merle saw that their bodies were of stone.

"They're waiting for something," said the Queen.

They are only statues.

"No. That they most certainly are not."

Merle had already seen that a single walk went straight
through the grill circle, from one side to the other. In its
center, and thus in the exact center of the dome, there was
a little platform, just big enough to offer places for several
people. At the moment it was empty.

On a rope from the platform dangled the body of an
Egyptian.

He wore golden robes, which were torn and charred in
many places. His head was shaved bald. A golden pattern
covered his scalp like a net.

She had seen this man just once, and that only from a distance. However, she recognized him at once.

Seth.

The vizier of the Pharaoh. The superior of the priests of Horus.

His body was twisting slightly, sometimes with his face toward Merle, sometimes his back. They'd hanged him with a coarse rope, which seemed strangely archaic in a place like this. She would have supposed that Burbridge would have more elaborate techniques at his disposal for putting a man to death.

Seth. The second man of the Empire. Burbridge had had him hanged like a street thief. As much as his death relieved her, it horrified her as well.

Always, when the dangling dead man turned his face toward her, his lifeless eyes skimmed over her. The same look as that time when he'd stared at her from the tip of the collector. A chill ran up her back like ice-cold fingertips.

"The Pharaoh sent him to kill me," said Burbridge. He sounded detached, almost a little astonished. "One could almost think Amenophis wanted to get rid of him. Seth never had a chance down here."

"Where did you catch him?"

"Over the city. He came far. But not far enough."

"*Over* the city?" she asked.

Burbridge nodded. "He flew. Naturally, not he himself." He pointed upward. "Just look up there!"

Merle's gaze followed his hand. She discovered two cages, which were hanging on long chains from a steel beam high over the mesh circle. The first cage was over the right half of the circle, the other over the left. It looked as if at any moment the chains would let them down—only there was nothing on which they could have been placed. Under them was only the glowing, curving upper surface of the Stone Light.

In one cage a mighty sphinx ran back and forth, back and forth, like a predator missing the freedom of the jungle for the first time. Powerful wings lay folded on its back. Merle hadn't known that there were winged sphinxes at all.

In another cage, very much calmer, almost relaxed, sat—

"Vermithrax!"

The obsidian lion awakened from his trance and moved his face closer to the cage bars. At this distance she couldn't see details, but she felt the sorrow in his gaze.

The sphinx saw that Vermithrax moved and snarled at him across the glowing abyss.

"No reproaches, please," said the Flowing Queen, but not even she could stop the quavering of her voice.

We brought him here, thought Merle. After all the years in the Campanile he was finally free, and now he's a prisoner again.

"You can do nothing about it."

The Queen intended to reassure her, but Merle would not accept it. They both bore the guilt for Vermithrax's fate.

She turned to Burbridge with trembling lips. The quivering of her cheeks betrayed that she was close to tears. But she still had herself under control. She wanted to scream at him, call him names. But then she pulled all her thoughts together and looked for the right words.

"Why are you friendly to me, but you imprison my friend?" she asked, controlling herself with difficulty.

"We need him. More than the sphinx, even."

Merle's eyes went to the sphinx, who, half predator, half human, was rampaging in his cage, frantic with fury. The steel box swung back and forth, but its strong chain was equal to the burden. Merle's eyes quickly turned back to Vermithrax. His long obsidian tail hung down between the bars of the cage and twitched slightly.

We have to free him, she thought.

"*Yes.*" This time the Flowing Queen had no objections. No suggestions either, however.

"An experiment," said Burbridge, "for which we've waited a long time."

"What . . . are you planning to do with them?" Merle asked.

"We're going to dip them in the Stone Light."

"What?" Merle stared at him.

"I've thoroughly considered whether I should show

you this, Merle. But I think it's important for you to understand. That you grasp what goes on down here. And why this world is the better one."

Merle shook her head dumbly. She understood nothing. Nothing at all. Why her especially?

"What's going to happen to him?" she asked.

"If I knew that, it wouldn't be necessary to try it," replied Burbridge. "We're not experimenting with this thing for the first time today. The first attempts were failures."

"You burn living creatures, only to see—"

"Don't you feel it?" he interrupted her. "The Stone Light gives off no heat. It cannot burn anyone. Including your friend."

"Then why do you want to dip Vermithrax in it?"

He grinned triumphantly. "In order to see what happens, of course! The Light changes every living creature, it *binds* itself with it and makes something new out of it. The stone hearts are part of the Light, small fragments, and they take the body's own will away from it. Afterward we can do what we want to with them. That has shown itself to be quite practical, especially with the resistant Lilim."

So, not all the Lilim had readily placed themselves under his rule. There were rebels. Potential opponents.

Merle and Burbridge were now standing at the inner railing of the round grill walk. Quite nearby was the first of the motionless stone figures that flanked the entire circle.

"We tried it with the golems," Burbridge continued. "Statues, bodies, hewn out of stone. We let them down into the Light on the chain and when we pulled them up again, they were *alive*."

Merle's eyes flicked over the endless line of stone figures. They had human shapes, certainly, but their proportions were too massive, their shoulders too broad, their faces smooth as balls.

The professor twisted the corners of his mouth. Then, loudly, he called out a word in a language Merle didn't understand.

All the stone figures made a step forward at the same time. Then they went stiff again.

He turned to Merle again with a smile. "Stone that becomes alive. A good result, one could say. In any case, a combat-effective one."

Was that supposed to be a threat? No, she thought, he didn't need to scare her with a stone army.

"And now," he said, "we come to a new attempt. A second experiment, one could say. Your friend consists of stone that is already living *before* he comes into contact with the Stone Light. What do you think might happen when we dip the obsidian lion into the Light? What will become of *him*?" There was a spark in Burbridge's eyes, and Merle realized that it was a part of the scientific curiosity he'd spoken of earlier. But it was a cold and calculating gleam. It had an alarming similarity to the Stone Light, and for the first time she wondered whether possibly she might be speaking not with Burbridge himself but with something that had gained power over him.

A heart on the hunt for a body, he'd said. One like his own? Was that the way the Light organized and directed whole societies and peoples? By giving a new heart to its leader first of all?

"We must get away from here," said the Flowing Queen.

Really?

"I feel something!"

Two figures approached over one of the walks to the circle.

One was a bizarre creature that looked like a human walking on all fours—but its chest and its face were pointed upward. Around its head, eyes, and mouth were wound thorny vines of steel.

The second figure was a girl with long, white-blond hair.

Impossible! Absolutely impossible!

And yet . . .

"Junipa!"

Merle left Burbridge standing and ran up to the two of them.

The creature took a step back and let the two girls fall

into each other's arms. Merle no longer kept back her tears.

When they pulled away from each other, Junipa smiled, her mirror eyes glowing in the light of the Stone Light. Very deep inside, very briefly only, Merle was horrified at this look; but then she realized that the mirror fragments only reflected the flickering brightness that was all around them.

"What are you doing here?" she asked breathlessly, asked it again, and yet again, shaking her head, laughing and crying at the same time.

Junipa took a deep breath, as if she must pull all her strength together to speak. She held Merle's hands, and her fingers now closed about them even more strongly, as if she never again wanted to let go of her friend, her confidante from the first days in Arcimboldo's mirror workshop.

"They have . . ." She fell silent, started over: "Talamar abducted me." With a wave at the grotesque thing behind her, she added, "He killed Arcimboldo!"

"*We must get away*," said the Flowing Queen. "*At once!*"

Merle stared at Talamar, saw the steel vine, which had distorted the face into a wasteland of scars. "Arcimboldo?" she whispered, disbelieving.

Junipa nodded.

Merle wanted to say something, anything—"*That's*

impossible! He can't be dead! You're lying!"—when a scream sounded behind her.

A scream of fury.

A scream of hate.

"Must get away from here!" said the Flowing Queen once again.

Merle whirled around and looked back, across the few yards to Burbridge and to the edge of the round grill walkway.

At first look, nothing had changed. The professor still stood there, his back to her, looking into the center of the circle. The golem guards were stiff as before. The sphinx rampaged in his cage, while Vermithrax sat motionless, gazing into the deep. Not at Merle and Junipa, and not at Lord Light.

The lion was looking down at the narrow walk that cut through the middle of the circle. At the platform in the center.

That platform from which the dead priest of Horus had been dangling.

The end of the rope now hung empty over the abyss. It was frayed, as if it had been bitten off.

Seth stood on the platform—*alive!*—with both arms raised and again uttered a scream.

"Iskander," he roared into the light-flooded emptiness.

The cage of the sphinx exploded as if the bars were glass.

And then Iskander descended on them.

13

THE FIGHTERS AWAKEN

THINGS HAPPENED TOO FAST FOR MERLE TO SEE IT ALL AT first. Only a little later did she succeed in grasping most of it, a movement here, a blur there, underscored by a cacophony of noise and screams and the rushing of powerful wings.

The sphinx shot out of the cloud of steel and iron fragments into which his prison had changed from one minute to the next. He raced down, faster than the remains of the cage plunging down around him, and reached the platform in no time.

Seth was waiting for him. He sprang agilely onto

Iskander's lion back, screaming out a string of orders in Egyptian. Immediately, the sphinx launched himself from the platform, stormed onto the round path and, with a single, clawed blow, beheaded three of the golem guards that stood in his way. Burbridge threw himself to the ground behind them, while other stone soldiers on both sides stomped forward to protect their master.

Carried on by his swing, Iskander had to fly a loop in order to renew the attack on Lord Light.

When the cage burst, Merle had instinctively thrown herself on Junipa and pulled her to the ground with her. She halfway expected that Talamar would tear her friend away from her. But instead, the creature jumped nimbly over Junipa and raced over to Burbridge and the golem soldiers, with the intention of defending Lord Light with his life.

Unexpectedly, Merle and Junipa were left unguarded.

Not that it was of much use to them. All they could do was lie flat on the ground, Merle protectively over Junipa, who, though only a year younger, seemed to her at that moment like a child who must be shielded.

"Too late!" whispered the Flowing Queen in her thoughts, but what she meant by it wasn't clear to Merle yet.

She lifted her head, first made sure that Junipa was all right, and then looked back at Burbridge. She was lying about ten yards from the place where the walkway entered the circle; ten yards from the place where Burbridge was taking cover behind a bunch of golem soldiers, while the sphinx with his rider—

Dead! Seth had been dead!

—flew in for a new attack. Two other stone men burst under a blow from Iskander's claw, while Seth bellowed further orders in Egyptian, clasped both arms around Iskander's half-human upper body, and kept his eye on the light-filled mist of the dome.

Merle didn't know how he'd managed to survive the execution, and perhaps it was better so. He was a high priest of Horus, one of the most powerful magicians in the Empire, and he must know how to raise the dead. Possibly that had been in his plan from the beginning: lull Burbridge into security and then be able to strike totally unexpectedly.

And he understood about striking, no doubt about it.

More golems shattered into pieces, proving that everything that Lord Light had expected of them had been in error. They might offer protection from humans and Lilim, but not against the anger of a sphinx, whose power and strength and cruelty were legendary among the peoples of the world.

Iskander was, as Merle saw at once, no ordinary sphinx. He was bigger, stronger, and in addition to that, winged. His long, bronze-colored hair had loosed itself from his neck and whirled wildly around his head, a net of fluttering strands like the tentacles of a bizarre water plant. He had claws not only on his lion feet but also on both hands of his human torso, and they were long and sharp enough to break even stone. Merle didn't like to imagine what would happen if they landed on soft flesh, muscles, skin, and bone.

Her eyes sought the second cage, in which Vermithrax was still imprisoned. The obsidian lion was no longer sitting there quietly but vainly trying to bend the bars apart with his paws. To no avail. Iskander's cage had been destroyed by Seth's magic, not by the muscular power of the sphinx, and Vermithrax's prison remained untouched by it. The steel box shook and jerked as Vermithrax ran around in it angrily, throwing himself against the bars repeatedly and bellowing something to Merle that she couldn't understand over the noise of the fight.

Why didn't any Lilim come to Burbridge's aid? He'd trusted in the strength of the golem soldiers. But wouldn't he have guessed what the sphinx was capable of doing?

Merle thought of the empty machine tunnels, the anxious creatures who took shelter from their master behind steel and smoke.

Only a single Lilim was ready to go to his death for Lord Light.

Talamar dared a desperate maneuver. When Iskander shot down once again from high altitude, the grotesque creature jumped from one of the railings and threw himself at the sphinx. Iskander crashed against him, lost his orientation for a moment, smashed into the opposite railing, and lost his rider. Seth was slung from the sphinx's back and thumped onto the walkway.

Talamar hung with his limbs entwined around Iskander's body and was carried high up with him, depriving him of sight: Talamar's scrawny body clung before the sphinx's chest and face. Iskander was confused for a moment. Then he seized the Lilim with both hands, tore him to pieces, and flung him into the abyss. Talamar's remains fell into the deep in a red cloud and disappeared in the glow of the Stone Light.

Iskander let out an angry scream, licked the Lilim blood from his claws as he flew, and ignored the calls of his master. Seth had pulled himself up to the railing with his unwounded arm; the golden grid inlaid in his scalp was sprinkled with damp red. Again and again he roared orders up to Iskander, but the sphinx didn't obey.

The winged creature screeched in wild triumph, shot away over Seth, and flew in a wide arc. His eye fell on Vermithrax and recognized in him a worthy opponent. He rushed at the obsidian lion's cage with brutish fury, leaped on it, fastened himself to the bars, and tore at them. Iskander was no ordinary sphinx. He was something artificial, bred through the black arts of the Pharaoh and his priesthood, a cross of several beasts, and Merle wouldn't have been surprised if somewhere in him there were also the traces of a Lilim.

Iskander rattled the bars of the cage again, while Vermithrax struck at him from inside. He wounded the sphinx on his legs and paws, but the pain only made Iskander angrier. The cage danced wildly on its chain, swung wide back and forth, twisted and circled, and the sound of grinding iron came down to the round walkway over the Light.

Merle and Junipa clung to each other; neither could do anything, and even the Flowing Queen stormed in Merle's thoughts in fear for Vermithrax's life.

Injured, Seth was still leaning against the railing, looking frantically from Iskander to Burbridge. The professor appeared very briefly behind the wall of his remaining golem soldiers to assess the situation, then took cover again and sent two golems in Seth's direction. The stone giants hurried forward with rumbling steps. The priest of Horus tried to hurl a magic spell against them, but when he opened his lips, only blood came out, red foam, which ran over his chin and soiled his chest.

"Iskander!" he cried in a long, drawn-out howl into the ever-present brightness. At the same moment the golems reached him, were about to seize him—and then suddenly Seth was gone, and a mighty falcon shot forward, wobbling, between the giant soldiers, turned a groggy circle over Burbridge, and then rushed upward, disappearing without a trace into the mist of light in the dome.

The sound of a metal grinding and rending alarmed Merle and Junipa and drew their eyes up to the cage.

Vermithrax had succeeded in splitting Iskander's face with a well-placed slash between the bars. The blow had torn a hand-sized piece of skin from the sphinx's head like old wallpaper. But Iskander's roar of pain was no different from the sound of his insane rage; his tearing and shaking grew even stronger.

The grinding sound came again, followed by shrill poppings.

Merle screamed. Junipa's hands dug into Merle's arms like pincers, clutching as hard as she could.

The chain parted, and for a fraction of a second the cage appeared to float in the nothingness, held like a cocoon by an invisible spiderweb.

Then it plunged.

The roaring of the obsidian lion was mixed with that of the sphinx. Iskander pushed himself off the cage just in time, before it could carry him with it to the depths. His wings whipped the air and caused a maelstrom in the haze of light. He wavered and swayed, then stabilized his position and looked down to where the cage was becoming ever smaller.

Merle tore herself loose from Junipa, rushed to the railing, and looked into the abyss.

"Oh, no," whispered the Flowing Queen, over and over again.

The cage rotated as it fell, like a child's building block. Inside it, Vermithrax was hardly still recognizable, only a black blur, which became smaller and smaller as it fell toward the brightness. Then the cage paled in the glowing mist over the curved surface; the chain, which had fallen behind it like an iron tail, vanished last of all.

Merle did not utter a sound.

The Queen was also silent.

When Merle finally turned around, with trembling knees and hands that were scarcely able to hold on to the railing, Junipa was beside her. Junipa with the mirror eyes, out of which the glow of the Stone Light looked at her with its own intelligence. The impression vanished just as soon as Junipa bent toward her and the reflection vanished from the mirrors.

Now Merle saw herself in them, with teary eyes and shining cheeks, and she was infinitely grateful when Junipa pulled her friend toward her, held her, and murmured soft words of sympathy in a tone that was soothing and cheering at the same time.

A resounding crash. The two girls whirled around.

Iskander was not being stopped by the obsidian lion's fate. Again he shot toward the catwalk in a nosedive, but this time he didn't rush away over the golems but landed among them. Blows that might have felled trees struck him from all sides, and already the skin under his fur was turning dark red. But he raged further among his antagonists. For every blow that struck him, he delivered several more, shattering golem soldiers in all directions. Splinters of stone flew everywhere, striking Merle and Junipa, and yet they had no choice, except to watch what happened next.

Now other Lilim were approaching from somewhere, winged creatures like those Merle had seen between the gigantic statues at the gate of Axis Mundi. But they were still far away, hardly more than tiny points in the brightness above.

Burbridge sprang among the stone soldiers shattering around him, both arms held protectively over his head, bent, now only a panicked man who feared for nothing but his life.

If the Stone Light had been in him, it had abandoned him now. Or was waiting to find out for itself how it was for a human to die. The search for new experience. Knowledge that made it easier for it to consume the next human, the next organism—or to become consumed by it, as a new heart, a new center of all things.

Iskander's power was ebbing, but his strength was still terrible enough to obliterate the last golem. Finally Burbridge stood alone on a heap of rubble, some parts still appearing human, others nothing but fragments of stone and sand.

Iskander hauled back for a deadly blow, when something shot up from the depths behind him, glowing bright like a meteor, only bigger, with a shape that resembled a lion. A deep roar overwhelmed Iskander's scream of rage and echoed back from the distant dome walls.

The sphinx turned, his movements slower than before, weakened by his battle and his own rage. And he recognized Vermithrax. Saw the light in which the obsidian lion was bathed, no, that shone through him, as if he himself had turned to light, light of stone, not hot, not cold, only different, strange, and fearsome.

Vermithrax seized Iskander by the head, tore him from the walkway, pulled him into the air, flung him up, and thus broke his neck.

The sphinx's wings fluttered one last time, held him in the emptiness for a moment, and then he would have plunged—had not the flying Lilim arrived at that moment. They caught up the body and carried it quickly away.

Burbridge laughed.

Laughed and laughed and laughed.

Vermithrax didn't bother with him; instead he rushed over to Merle and Junipa and landed beside them on the walkway. The grill rattled under his paws, as if his weight had multiplied at one stroke.

"Come," he cried in a voice that sounded a little more rumbling than before, "get on!"

His body was no longer black. He glowed, as if someone

had poured lava into the shape of a lion, and he was bigger, his feathered wings wider, his head heavier, his teeth and claws longer. In the midst of her relief, Merle wondered if that was all the Light had done or whether there were other changes, ones that she couldn't see now, which might appear later when no one was thinking about it anymore. She remembered the spark in the professor's eyes and saw a dissimilar, brighter glow in Vermithrax's eyes, two beaming points like stars implanted in his face.

But she was also happy, so happy, and she hugged the glowing lion's head and patted his nose before she sprang on his back with Junipa and held on tight.

"He is still the same old Vermithrax," said the Queen in her head, and at the moment, Merle believed her. *"Still the same old Vermithrax."*

Vermithrax took off and rushed over the bunch of Lilim clustered around the dead sphinx. They let go of Iskander's body; not much was left of him. Burbridge bellowed orders, and one of the Lilim shot over to him and waited until his master sat down on him—a serpentine creature that bore some likeness to a dragonfly, spiraled like a corkscrew, with massive wing shells like those of a beetle, three on each side, and a head that looked like a swirl of teeth.

The Lilim rose up, placed itself at the head of the flying pack, and took up the pursuit of Vermithrax. Burbridge yelled something, but his voice was too shrill to understand.

So they rushed after the glowing lion, the first living creature of stone that had been dipped in the glow of the Stone Light.

"*They are afraid,*" said the Flowing Queen. "*They are afraid of Lord Light, but also they are afraid of Vermithrax and what he is now.*"

What is he, then? Merle asked in her thoughts.

"*I do not know,*" said the Queen. "*I thought I knew much, but now I only know that I know nothing.*"

Junipa was sitting behind Merle and had flung both arms around her, holding on desperately and trying frantically not to look down into the abyss. Vermithrax was mounting more and more steeply, and it cost Merle all her strength to cling to his glowing mane. It was lucky that Junipa was thin, almost emaciated; it was all that allowed Merle to keep both their weights on Vermithrax's back.

Vermithrax was faster than before, as if the Light had doubled the strength of his wings. But he lost a portion of his valuable head start when he was compelled to circle under the highest point of the dome before he discovered an opening to the outside, a sort of gate, which was guarded by two winged Lilim. Both drew back anxiously when they saw him coming toward them, a beaming fury, a living, breathing, roaring comet.

Vermithrax bore Merle and Junipa out of the haze of light, broke out of the brightness with them, and shot out into the eternal red dusk of Hell. After the extreme glitter of the interior of the dome, the diffuse lava light of the rock ceiling over Axis Mundi seemed to Merle dark and uncanny. Her eyes needed a while to get used to it.

She imagined how Vermithrax must be affecting the Lilim who'd gathered in streets and on piazzas: a glowing tail of light against the rock sky, a creature that hadn't yet been seen in Hell.

She glanced back and saw again the growing swarm of their pursuers, which shot out of the dome not even a hundred yards behind them, pulling a thin veil of light along with them before it paled and dissolved into glowing dust.

Lord Light sat on the back of the foremost Lilim, with fluttering coattails and streaming hair, his face twisted; some blows of the sphinx had grazed him and torn red furrows in his hair and clothing.

"*He wants Vermithrax,*" said the Queen. "*More than anything else, he wants Vermithrax.*"

And as if Junipa had heard the words in Merle's head, she contradicted the Queen: "He wants you, Merle. He's after you." After a moment she added, "And after me. My eyes."

"Your eyes?" cried Merle over her shoulder, while deep below them the towers and roofs and domes of Axis Mundi moved past and Vermithrax neared the gap in the rock wall.

"Yes. He ordered Arcimboldo to implant them in me."

"But why you?"

"You know how I began to see with the mirror eyes? First only outlines and shapes, then your faces, and then everything? And how I began to even see in the dark? I can *always* see, no matter where and when, whether I want to or not."

Merle nodded. Of course she remembered that.

"It didn't stop with that," Junipa said.

"How do you mean?"

"I can see even farther." She sounded sad. "Always farther. Through things and . . . other places."

Merle looked back at the Lilim. Vermithrax had increased the distance again, but the number of pursuers had grown to fifty or sixty.

"Other places?" she repeated.

"Into other worlds," said Junipa. "That's the reason why Lord Light needs me. I'm supposed to look into other worlds for him . . . into worlds that need a new heart, he said."

Merle shivered and thought of Winter. She was suddenly overcome with remorse because she hadn't thought about him the whole time. He'd fled, Burbridge said. In silence she wished him the best of luck. He'd been going through Hell alone before they met him, and he'd probably manage from now on.

"Where are we flying?" she roared into Vermithrax's glowing ear.

In front of them the gap now yawned, like a chasm in the rocks of Hell. "Out of the city, first," cried the lion. "And then we'll see where our leader takes us."

She didn't understand. "Our leader?"

Vermithrax's mane vibrated as the powerful lion head nodded. "Look straight ahead!"

Merle peered forward over the glowing head. The gap was darker than its surroundings, and it was hard to make out anything in it. There were a few flying Lilim, but most turned aside when they saw Vermithrax coming toward them.

But then Merle saw what he meant: a tiny dark dot that was flying some distance ahead of them. She just caught sight of it before it disappeared behind the first bend of the rock gap. It looked like a bird, like a—

A falcon!

"We'll hope that Seth knows how we're going to get out of here," cried Vermithrax.

"*Quite possible,*" said the Queen, and finally she sounded like herself again. *"Perhaps we really will manage it."*

The walls of the rock gap grew rapidly toward them along both sides. Vermithrax rushed between them at breakneck speed. Projections, ledges, and spines blurred in the corners of Merle's eyes to a brown-red fog.

They had almost reached the last curve when a shudder ran through the rock walls, a shaking and explosion, followed by dust and an avalanche of rubble that plunged down to the bottom to the right and left of them. The vibrations appeared to come toward them, as if the structure of the rock walls were falling in waves, which rolled toward them, grinding and thundering. The rockfalls became stronger, ever more pieces broke out of the rock with such force that they were carried far out into the pass. Sometimes Vermithrax made a swift turn to the side in order to avoid them, but even he couldn't prevent his riders from being repeatedly struck by small stones, which smacked painfully against them like shots.

The end of the gap came into view in front of them, and their worst fears were confirmed.

The gate to the city was impassable.

The Eternal Fighters were alive—awakened, as all here was awakened, by a light of stone.

The two mighty statues had begun their wrestling, bent forward and wrapped around one another like two children in a fight over a toy. Their wrestling was so dogged, they were so evenly matched, that their positions changed constantly. Again and again, they crashed against the rock walls in the narrow mouth of the gap and caused further tremors. Merle saw a Lilim hit by a piece of stone and thrown down into the depths. Some barely caught themselves, others crashed against the walls or to the ground.

But the stream of pilgrims and travelers between the

feet of the rock giants were getting the worst of it. The endless ribbon was frayed. In panic, those who'd managed to get inside the gap streamed forward, plunging and stumbling over one another, pulling themselves up, running on two, four, and more legs; some emitted screams that sounded almost human, others high whistles, scratchy growls, or sounds for which there are no words and no descriptions.

Even if the two battling stone giants did not completely fill the gap, anyone daring to run between them ran the danger of being ground up on the spot. It was suicide to fly through the gate.

"I'm going to try it," cried Vermithrax.

Merle looked over her shoulder again, nodded encouragingly to Junipa first, then looked at their pursuers. The Lilim were relentlessly on their heels. Vermithrax was flying more slowly on account of the fighters, and the Lilim had caught up to them a little. Lord Light still rode at their head. She wondered how he'd succeeded in waking the fighters from a distance. Before, when it had looked as if the sphinx would kill him, Merle had assumed that the Stone Light had withdrawn from Burbridge. But now it appeared to be back, perhaps stronger than ever; there was no doubt that the Light, with its power over stone and rock, had called the Eternal Fighters to life. Suddenly Merle had the thought that possibly this whole place, perhaps the whole of Hell, was already possessed by the

Stone Light. And she wondered if it hadn't been a mistake to look at the Egyptian Empire as the greatest danger for the world. Perhaps they'd deluded themselves; perhaps the Pharaoh or even Lord Light or Hell were not the ones who were the worst threat to them all. Perhaps an entirely different war was taking place here in concealment. The Stone Light strove for more. First Hell. Then the upper world. And then, with Junipa's help, all the other worlds that might exist somewhere behind the walls of dream and imagination.

Vermithrax suddenly pulled in his wings and let himself drop. Something gigantic rushed away over them and cracked with deafening thunder against the rock wall—the elbow of a fighter as big as a church tower.

Junipa's hold around Merle's waist was so tight that she could hardly breathe, but it didn't matter, for she was almost forgetting to breathe with the tension. Stone splinters rattled down on them, and it was thanks to Vermithrax's speed alone that they weren't struck by any of the larger pieces. Suddenly everything else was meaningless. They dove into the middle of the fight between the two titans, and now saw nothing more but high stone walls and ramparts that relentlessly shifted, grinding and cracking, rubbing against each other and sometimes slowly, sometimes with lightning speed, moving toward or away from them. Vermithrax flew hair-raising maneuvers to avoid the bodies of the fighters, his wingtip sometimes touching the curve of a muscle here or the crest of a rib there.

Then, just as abruptly as the fighters had popped up, they were behind them. Vermithrax carried the two girls out of immediate danger, past the edges of the rock gap, and out into the breadth of the plain, high over the heads of scattered Lilim hordes, who flowed fan-shaped in front of the fighting place of the stone giants and sought their safety in flight.

"Have we made it?" asked Junipa in Merle's ear. The words sounded breathy, tired, and feeble.

"At least we're out of the city." Was that any ground for relief? Merle didn't know, and she was sorry that she couldn't be more encouraging for Junipa.

Before Lord Light's swarm reached the fighters, the two titans froze, closely intertwined with one another as before. The flying Lilim, headed by the one carrying Lord Light, shot unhindered between the bodies. The fighters had crushed hundreds of Lilim under their feet, and the survivors were still fleeing in all directions; it would be a long time before anyone dared to come here again. Yet Merle saw a few Lilim stop on the ground and gesticulate toward the red sky with a multitude of the most various limbs at Lord Light and his companions. Then Vermithrax strengthened the beat of his wings, and his speed became so fast that Merle had to blink to keep the headwind from making her eyes burn.

The falcon had flown through the rock gap and the bodies of the fighters much more quickly than Vermithrax. But now Vermithrax caught up again and soon was staying just in sight of the bird. He was their only chance. On their own, they'd never find the gateway they'd used to enter. No one could have committed to memory the route the heralds had used, and so they knew neither where to find that entrance nor how long it would take to get there.

Seth must know another way out of Hell.

Merle had hundreds of questions she would have liked to put to Junipa. But they were both completely exhausted. Her curiosity could wait.

The wasteland seemed even more monotonous to her now than during their flight with the heralds. The jagged rock fans and fissures, the cracks in the ground, the pointed rock promontories, and long-solidified lava glaciers repeated themselves over and over and over again, as if they had in truth been flying in circles for an eternity. Only small variations, differing formations here and there, confirmed to Merle that they were always going straight ahead, that Seth wasn't fooling them.

At some point, long after Merle's sense of time had failed and she was having trouble not losing her grip with weariness, an outline peeled itself away from the red glow on the horizon. At first she thought it was a wind spout, perhaps of a cyclone. Then she realized that it was massive and didn't move from the spot.

A column. Miles high, so that it linked the floor of Hell with the ceiling.

As they approached they could make out openings, irregularly arranged, but all the same size. Windows.

"That's no column," whispered Merle in astonishment. "That's a tower!"

"The falcon is heading straight for it," said Vermithrax.

"Is that the exit?" asked Junipa, her voice weak.

Merle shrugged her shoulders. "Seth at least seems to think it is. Anyway, he's led us here."

"Yes," said the Queen, *"but not us alone."*

Merle didn't have to look back to know that the Queen spoke the truth. The swarm of Lilim was still behind them, flying just as tirelessly as Vermithrax and the priest of Horus.

"This could become exciting," she murmured.

"And shortly," said Junipa, who, unlike her, had looked back.

Now Merle couldn't resist either and looked behind them.

The Lilim were barely fifty yards away.

She could see Burbridge's smile.

14

FLOTSAM

THE SEA TURTLE SHELL DANCED ON THE WAVES LIKE AN autumn leaf sailing down from a tree. Serafin's stomach had been cramped for hours, as if he were actually falling, an endless drop into an uncertain chasm, and something in him seemed to be tensing for the impact—for *something* that would put an end to the monotony.

He'd already been looking out at the unchanging sea for so long that he saw its image when he closed his eyes: a sky hung with clouds, and under it the gray, wavy desert of the sea, stirred up but not stormy, cold but not icy, as if the water itself couldn't decide what it wanted. There was no land to be seen anywhere. Their condition hadn't grown any more hopeful a while ago, when the mermaids who'd been pulling them had vanished without a trace. They'd dived away from one moment to the next, and he had only to look into Eft's eyes to read how perplexed she was.

Eft sat between Dario and Tiziano in one of the horn segments of the sea turtle shell, holding the knapsack containing Arcimboldo's mirror mask pressed firmly against her. Serafin grieved with her, certainly, but in spite of all that, he'd have appreciated it if she'd pushed away her despondency for a while and given a few thoughts to the future. The immediate future.

It didn't look good. Not by any means.

Aristide had given up babbling to himself, though. Serafin had been afraid that either Dario or Tiziano would throw the boy overboard, but by daybreak, Aristide had finally grown quiet. Now he stared numbly ahead of him, didn't answer when spoken to, but nodded occasionally or shook his head if someone asked him a question.

But strangest of all was the way Lalapeya was behaving. The sphinx, in her human form, crouched half over the edge of the shell and let her hand dangle in the water up to her wrist. Someone—Serafin thought it was Tiziano—had remarked that perhaps Lalapeya hoped to catch a fish for breakfast, but no one laughed. And anyway, by now the time for breakfast was long past.

The sphinx's silence filled Serafin with anger, almost more than the situation into which Lalapeya had brought them. After endless hours on the water, first in darkness and now in the bright daylight, she still hadn't considered it necessary to explain the experiences of the night to them. She brooded to herself, gazed into emptiness—and let her hand hang in the water as if she were only waiting for someone underneath to grab it.

But whoever she might be waiting for refused her the favor.

"Lalapeya," said Serafin for the hundredth time, "what happened on San Michele? How long had that . . . that thing been lying there?"

He thought, She will say "a long time."

"A long time," she said.

Dario shifted backward and forward against the horn wall at his back, but he didn't find the comfort he was seeking. "That was no ordinary sphinx."

"Oh, really?" Tiziano made a face. "As if we hadn't noticed that ourselves."

"What I mean," said Dario sharply, staring angrily at his friend as he spoke, "is that it wasn't just a *large* sphinx. Or a *gigantic* sphinx. That thing lying buried under San Michele was . . . more." The appropriate words failed him; he shook his head and was silent again.

Serafin agreed with him. "More," he said shortly, and after a pause: "A sphinx god."

Aristide, confused, silent Aristide, looked up and said his first words in many hours: "If it was a god, then it was an evil one."

As if Lalapeya had suddenly awakened from a trance that had carried her far from the boys and the sea turtle shell, even from the sea, she said: "Not evil. Only old. Unimaginably old. The first son of the Mother." She took her hand out of the water, stared at it for a long moment, as if it belonged to someone else's body, then went on, "He was already lying under there before there was Egypt—and I mean the *ancient* Egypt! At a time when other powers ruled the world, the suboceanic cultures and the lords of the deep and—" She broke off, shook her head, and began again: "He lay there a long time. At that time no humans lived in the lagoon, and he was brought there so that no one would disturb his rest. He *was* a god, at least by your measures, even if at that time no one called him that. And they wanted to be sure that he would remain there undisturbed forever. Therefore, guards were put in place to watch over him."

"Guards such as you," said Serafin.

The sphinx nodded, looking infinitely beautiful in her grief. "I wasn't the first, but that isn't important. I watched the lagoon for so long that I gave up counting the years. I came here when there was still no city, no houses or fishermen's huts at all. But then I watched men come, take possession of the islands, and settle there. Perhaps I ought to have prevented it, who knows? But I always liked you humans, and I saw nothing wrong with your living there where *he* lay buried. I did what I could to protect his honor and rest. It was I who saw to it that San Michele would also become a cemetery for you humans, too. And I took pains to be a friend to the mermaids, for they are the true masters of the lagoon—or at least they always were until the humans made a sport of catching them and killing them or hitching them before their boats."

Eft had been listening attentively for some time, and now she nodded in agreement. "You gave us the cemetery of the mermaids. A place that the humans could not find. To this very day."

"I've only done what I could do best," said Lalapeya. "I've watched the dead. Just as I have done for thousands of years. And it was easy. At first I had only to be there, only wait. Then it was time to build a house, finally a palace, all in order not to attract attention, to give no one reason to mistrust." She dropped her eyes, and for a moment it seemed as if she were about to put her hand into the water again, almost mournfully, guiltily. "When the lagoon was still uninhabited, the loneliness didn't bother me. That only came later, when all the others turned up, the mermaids and the humans. And naturally, the Flowing Queen. I had to see how it was to have friends, to trust others. Therefore I gave the mermaids a place for their dead, but they avoided me too."

"We honored you," said Eft.

"Honored!" Lalapeya sighed softly. "I wanted friendship and instead I got honor. One has nothing to do with the other. I was always lonely and would have remained so, if not . . ." She fell silent. "When the great war began, when the Egyptians conquered the world, I knew that it was time to act. I heard that they possessed the power to awaken the dead and to enslave them—and then finally I understood that I, without knowing it, had been awaiting this moment down all the ages. Everything suddenly made sense. If the Egyptians succeeded in making the *god,* as you called him, be their tool . . . if they actually succeeded in that, yes, then they would truly be masters of the world."

"But where do the sphinx commanders come into it?" asked Dario.

"I no longer doubt that the Pharaoh has been merely a puppet of the sphinxes for a long time," said Lalapeya thoughtfully. "The commanders are young, in comparison to me and some others of my people, and they have no respect for the old laws and customs anymore. They recognized the power that the god would give them. Had it not been for the Flowing Queen, they would have reached their goal much earlier."

Serafin nodded slowly. So that was it. The sphinxes had worked in the background all those years to make the old god of their people into their slave. For that, they first needed the Pharaoh, then the priests of Horus with their power to subjugate the dead. Not much longer and they would rule the Empire with the help of the old god.

Lalapeya continued. "So I began to take precautions. All the millennia, all the waiting . . . now finally I realized that it hadn't been for nothing. And so I tried all that was in my power." She dropped her eyes. "And I have failed. Such a long time, and then a defeat. The son of the Mother is lost."

Serafin had said not a word. But now he had to accept the responsibility: Her failure wasn't her fault. He was the one who'd prevented her from stopping the collector; he'd wrecked all that she and her predecessors had been await-ing for eons.

But that also didn't change the fact that Boro had had to sacrifice his life.

Serafin didn't feel guilty. He wanted to, but he could not. They had both made mistakes, Lalapeya and he, and now they must both bear the consequences.

"We're dying of thirst," said Tiziano, as if Lalapeya's confession hadn't taken place at all. Perhaps he hadn't been listening to her.

Serafin stared at the sphinx and now she returned his look, and for a fleeting moment he thought he'd seen those eyes once before, but not in her.

"Land!" Dario's voice shattered the silence. "There's land over there!"

All looked in the direction he was pointing. Even Lalapeya.

Tiziano leaped up, and at once the shell began to rock and tip, and suddenly water splashed over the edge, an entire wave, and then they were sitting up to their ankles in wetness.

"Sit down, damn it!" Dario raged at him.

Tiziano, completely in thrall to his euphoria over the light-colored mound in the distance, stared at him for a moment as if he didn't understand what Dario wanted of him. But then he sank back into his place without taking his eyes off the gray hump that had broken through the surface of the sea some distance away, like the hump of a whale.

The mound must have been visible for quite a while before Dario had discovered it, but its color was hardly any different from that of the sea or the sky.

"That isn't land," said Serafin, and no one contradicted him.

There was tense silence for a while, then Dario said aloud what all were thinking: "A fish?"

And Aristide: "A whale?"

An icy shiver ran down Serafin's back. He shook his head. "If it is one, then it's no longer alive. The thing doesn't move. Eft?"

When she looked at him and he looked into her eyes, he immediately wished that he'd kept back the question. But it was too late for that now.

"You won't want to hear it," she said softly.

"*I* want to hear it," said Dario in irritation.

"Me too," Tiziano added quickly.

Serafin was silent.

Eft didn't take her eyes off him as she said, "We're sinking."

"What?" cried Tiziano in horror. Again he leaped up but was immediately pulled back into his place by Dario.

"That's only a little water," said Dario quickly, letting a little of the saltwater on the floor run through his fingers. "Not bad. And I don't know what that has to do with that thing out there—"

"We're going under," said Eft once more. "Have been for quite a while now. Very, very slowly. We can't stop it. And the only place we can go is that thing over there." She pointed to the light-colored elevation in the sea without looking toward it herself.

"Why didn't you say anything before?" Serafin asked.

"What difference would it have made?"

Aristide looked frantically from one to the other. "We're sinking? Really?"

Dario closed his eyes for a moment and took a deep breath. "That's what she said, yes."

"Hairline cracks," said Serafin, and for the first time he examined the water level inside the sea turtle shell. They'd all been wet through since they'd left Venice, and no one had paid any attention to the dampness on the bottom of the horn shell. But now it dawned on him that they had in fact been sitting in water before Tiziano had almost caused the shell to capsize.

"Hairline cracks?" Tiziano splashed around in the dark water, as if he could feel them with his bare fingers and stop them.

Dario became very calm. "Good. So we're going under. But up there ahead is land . . . or something like it. And you, Eft, know exactly what it is."

She nodded. "If everything doesn't deceive me, it's a body. And a very special one, at that. The mermaids sensed it, so they swam away. They were afraid."

"A . . . a body?" stammered Tiziano. "But . . . that thing is at least . . . at least seventy, eighty yards long. Isn't it?" When no one answered, he said once more, louder this time, "Isn't it?"

Now they floated nearer to the light gray mound. And gradually, very gradually, Serafin distinguished an outline.

"The cadaver of a sea witch," said Eft.

Serafin's heart beat faster.

"Sea witch," repeated Aristide, and now it was he who was about to stand up. Dario pulled him back with such force that Serafin briefly considered remonstrating with him.

He let it go and turned to Eft. "How long do we have?"

She slowly moved her right hand through the water

inside the sea turtle shell. "Three hours. Maybe four. Possibly the shell will break apart sooner."

"Can we reach land in that time?"

"I haven't the least idea where we are."

Serafin nodded. Nothing could surprise him anymore. "So we have to leave the shell?"

"Yes."

"And climb up on that thing?"

"She's dead," said Eft. "She can't do anything more to anyone."

"One moment!" Dario rubbed the palm of his hand across his eyes, then massaged his temples with a slow movement. "You're suggesting in all seriousness that we climb onto a dead *sea witch*?"

Eft sniffed the wind. "She hasn't been dead long. She'll float for a few days."

"Longer than three or four hours," Serafin heard himself agree, even if he couldn't grasp that he was accepting this madness.

"I'm not going up there," stammered Aristide.

Tiziano said nothing.

"I'm certainly not going up on that." Aristide's voice sounded higher now, almost panicked.

"She can't be dangerous for us anymore," said Serafin soothingly. "And she's our only hope."

Tiziano came to his aid. "Imagine it's a dead fish. Then you'd probably even eat it."

Aristide stared at Tiziano for a long moment, speech-
less, then his features contorted, and his voice was a shrill
howl. "You're all completely crazy! Completely mad!"

Dario ignored him. "The current is driving us straight
toward it. Just a few minutes." When Aristide tried to
protest again, Dario silenced him with a look that could
have turned him to stone. His eyes narrowed as he again
looked over at the floating body of the sea witch. "Is that
her face there?"

All stared at the place he indicated.

"Yes," said Eft. All at once she turned pale and said
nothing more. No one except Serafin noticed it. But he
asked no more questions; there was time for that when
they were sitting safely on the corpse.

The wind turned, and from one breath to the next it
stank as terribly as the Venetian fish market on a summer
day.

The witch was floating on her back. As far as Serafin
could see from here, she had the body of a gigantic old
woman—as far as the hips. From there her body continued into a powerful fish tail, such as the mermaids had,
only the witch's was as long as a ship. Her hair floated like
a gray carpet of algae, spread out in a fan on the waves.
They'd have to be careful the sea turtle shell didn't catch
in it; if they were forced to leave the shell while it was in
the middle of this flood of hair, they'd be hopelessly
tangled in the long strands and drown.

Serafin expressed this thought aloud, and immediately they all tried to propel the shell with their hands and steer it in another direction, toward the scaly tail, where it would be simplest to climb onto the sea witch. Even Lalapeya helped, though Serafin wasn't certain if she was merely taking the opportunity to dip her hands into the water again to feel for heaven knew what.

Only two yards.

Only one.

The turtle shell bumped against the witch's fish tail. The scales were as large as wagon wheels, overlaid with seaweed, slime, and algae that had settled into the cracks. The stink took their breath away. The boys swallowed and fought with their nausea until their noses and stomachs gradually got used to it. Only Eft and the sphinx seemed to be immune to it.

No one wanted to be the first to lay a hand on the scaly tail. Even Eft, deathly pale, stared at the dead witch, although Serafin suspected that she had other reasons for that. Later, he said to himself. Not now. Not one single worry more.

He took heart, grasped Dario's shoulder, balanced a long moment in the rocking shell, and then grabbed the edge of a scale with his right hand. The scabby horn plates were arranged like roof tiles, overlapping one another, and offered enough grip for fingers and feet. Had there not been the horrible stench, Serafin would almost have felt at home: In his lifetime, he'd already climbed up and down so many roofs that climbing a fish tail was child's play.

Once on top, he turned and looked along the curve to the sea turtle shell. From here it was even more clearly visible how low the shell already lay in the water. Eft's estimation had been more than generous. Serafin doubted that the shell would have stayed afloat for more than an hour longer.

He couldn't help the others, could only watch as, one by one, they climbed over the edge of the shell, grabbed onto the scales with trembling hands, and tried somehow to get a grip on the slippery surface. The tangle of dead water plants was as slippery as soft soap, but somehow they all finally succeeded in reaching the highest point of the bulge of the tail. Eft was the last to leave the shell. Serafin and Dario reached down to pull her up.

The sea turtle shell rocked for a while longer beside the body, then it was seized by a current and carried away. Aristide and Tiziano watched it go, but Serafin's attention was now entirely devoted to the gigantic body on which they were stranded.

He'd overcome the nausea, but the disgust remained. Never in his life had he seen anything so repellent. He stood up carefully and managed several steps over the rounded top of the fish tail in the direction of the upper body.

A hand was placed on his shoulder from behind.

"Let me go first," said Eft, walking ahead of him and taking over the lead. The others, including Lalapeya, stayed back on the tail. As long as the cadaver lay quietly in the water, nothing could happen to them there, and for a moment Serafin enjoyed the quiet at the side of the silent Eft.

As soon as they'd left the scales, the consistency of the surface under them changed. The belly of the witch was soft and spongy; with every step the indentations around Serafin's soles filled with fluid. He'd often walked through Venice's piazzas when markets there had been dismantled; then the pavement was overflowing with an ankle-deep layer of rotten fruit and vegetables—this felt very similar under his feet.

They meandered through the hollows between the ribs. Water had collected in long puddles, with all kinds of small animals darting about in them.

From here Serafin could make out the witch's chin, a pointed triangle above several broad swellings. Behind it the nostrils were visible, two cave openings under a sharp ridge of skin and cartilage.

A wide scar divided the chin, overgrown by proud flesh. Eft saw it and stopped.

"What's wrong?" Instinctively, Serafin looked all around him. There was no threat of danger, at least nothing he could name.

Eft's face, despite the taxing walk, was chalk white.

"Eft," he said imploringly, "what's the matter?"

"It is she."

He frowned and at the same time felt his stomach lurch. "She?"

Eft didn't look at him as she spoke, only stared at the ugly scar, which was as long as a team of horses. "The witch who took my kalimar from me."

"Your scaled tail?"

She nodded. "I begged her to do it, and she gave me the legs of a human for it."

"Why?"

Eft took a sharp breath in, then out. Then she told Serafin the story of her first great love; of the merchant's son who'd sworn everlasting faithfulness but then had shamefully betrayed her; of the witch's warning that she could of course change Eft's legs but not her broad mermaid's mouth with the needle-sharp teeth; of how a few men had beaten her half to death while her lover looked on; and how Arcimboldo, at that time still a boy, had found her, cared for her, and taken her in.

"Merle knows the story," she said finally. "She was the first after Arcimboldo to whom I told it. You're the second." Her tone remained expressionless with these words; they were not meant as a distinction, not as a warning, only as a declaration.

Serafin looked from her over to the gray landscape of the witch's face. "And now that she's dead, that means—"

"That I must forever remain what I am today," she said with a thick voice. "Not human, not mermaid."

He looked for a solution, a few hopeful words. "Couldn't another witch—"

"No. The magic of one witch can only be undone by her alone." Her eyes mirrored the bleak sea. "By her alone."

He felt helpless and wished he hadn't come with her, had left her alone with her sorrow.

"It cannot be changed." She didn't sound really collected, but she was trying hard. "We'll go back to the others."

Dejected, he trotted along beside her and imagined how this gigantic creature once had lurked in the depths of the sea, a hideous giantess who hunted for fishing boats and merchant ships—and, in passing, plunged a mermaid in love into unhappiness. He admired Eft's courage: She'd left her home, had swum out into the open sea, into unknown regions, which alone must be creepy for mermaids, and had *begged* a sea witch for something. He knew very well he wouldn't have done it. Not for all the love in the world.

Not even for Merle?

He quickly repressed the thought, but it was hard. He still couldn't imagine what had happened to her. The uncertainty gnawed at him, even when he really wasn't thinking of Merle at all—or other things were more pressing. Surviving, for instance.

The others were sitting where Serafin and Eft had left them. Only Lalapeya had stood up and removed herself from the boys a little, in the direction of the broad tail fin, which floated on the waves like the sail of a sinking ship. She stood alone down there, her arms crossed, and looked out to sea, out into the emptiness.

Dario got up when he saw Serafin and Eft and came to meet them. He was about to say something, perhaps to ask what they'd done, when suddenly Aristide let out a cry.

All faces turned in his direction.

It had not been a call, only an inarticulate sound, born of fear and sheer helplessness.

"What—" Dario fell silent. He saw it too. Just like all the others.

The water surface on both sides of the tail was no longer empty. Heads had appeared, narrow women's faces with long hair that floated, shimmering, on the waves.

Eft took a step forward, hesitated only a moment, then called out in the language of the mermaids. Immediately all the faces in the water turned in her direction. A remarkable chatter arose, sounds of surprise when the mermaids looked into Eft's features, recognized the sharp-toothed mouth, and obviously asked why one of their people walked on legs like a human being.

"I guess those aren't the ones who brought us here?" Serafin's statement was expressed as a question, but he expected no answer.

Eft climbed down over the curve of the tail until the water lapped at her feet. One of the mermaids came closer, and then minutes passed while the two of them spoke with each other in the language of the ocean, entirely without gestures, only with words and tones and strange syllables.

Finally Eft came back to Serafin, and together they went to Dario, Tiziano, and Aristide. Lalapeya also joined them.

"To make it short," said Eft, "there was a fight between two enemy sea witches. The older one lost—we're standing on her right now. The other, a young witch, although she's older than we all are—excluding Lalapeya, of course"—Eft gave the sphinx a half-hearted smile—"the younger therefore claims this part of the undersea as hers."

Undersea. Serafin was hearing this term for the first time, and it called up pictures of the suboceanic kingdoms, images that no human had ever seen and yet everyone knew in his imagination. Images from legends, from fairy tales, from ancient myths.

"We've intruded on her territory." Eft looked nervous, although she sounded calm. "And now she wants to speak with us. Not with all of us. But she wants two of us to go with the mermaids to speak with her and give an account of ourselves."

A murmur ran through the group. Only Serafin and Lalapeya were silent.

"To be honest," said Eft, "I'm really astonished. Sea witches aren't known for dealing with humans. They eat them or do far worse things with them. But they don't talk with them. At least not until today."

"Eat them," Tiziano repeated softly, and Aristide turned ashy.

"What do you suggest?" asked Lalapeya.

"We obey," said Eft. "What else?"

Dario looked out at the good dozen heads dancing on the waves like flotsam. "They couldn't come up here, could they?"

"No," said Eft. "But they could pull the cadaver under. Or ask a hungry whale to eat it out from under our feet."

Dario blanched.

"I'll go with them." Eft's decision was firm. "They have diving helmets with them."

Lalapeya sighed. "I'll go with you."

"No," said Eft. "Not you."

And then she looked Serafin firmly in the eye.

He looked down at the water, then back at the friends—Dario, Tiziano, Aristide—who were staring at him, and finally he again met Eft's gaze.

"I?" He wasn't even certain if he asked the question aloud or if it was merely echoing in his head.

And again images: a mighty shadow, eighty, a hundred yards long; a white body that gradually separated itself from the night-black darkness; eyes that had seen more than fish in the depths; in them infinite wisdom, infinite guile.

Slowly Serafin nodded.

15

FRIENDS

Winds smelling of tar swept around the sides of the tower and whistled in openings and cracks, singing with the voices of the lost. For the first time, Merle thought that perhaps this *was* the Hell of the Bible and not merely a hollow space in the interior of the earth: the truth of the myths under a crust of rock and sand and dusky light.

The tower had three walls, which gradually tapered toward the top, like a mighty lance point that someone had planted in the wilderness. Its edges were correspondingly sharp. When Merle looked inside through one of the windows, she could make out steps of stone in the half-dark. She wondered how angular a staircase with a triangular base would have to be and was glad that Vermithrax was taking them up on the outside.

The obsidian lion stayed close to the wall, only a few yards away from the dark stone. Merle saw insects zigzagging over it and other, larger creatures whose skins matched the background like chameleons; they remained motionless, sunbathing reptiles in a land without sun.

"Merle," said the Flowing Queen, *"do me a favor and look at the falcon. I want to know exactly where he is flying."*

She dutifully turned her eyes upward. The bird shot up close to the tower wall, much more steeply than Vermithrax could. The lion had to take care not to get too vertical or he ran the danger that Merle and Junipa would fall off his back. Also, Merle's arms would hurt even more from the burden, because she had to hold Junipa's additional weight.

For various reasons, the Lilim at their heels were also not flying up the wall any more steeply than Vermithrax. Most of them had broad wings, which bore them forward with great speed; but when it was a matter of climbing upward, they fluttered like the fully fed doves on Venice's Zattere quay.

Earlier, before they'd reached the tower, Burbridge had called something to Merle and Junipa, but they couldn't understand him because of the screaming winds and the noise of many pairs of wings. His smile confused her and frightened her more than she wanted to admit. It wasn't a smile confident of victory, or of premature triumph—no, she almost had the impression that he was again showing his friendliness and kindliness.

Stay with me, I am your friend. Give up, and everything will be fine.

Never in this life!

She could only vaguely estimate how high they were by now. The rocky wastes had long ago melted to a uniform orange; details were no longer discernible. At this height, the tower walls measured around a hundred yards from one corner to the other, and at that, they were only half as wide as those down at the bottom. Merle estimated that they had about half the ascent behind them, at least a mile and then some. The idea of falling off Vermithrax's back at this height was anything but uplifting, and she was aware that her hands instinctively dug deeper into his glowing mane. At her back, Junipa was more silent than ever, but at the moment that was all right with Merle. She wasn't in the mood to talk. Anyway, her breathing was so fast, it was as if she was carrying the others up, not Vermithrax.

"Merle! The falcon!"

The Flowing Queen's cry cut through her thoughts like an axe. It would have made her wince if her muscles hadn't cramped into hard knots long since.

She looked up just in time to see the falcon fly outward, away from the tower, in a gentle arc, turning as he flew, and then, exactly horizontal, disappear into one of the window openings.

Vermithrax reacted immediately, if also quite a bit less nimbly. He moved away from the wall of the tower, turned in a broad spiral, and followed the bird inside. His wings were too wide, and he had to land on the windowsill.

"Pull your heads in!"

He squeezed through the opening as Merle and Junipa pressed as close to him as possible in order not to crack their skulls. But finally they were through, and immediately the glowing body of the lion filled the tower with light.

It was the staircase that Merle had correctly discerned from the outside. It was broad enough to offer room for an army and, because of the triangular form of the tower, even more angled than she'd imagined. The steps were of differing heights; some were slanted, others even curved. They weren't created for humans but for something that had longer and *more* legs. The walls were covered with strange signs, with lines and circles and loops.

"Those are not signs," said the Flowing Queen, as Vermithrax took off again and now began flying up over the steps, a dizzying ascent that almost turned Merle's stomach. Back and forth, in a wide left-hand curve, now

and again interrupted by daredevil maneuvers when a wall appeared unexpectedly behind a curve and Vermithrax only narrowly escaped a collision.

"What do you mean, not signs?" asked Merle.

"They are tracks."

"Things ran along the walls?" She thought of the barbs on the legs of spiders, remembered the Lilim in the Hall of the Heralds, and shuddered. "How old is this tower?"

"Very old. It comes from a time when the lords of the depths were at war with the suboceanic kingdom."

"It's time you told me about that."

"Now?"

"No." Merle pulled her head in between her shoulders as Vermithrax came alarmingly close to the ceiling. "Not now," she said. "But sometime, you won't be able to get out of it anymore."

The Queen was quiet again, but Merle realized why a moment later. Behind them the noise had grown loud, as Burbridge and the Lilim followed up the stairs. The humming of insect wings and the slow rushing of leathery wings echoed from the walls and rebounded a hundredfold on the steps and edges; it sounded as though Burbridge's troops had gained unexpected reinforcements.

"They're going to catch us." Junipa's words were not directed at anyone except herself, but Merle heard them nevertheless.

"No," she countered, "I don't think so." And in fact,

she was suddenly no longer afraid of Lilim. As long as she didn't have to see Burbridge's smile, now concealed behind a corner of the stairwell, the Lilim were, in her mind, only a crowd of clumsy monsters, who were no match for either Vermithrax's strength or his skill. In truth, it was Burbridge alone whom she feared. Burbridge and the Light in him.

The same Light that now also caused Vermithrax to glow, that penetrated him, filled him, that made him bigger, stronger, and more dangerous.

More monstrous?

Perhaps.

Seth—or the falcon he'd become—was no more to be seen, but now there was no further doubt that he was seeking the fastest way up, to an exit used millennia before by those beings the Queen had termed the lords of the depths. The enemies of the suboceanic cultures. The ancestors of the Lilim, whose kingdom had perished when the Stone Light smashed their city.

The farther they got from the floor of Hell, the cooler it became. Perhaps it was because of the shadows inside the tower, Merle thought; perhaps also because of the sweat on her skin and the powerful headwind blowing through her clothing and hair. A look at Junipa's narrow hands on her waist showed Merle that she had gooseflesh too. Of course, Vermithrax was glowing like a powerful lantern, but the glow gave no warmth at all, just like the light inside the dome. He'd bathed in the Stone Light, and no one knew yet what consequences that would have for him and for them all.

"Do not think about it," said the Queen. *"Not now."*

I'm trying not to.

Another corner, another turn of the stairs. Steps in the most unusual forms, which repeated at certain intervals, as if the higher ones were made for large creatures, the lower ones in between for smaller ones. Before Merle's eyes arose the picture of a seething mass of beings shoving and squeezing themselves up the steps, while creatures with many bent stilt-legs stalked over them, and other, still stranger creatures ran along the walls and ceiling effortlessly.

She shivered, and this time the cold wasn't the reason.

"What will he do with us if he catches us?" she asked the Queen, before she realized that she'd spoken the words aloud.

"The same as with me," said Junipa.

Merle felt the Queen's amazement, but still the voice inside her said nothing. Waited.

"What do you mean?" she asked, this time turning directly to Junipa.

"I said, he'll do the same thing to you as he did to me."

Was the throbbing and whirring of wings behind them closer? Or was it only a trick of the acoustics that made it sound louder, more threatening?

"I understood that," said Merle. "But what exactly . . . I mean, if you don't want to talk about it, I could—"

"*No.*" The Queen sounded unusually firm. "*She should say it.*"

But it wasn't necessary for Merle to repeat the question.

"You can feel it if you want," Junipa said softly. Her hand moved from Merle's waist to her right underarm, as if Junipa wanted to loosen its hold on the lion's mane.

"Feel?" asked Merle.

Vermithrax flew a loop. The girls on his back were thrown to the left, and Merle almost lost her grip. She dug her hands into the mane and pressed her knees to the lion's flank. Her heart stopped for a moment.

"Later," she got out between clenched teeth.

Junipa said nothing more, and the Queen also remained silent.

"We must be getting to the top soon!" Vermithrax's words rebounded from the walls, rumbling through the stairwell like rolls of thunder. His light beams passed over the walls like an army of fluttering ghosts.

They'd lost sight of the falcon a long time ago. If there was an exit up there, and Seth reached it first and perhaps attacked them from the front . . .

"*Do not think of anything like that,*" said the Queen.

Merle shivered more and more. The cold was increasing, not only inside her.

"Not much farther!" Vermithrax beat his wings faster, his loops around the sharp bends became ever more headlong.

"They're catching up," Junipa whispered into Merle's ear.

Merle looked back, but she couldn't make out anything in the shine of Vermithrax's body. The stairwell at their backs was empty. The sounds of those coming up from below, however, betrayed clearly that their pursuers hadn't given up.

"They're catching up." Once more. Still softer.

Merle shook her head. "I don't think so."

"Yes. Soon."

You can feel it, Junipa had said.

Merle was worried, and all of a sudden, not only because of Burbridge and his Lilim.

An icy wind blasted against them, made her hair flutter, and poked a thousand needle pricks through her clothing. Behind them, in the depths, an angry yell sounded.

"What was that?"

"*Only wind,*" said the Queen.

"I mean the yell."

"*Lord Light.*"

"But why?"

"*Perhaps his Lilim cannot take the cold.*"

"Seriously?"

"*I do not think it is ever cold in Hell. They are not used to it.*"

The ice-cold wind was now blowing down steadily from above.

"How far now, Vermithrax?"

"It's getting lighter. There's an exit over us somewhere."

Lighter? She saw only the light that streamed from the lion. It felt as if they were riding on a meteor through the dark shaft. His light flitted over the coarse walls, producing wandering shadows and awakening the furrows and scratches to life; like the creatures who'd left them behind, the tracks appeared to crawl over the walls on spindly legs.

When Merle looked more closely, she realized that the light was reflected, as if the walls were covered with glass—or with ice.

In fact, there were ice ferns on the stone.

From one minute to the next, the cold seemed to her to become even more severe.

In her mind, she turned to the Queen: I take it you don't know where this exit leads either?

"*No.*"

Not into everlasting ice, I hope.

"*I do not believe that we have flown so far. Not in such a short time.*"

Was she deluding herself or was the fluttering of wings from the deep becoming fainter? She heard Burbridge's angry bellow once again, but the shaft behind them remained empty.

Junipa's hands clenched.

"We've just made it," said Merle to cheer her up.

She felt Junipa nod; her chin struck against Merle's shoulder.

The steps under them were now evenly coated with a thin layer of ice. Vermithrax's glow made the surface sparkle in a variety of colors.

Junipa's hands clenched even more tightly around Merle's waist, pressing painfully into her side. She trembled pitifully.

"Not so tight," Merle called behind her. "That hurts."

Junipa must not have heard her, for the pressure remained the same, even increased.

"There, ahead!" Vermithrax glowed even brighter for a moment as the steps fell away under them and they rushed out into a broad hall. The ground plan was triangular, like that of the tower. The slanting walls met high above them at a point in the half-dark, beyond Vermithrax's light.

They'd reached the tip of the tower.

Rubble formed mountains and valleys on the floor of the hall. At some time there'd been a ramp here, but now only the remains of it were discernible. It had led to an opening to the outside, which from afar looked strangely irregular, until Merle realized that it had once been very much wider and today was closed except for a slanting hole. The cold inside the hall was noteworthy; here, too, ice glittered on the rubble and walls.

In front of the opening, under a gray, cloudy sky, there was a balustrade, half destroyed and without railings. But it was wide enough for Vermithrax to be able to land on it. From there they would, hopefully, be able to see what awaited them outside.

The beat of the Lilim wings had faded. Perhaps the Queen was right: The cold had forced them to give up. It was also possible that the sound was merely lost in the breadth of the hall.

Merle tried to wrench herself out of Junipa's painful grip, but the girl's hands were clenching her sides desperately. "Not so tight," she cried once more, again without result.

While Vermithrax was mounting to the balustrade, Merle looked over at the entrance to the stairwell. From above, she could see that a heavy stone slab lay over it, as large as a Venetian piazza. A broad crack had split it from one side to the other; that was the opening through which they'd flown out into the hall. Someone had done everything imaginable, presumably a long, long time ago, to bar the Lilim's way to the upper world. In vain.

The crack gaped like a black mouth in the floor of the hall. Still, none of their pursuers were to be seen.

"We've—"

—shaken them, she was about to say. At that very moment, Junipa pulled her backward.

Merle's stiff, frozen fingers lost their grip on Vermithrax's mane, the Queen screamed something in her thoughts, the obsidian lion's back slid away under them, and then they fell.

Fell down into the darkness.

For a moment Merle believed that she'd fallen through the crack straight back into Hell. But they were way too far away from the stairwell. Instead, the fall ended after a few moments on a slope of loose rubble, a remnant of the ramp, about half the height of the hall. Merle fell flat on her back. It felt as if her back had smashed to pieces. Then she tumbled onto her side, rolled a few yards, and was stopped by a flat piece of stone. It was under an overhang of ruins, so that she couldn't be seen from above.

Junipa landed beside her, cracking against the stone like a bundle of loose bones. But in contrast to Merle she didn't cry out. Didn't utter a sound.

You can feel it. . . .

Merle looked up, peered out through the gap under the overhang, and discovered Vermithrax, glowing like a star in the darkness, much too far away. He flew a loop and looked for her. She tried to call him, but only a croak came from her lips. There was sand in her mouth, grit between her teeth. Her breath steamed white, like smoke. The ground under her was so cold that for a moment she was afraid that her palms would freeze to it. She wasn't used to such cold, not at this time of year, especially not after the warmth of the inner earth.

Junipa.

Merle looked searchingly around for her friend, intending to creep to her to help her. She shrank in horror as Junipa suddenly stood beside her and looked down at her impassively. Her mirror eyes reflected nothing but darkness; they looked like empty holes.

Junipa was bleeding from a wound on her knee, and her palms were scraped, but she seemed not to feel the pain.

Just stared at Merle.

Stared with black mirror shards. With eyes that saw through everything. *I should look into other worlds for him. Into worlds that need a new heart.*

"We must get away from here," said Merle, levering herself up.

Junipa shook her head. "We wait."

"But—"

"We wait."

"Do you not understand yet?" asked the Queen.

Of course Merle understood—but she didn't want to admit it. Impossible. Not Junipa.

"That was no accident," said the Queen. *"She did it on purpose."*

The obsidian lion flew another loop in the darkness and passed the opening through which Merle was able to look out under the overhang. He'd never find her under here, unless somehow she managed to crawl out from underneath it.

But there stood Junipa, right in her way.

"Let me through," said Merle. Her right ankle hurt and hardly bore her weight.

Junipa didn't move. Just stared.

"Let me through."

It was dark under there; the only shimmer of light came from the opening high over them and from Vermithrax. He now called Merle's name, and this time she answered him. But she doubted that her voice made it out from under the overhang all the way up to the lion above.

Junipa took a step toward her. The darkness in her eyes came nearer.

"What did they do to you?" asked Merle.

"You can—"

"Feel it, yes, I know. But I want you to say it to me."

Junipa briefly tilted her head, as if she were considering what Merle meant by that. Then she began to open the placket of her dress. Her flat chest, bony like all the rest of her, shone silvery, as if her entire body had begun to turn into a mirror. But that was only a deception. Only her white, smooth skin.

"Here," she said.

In the darkness, the scar was hardly more than a line, a shadow.

Cross-stitch.

Merle's voice sounded as far away as the rushing of Vermithrax's wings. "You were in the Heart House."

Junipa nodded.

"But why don't I see anything? The wound . . ."

Junipa buttoned her dress again. "A heart of Light heals all wounds." It sounded memorized, a line from a bad poem. But then Merle saw that the wounds on Junipa's knees had closed. Now only a dark spot and a few stripes of dried blood remained.

She looked for rage inside her, for hatred of Burbridge, of the surgeon, of the whole accursed brood. But instead there was only sadness and infinite pity for Junipa. A blind orphan girl in whom cold mirror glass had been set for eyes, and now, on top of it, a new heart. A heart from the Stone Light. She was manipulated and changed at someone else's discretion. And in so doing, he took from her all that was *her own self.*

"*You cannot help her,*" said the Queen.

She is still my friend.

"*Lord Light controls her. Just as the Stone Light controls him. Or them both.*"

She is my friend. I cannot give her up.

"*Merle.*" The voice of the Queen sounded imploring but also sympathetic. "*You cannot rip the heart out of her chest again.*"

Not I. But perhaps someone else. We must try it.

"*You intend to take her with you?*"

Merle gave no answer. Instead she grasped Junipa's hands and was surprised that the girl let it happen. Perhaps a good sign. "Junipa, listen. You don't need to obey him. No matter what he threatens you with. We will find a way to help you."

"Threaten?" Junipa frowned, not understanding. "But he doesn't threaten me at all."

Merle took a deep breath. In the distance she saw Vermithrax's light gliding over the hall walls. But she didn't want to call him for fear of losing Junipa completely. At least Junipa had kept on talking with her and hadn't tried to grab her. Perhaps there was more of the old Junipa still in her than the Queen believed.

Merle forced herself to smile. "Let's get out of here."

"We wait," said Junipa.

"Junipa, please."

The girl drew her arms back, looked blankly from one hand to the other for a moment, then came toward Merle.

With a cry Merle reeled back and crashed against rock. Junipa grabbed her arm, but she was able on her side to grab Junipa's wrist. Merle's instinct commanded her to let go, withdraw, run away, and call out to Vermithrax; the Flowing Queen was also talking at her, pleading with her to give Junipa up, to flee, to get them to safety.

But the girl in front of her was her best friend. And she couldn't help what had happened to her.

Merle wriggled out of Junipa's hold. It wasn't a serious attack, not one that was supposed to injure her. Junipa wanted to hold her, perhaps only for a few seconds, a few minutes. Long enough for Burbridge's Lilim to overcome the cold and retrieve their victims. She couldn't see the crack from here, didn't know if Burbridge was already in the hall. But then she saw Vermithrax's light again and told herself that he wouldn't be there over her if the enemy were already in the vicinity.

Suddenly she received a blow from Junipa that knocked her to her knees. She immediately sprang up again and flung her antagonist against the rubble. Junipa's head cracked on the hard stone and bounced back like a volleyball—then she collapsed and lay motionless. Before Junipa could get up, Merle slid her knapsack from her back, looked for something, anything with which she could defend herself, threw water bottle, mirror, hen's claw carelessly on the ground. And gave up.

What had she expected? To be able to snatch Junipa from this nightmare with cold water? Slowly Merle turned to her, in the certainty of defeat, sensing that Junipa wouldn't give up, not before Burbridge had achieved his goal. And was corrected.

For Junipa still lay stretched on the ground, motionless and with no sign of life. Her mirror eyes were open. They stared into Merle's little hand mirror, which was lying before them on the rocks.

Merle bent for the mirror and the claw and shoved both into her pocket, then she ran, leaping over rubble and fissures, finally emerging from under the overhang. She waved both arms and bellowed Vermithrax's name as loudly as she could, and after a few seconds, she saw the light turn toward her. The obsidian lion shot down out of the darkness. His glow illuminated her surroundings, creating shadows behind angled pieces of debris.

"Where's the girl?" he asked as he landed next to her.

"Wait!" Merle stormed back under the overhang and came back with Junipa a moment later, carrying her like a child in both arms, with wheezing breath and a pain in the small of her back. Junipa was moving her lips, but Merle didn't understand what she was saying.

"We have to take her with us." She was about to say something else, but now her mouth opened without her help, as the Queen took it over. "She belongs to Lord Light! She has betrayed us!" Merle would have liked to bellow with rage, but she couldn't even do that as long as the Queen was controlling her tongue. She pulled all her will together, balled her anger like a fist—and discharged it with a wild yell.

She felt the Queen's astonishment. Her deep uncertainty. Felt how she withdrew, deeper into her interior, shocked at Merle's sudden strong-mindedness.

Don't you do that again! Merle thought furiously. Not ever again!

And she thought, We never once asked him . . . for help for Venice, for Serafin and Junipa and all the others . . . never once asked. In truth, you never intended to, right?

You wanted to be sure you were right about something. That's why we came down here. Was it about Burbridge? Or the Stone Light? No, she thought icily: Basically it was always only about *you*.

Contempt and a deep sense of injury were suddenly her only feelings. And at the same time she realized that the secret around the Flowing Queen was much larger, much more incomprehensible than she could grasp at this moment.

The Queen was silent and Vermithrax, surprised, allowed Merle to load Junipa onto his back. Then she climbed on behind her, wedged the lifeless Junipa backward between her and the lion's neck, curled her hands into Vermithrax's mane, and gave him the signal to take off.

The obsidian lion rose with a mighty flap of his stone wings and flew up to the opening.

Junipa's lips moved more and more vehemently, but Merle dared not put her ear closer to the girl's face, for fear it could be a trick to force her to Burbridge.

But then, very briefly, she did think she understood something that sounded like a word. Something that didn't belong here at all.

"Grandfather," said Junipa.

And then, more clearly: "He is your grandfather."

Merle stiffened.

"He is not," said the Queen. *"She is lying. He is lying."*

Junipa's eyes opened slowly, and in the mirror eyes Merle saw herself, lit from below by the light of the lion, white as a ghost.

Junipa's features slept, only her eyes remained open, looking through Merle, the shadows, the world. Somewhere into the land of lies, the land of truth.

"Grandfather," murmured Merle.

"Do not do that! That is exactly what he intends. Burbridge is only using her; he invents lies to weaken you."

Merle stared a moment longer into the mirror eyes, at her two white likenesses, then gave herself a shake.

"It wouldn't change anything," she said, but in her head the thoughts were buzzing like a swarm of hornets. "Grandfather or not, he's to blame for what happened to Junipa . . . and all the others."

The Queen must have been feeling what was going on in her, but she restrained herself and kept quiet.

Vermithrax had almost reached the destroyed balustrade when Merle spoke a thought out loud. "Why can he control Junipa but not Vermithrax? Vermithrax has much more of the Stone Light in him than she does."

The lion landed on the broken ledge not far from the opening to the outside. A drifting of snow had blown in and trailed off into ever-thinning white on the dark stone, like feathers from a burst down cushion.

"It doesn't rule me." Since his bath in the Light, the

voice of the lion sounded even more awe-inspiring. "It is mine, but I am not its."

His eyes said: Not yet.

Perhaps it was only an illusion, vanished in a blink. Please, please, please, thought Merle.

Behind him wings whirred in the darkness, slowly, torpidly, and as Merle and Vermithrax looked around, Burbridge on his Lilim hovered in the half dark. The spiral body of the creature wavered and trembled, its eyes glittered even more than before, and Merle saw that it was coated with ice.

You were right, she thought. The Lilim is freezing.

"Of course," said the Queen.

The creature came no nearer, held itself in the air with difficulty, barely twenty yards away from them, and on a level with the balustrade.

Burbridge only looked at her. All the friendliness had departed from his features. The rest of his Lilim troops had not come with him. It must be clear to him that he was running the danger of being attacked by Vermithrax.

However, he was here.

"Merle," he said to her. "Do you know your name? I can tell you your name."

Whose name did he mean? The name of the Flowing Queen? But what—

A gust of wind made the snowdrift swirl up. White flakes, frozen hard like glass splinters, drove over the ragged edge of the balustrade down deeper into the darkness. The Lilim trembled and pulled back.

Burbridge said nothing more, only slowly shook his head. Merle had the feeling that the gesture had nothing to do with the Lilim. Only with her.

Then he kicked the creature in the flanks, and the slender body turned heavily and sank back into the deep, to the crack in the floor, and through it into the stairwell.

Merle detached her gaze from the abyss and looked again into the face of the unconscious Junipa. Her lids were closed now, but through two tiny cracks there was a shimmer of silver. Merle's hand wandered to Junipa's chest. No warmth, no heartbeat. But for a moment she had the impression that light streamed through her fingers, a fan of brightness. However, it paled before she could be certain it wasn't an illusion.

She would help Junipa. Somehow she would help her.

What could Burbridge have meant? *Your name . . .*

Vermithrax bore her outside.

Glowing brightness awaited her, as if the Stone Light had also seized the upper world. But it was only the white of the landscape and the white of the sky. Snow clouds covered the sun. The plain that stretched far below them was buried under a deep layer of snow.

"Winter," whispered Merle.

"In the middle of summer?"

"Winter. He's here."

The Queen hesitated. *"You think . . . ?"*

"He spoke the truth. He arrived here before us."

They stood high over the icy plain, and the wind bit painfully into Merle's face. She'd long since been frozen through and thought it couldn't get worse. But now she felt that the cold would kill her if she couldn't warm up at a fire soon. Her hands shoved themselves into the pockets of her dress on their own. Her right hand touched the oval frame of the mirror, but it was also cold as ice. Only the water inside felt reassuringly warm, as always.

She'd assumed they were standing on a mountain, several dozen yards over the plain. But now as she looked around, she realized that was wrong. The snow-covered surface was smooth, but it was no balustrade as on the inside of the hall.

It was a step. The incline, as she looked down, consisted of a dozen such steps, each several yards high.

"Merle!" Vermithrax's voice made her look up. "On the horizon."

Blinking, she followed his gaze, blinded by the endlessness of the snow. After her eyes had become somewhat accustomed to the brightness, she made out shapes in the distance. Too pointed and symmetrical for mountains. They were constructed of the same steps as those on which they stood.

Merle turned her head and looked up behind her. The stepped incline grew narrower above, ending in a point.

"*Pyramids,*" said the Queen.

Merle could scarcely breathe for cold, but also because she realized where they were.

Egypt.

And the desert was three feet deep in snow.

Merle's hand felt for the water mirror, slid in, into gentle, comforting warmth. And while her eyes kept skimming over the ice, over to the snow-covered pyramids, slender, feminine fingers grasped her own inside the mirror, clasped them, stroked them.

Mother, thought Merle numbly.

The mirror phantom murmured, whispered, murmured.

And somewhere, on the tail fin of a floating sea witch, the sphinx Lalapeya crouched by the water, her hand plunged deep into the sea, and shed silent tears.

COMING IN FALL 2007

The Glass Word

THE FINAL VOLUME IN THE
DARK REFLECTIONS TRILOGY
BY KAI MEYER

Merle and Serafin are reunited in the final battle with the forces of the pharaoh and his sphinx commanders for control of all the worlds. Will they be able to outwit the Egyptians—and what price are they willing to pay for victory? Events are moving at breakneck speed as all the threads pull together in this thrilling conclusion to the spellbinding tales found in the Dark Reflections Trilogy.

ABOUT THE AUTHOR

Kai Meyer is the author of many highly acclaimed and popular books for adults and young adults in his native Germany. The first book in his Dark Reflections Trilogy, *The Water Mirror*, was a *School Library Journal* Best Book, a Book Sense Pick, a *Locus* Magazine Recommended Read, and a New York Public Library Book for the Teen Age. It also received starred reviews in *School Library Journal* and *Publishers Weekly*, and has been translated into sixteen languages. Kai Meyer lives in Germany.

ABOUT THE TRANSLATOR

Elizabeth D. Crawford is the distinguished translator of the Batchelder Award–winning novels *The Robber and Me* by Josef Holub and *Crutches* by Peter Hartling. She lives in Orange, Connecticut.